I0544162

The Darkness Between Us

Gwendoline Vale

ISBN: 978-1-7642709-9-1

First Edition, 2025

DEDICATION

For the dreamers, the seekers,
the ones who step into the dark to find their own light.

For every heart that has carried questions
and kept walking when the way was uncertain.

For those who trust the quiet pull of wonder,
and for those who dare to believe that even in shadow
a new beginning waits.

CONTENTS

ACKNOWLEDGMENTS

This book would not exist without the love, encouragement, and patience of those who walked beside me through its creation. To my family and dear friends, thank you for holding me steady when I faltered, and for reminding me of the light when the shadows felt overwhelming.

To Betty - Betz - for guidance that lit the path when I felt lost in the dark, and for the gift of friendship that made the journey brighter. Your support shaped not only these pages, but the heart behind them.

To the readers who step into this story, thank you for carrying it forward. May it remind you that even in the darkest places, there is always a light waiting to be found.

1
THRESHOLD OF SHADOWS

T he city rose like a mirage, its jagged skyline piercing through the thick, silver mist of a dreary London afternoon. The train clattered along the tracks, carrying Cassandra Moore from the stillness of the English countryside into a restless expanse of metal and glass. Green fields had receded behind her, replaced by the city's worn edges. Industrial estates passed in a blur, their rusted fences leaning under the weight of graffiti and soot. The change seemed sudden, like crossing some invisible border into a world both unfamiliar and unapologetically alive.

Inside the carriage, the air shifted. The murmur of passengers sharpened into louder voices, accents rising and mingling with the forward pull of the train. Cassandra pressed her forehead to the glass, her breath leaving a faint mist as she watched the city unfold. The scent of stale coffee and damp coats filled the space, clashing with the cleaner, eucalyptus-scented breezes she'd known back in Melbourne. It was overstimulating yet exhilarating. The kind of awareness that whispered her journey had only just begun.

The train moved faster now. The soft rhythm of the countryside gave way to the harder tempo of the city. Rows of brick buildings stood in silent formation; chimneys blackened by time. Warehouses crouched behind wire fences, windows opaque with grime. The sky was a sheet of grey, pressing low, casting everything in muted tones. It wasn't the warm brightness of home. But it held its own kind of electricity.

As the train pulled into King's Cross, her pulse quickened. The platform stretched beneath a ceiling of arched steel and glass, the structure intricate and endless above her. She stepped down, her suitcase bumping along behind her, too full and awkward. The sounds here were harsher than she'd expected. Announcements echoed from the speakers. Shoes struck tile. Someone shouted into a phone. Another laughed too loudly. She paused, inhaling the sharp scent of diesel mixed with roasted coffee, and for a moment, it all felt like too much.

Then, a gust of damp wind swept through the station, lifting strands of her dark auburn hair. Rain clung to the ends in delicate droplets. She stepped outside and raised her arm, fingers trembling as she hailed a cab.

Sliding into the backseat, she gave the driver the address. "Bayham Street, Camden, please."

He glanced at her in the mirror. His Cockney accent was thick, but friendly. "First time in London, Love?"

She nodded. "Yes. Just moved here."

"Well, enjoy the Madhouse," he said as they joined the traffic. "Camden's something else. Bit posh in parts now, but still rough around the edges. Punk and banker on the same footpath, know what I mean?"

She managed a soft smile and turned back to the window.

The city blurred past in shades of silver and red. Glass towers shimmered beside soot-darkened churches. Buses lumbered through intersections. People moved in every direction, always just out of reach. The rhythm was different here. Faster. Louder. But under it, something pulsed.

As they entered Camden, the city's voice changed again. The streets were tighter, lined with signs in bold fonts and garish colours. Tattoo parlours, vintage shops, vegan cafes, and record stores jostled for attention. The energy was sharper than that of Melbourne's Fitzroy. More urgent. More worn in.

The cab stopped outside a modest brick building.

"Here we are," the driver said. "Keep your wits about you, and you'll be fine."

Cassandra stepped out into the drizzle. The building loomed quietly; Its bricks streaked with old rain. Not imposing but, not inviting either. She pulled her suitcase to the entrance and climbed the narrow stairwell to the second floor.

The door opened before she knocked.

"There she is," Miranda said, tugging Cassandra into a huge hug. "Welcome to chaos, I can't believe that you're finally here!" Then she added, "Let the adventure begin."

The flat was small but inviting, warmed by mismatched furniture and the scent of lavender drifting in faint trails through the air. A bookshelf sagged under the weight of paperbacks, stacked two-deep. In the corner, a pile of records leaned precariously, a few spilling out of their sleeves. It looked lived-in and lovingly neglected, like a place where stories happened without planning.

Miranda pulled Cassandra's suitcase inside and dropped it by the couch. "You'll love it here. Just don't expect London to love you back. Not at first, anyway."

Cassandra laughed, accepting the steaming mug of tea Miranda handed her. The warmth seeped into her palms, grounding her.

"Thanks for letting me stay."

Miranda flopped onto the couch with a soft thud. "What are old friends for?"

They had known each other for years, their first meeting blurred in memory, but what had lasted was Miranda's wildness, her irreverent humour and fearless heart. She was the kind of girl who had talked Cassandra into rock climbing with no experience, then laughed at the top until they couldn't breathe. That memory, of suspended joy and adrenaline, clung to Cassandra now like something important.

They stayed up for hours, the conversation winding through updates, old stories, and laughter thick with wine. Miranda's voice was quick and clever, her presence filling the room with ease. For the first time in days, Cassandra felt something close to comfort.

Later, as the night softened and the city hummed in the background, Cassandra curled under a thick blanket on the couch. The fabric smelled faintly of jasmine and sleep. Her phone buzzed once on the coffee table, lighting the room with its screen.

She reached for it. The name glowed through the dim light: Ethan.

Did you make it to London safely?

Her heart lifted. She opened the message, the warmth of his voice threading through the words in her mind. Quickly, she typed her reply.

I did. London is overwhelming, but incredible. I've barely scratched the surface, but it's everything I hoped for. You'd love it here.

She paused, then added:

I miss you so much already.

The response came fast.

I miss you, too. I can't wait to hear all about it. Just promise me you'll take care of yourself, okay?

She exhaled slowly, the ache of missing him settling like a stone in her chest. She could see him so clearly, still at the old kitchen table, coffee in his hands, the early light brushing his face.

I promise. I'll call you soon. There's so much I want to share. It's not the same without you. Wish you were here.

She hesitated before pressing send, adding a small heart at the end. Something to carry what she couldn't quite say aloud.

The reply arrived almost instantly.

I'm always with you, Cass. Remember that. No matter where you go. We can face anything together when you are ready.

Her throat tightened. She pressed the phone against her chest, eyes burning.

"I know," she whispered.

Then she typed:

Goodnight, Ethan. Sweet dreams.

His last message came just as her eyelids began to flutter closed.

Goodnight, Cass. Sleep well xox.

She placed the phone back on the table, pulled the blanket tighter, and let herself drift. Outside, the city breathed its strange lullaby, and inside her chest, Ethan's voice lingered like a thread of light.

The morning arrived quietly, with pale light stretching through the curtains in silvery threads. Cassandra blinked awake, her limbs heavy from travel, her thoughts floating between sleep and clarity. She hadn't made it to the bedroom. At some point in the night, she'd fallen asleep on the couch, still wrapped in the blanket that smelled faintly of jasmine and rest.

For a moment, she wasn't sure where she was. Then came the sound of humming from the kitchen, followed by the soft clink of cutlery, and it anchored her in place.

She sat up slowly. Morning light gentled the flat, as if it had softened overnight to welcome her.

She padded quietly into the kitchen, drawn by the smell of coffee.

"Morning, Sunshine," Miranda said, sliding a mug across the counter. "Thought I'd better feed you before you go full London freelancer."

Cassandra stretched, easing the stiffness from her shoulders. "You're a lifesaver." She took the coffee and perched on the stool.

They ate in easy silence. Toast, eggs, and Miranda's dry humour made the city outside feel a little less overwhelming. Sounds of life rose from the street below, muted conversations, the occasional horn, footsteps along the pavement.

Cassandra dressed, packed her notebook, and double-checked the map. When she turned, Miranda was already leaning in the doorway with a crooked grin.

"Remember, Cass. You've got this. And if anyone gives you trouble, call upon your inner rock climber. Grip tight. Keep moving. Don't look down."

Cassandra laughed, slipping on her coat. "I'll try."

She stepped into the morning. The air held a clean chill, sharp enough to wake her fully. She hailed a cab, nerves fluttering as the city blurred past the window. In daylight, London looked different.

It was less cinematic, more tangible. Real in a way she hadn't expected.

When the car pulled up to the glass-fronted building, she hesitated.

Vanguard Publishing rose before her, all clean lines and reflective surfaces. Sleek. Curated. Quietly intimidating. The entrance gleamed beneath a row of sculpted hedges, as if even the plants had been told to behave.

She stepped inside. The lobby was bright and still, humming with the low thrum of distant conversations and elevator chimes.

Cassandra gave her name at reception, her voice steadier than she felt, and moved toward a sculptural bench tucked beneath a living wall.

She gripped the strap of her bag with both hands, grounding herself in its weight, in the shape of something familiar.

A woman approached with measured strides.

"Cassandra," she said, offering a hand. Her voice was Australian, crisp and unhurried. "Lydia Hart. Welcome to Vanguard."

Lydia was striking in that intentional, effort-left-nothing-to-chance way. Dark hair pulled into a sleek ponytail. A sharp blazer, trousers tailored within a millimetre of precision. Steel-blue eyes that flicked over Cassandra like a quiet assessment, cool but not unkind.

Cassandra returned the handshake. "It's great to meet you in person."

"Come," Lydia said, already turning.

They moved through an open-plan office that gleamed with glass and clean lines. Abstract art hung like punctuation on otherwise immaculate walls.

The energy felt charged but controlled. Editors murmured into headsets, designers gestured at glowing screens, writers hunched in quiet intensity over keyboards. Creative. Composed. Curated.

Lydia led her into a corner office with wide windows and a minimalist interior. A single fern, a few stacked books, and a line of awards offered the only colour.

"So," Lydia said, as they sat. "What made you say yes to this?"

Cassandra took a breath. "Ambition. Curiosity. And a need for something different. I've always loved London's creative scene. Vanguard felt like the right place to begin."

Lydia nodded slowly. "I get that. I moved from Sydney years ago. Same impulse. It's not an easy path, but if you're good and willing to work harder than most, it's worth it."

They spoke for a while, their words circling everything that wasn't said. Something passed between them, quiet but understood. Shared country. Shared hunger. Lydia came across as exacting, but there was a kind of precision in her gaze that felt less like judgment and more like expectation.

"Freelancing takes grit," Lydia said, watching her. "But your work shows promise. If you can keep up, we'll get along."

"I'll do my best," Cassandra said, quieter now.

Lydia held her gaze a moment longer, then gave a wry smile. "God, I miss the heat. London winters still hit me like a betrayal."

Cassandra laughed softly. "I've already stopped feeling my toes."

Lydia smiled. "You'll adapt. Or grow very good boots."

She slid a folder across the desk. "Your first assignment. Winter fashion. What's new, what's recycled, what's being reimagined? Focus on contrast. London lives on contradiction. Especially Camden."

Cassandra opened the folder. Mood boards spilled out, filled with oversized silhouettes, clashing textures, and jewellery shaped like sculpture. Her pulse lifted.

"Camden?" she asked.

"Intentional," Lydia said. "It's raw and rich. Edge meets elegance. You'll find everything you need there. Start local. Make it your own."

Cassandra nodded, ideas already forming.

Lydia stood. "One more thing."

Cassandra looked up.

"Don't just observe. Immerse yourself in it completely. Fashion isn't about what people wear. It's about why they wear it."

The words settled into her like a thread pulling tight. She thanked Lydia, gathered the folder, and made her way out through the polished quiet of the office.

The moment the glass doors released her, the city rushed in. London pulsed around her, messy and enormous and alive.

The cab ride back to Camden blurred into fragments. Streets flickered past the window, distorted by light and movement. Crosswalks swelled with crowds layered in winter tones. The sharp red of buses bled into her periphery like a warning or a promise. Her thoughts spun with colour palettes, mood, and texture. Threads she hadn't realised she was collecting.

There was so much to take in. It thrilled her. And unsettled her. Both at once.

At the flat, the familiar scent of lavender drifted out to meet her, soft and grounding. Cassandra exhaled. Something in her chest uncoiled.

Inside, Miranda was curled on the couch, one leg tucked beneath her, a wineglass cradled in her hand. The room was dim and warm, a low playlist murmuring in the background.

"Back already?" she asked, not looking up. "How was the Dragon Lady?"

Cassandra dropped her bag by the door with a thud that echoed more than she expected. "Tough, but fair. I think I survived."

Miranda raised her glass in a lazy salute. "That's a win. What's the first assignment?"

"Fashion trends. Winter. Camden focus."

Miranda whistled softly. "Camden's a baptism by fire. You'll love it. It has grit and glamour in strange amounts. And a touch of darkness that never quite lifts."

Cassandra moved to the couch and sank into the cushions beside Miranda, folding her legs beneath her. The warmth of the room wrapped around her like a second skin.

"Got any local tips?"

"Go early if you want the best of the market," Miranda said, swirling the last of her wine. "The vintage stalls vanish quick. And check the side streets. That's where the stories hide. You'll find everything from antique brooches to boots with a past. Half the vendors look like they wandered in from another decade."

Cassandra smiled, pulling the blanket across her lap. "Comfortable shoes, then?"

"Obviously. Your heels are for looking, not walking," she grinned.

The next morning unfolded in a hush of pale light. A cool grey hung over the street, softening the edges of the city. Cassandra dressed slowly, choosing dark jeans, a tailored coat, and sturdy boots.

The kind that would survive Camden's uneven streets. She slipped her notebook and camera into her bag, then paused by the window.

Below, London stirred awake in fragments. Headlights blinked through mist. A cyclist passed, scarf trailing. Somewhere, a kettle shrieked in another flat. Cassandra pressed her fingertips to the glass. The day waited. And something in her felt ready to meet it.

Camden Market was already alive. The stalls spilled colour into the grey morning, scarves and jackets layered in bright defiance against the muted sky. Vendors called out to early passersby.

The scent of warm bread and cardamom drifted on the air, weaving between the crush of voices and footsteps.

Cassandra moved slowly, letting the place unfold around her. Her camera clicked in rhythm with her breath. Her pen scratched brief impressions into the notebook curled in her hand. She watched. She listened. She let the textures reach her.

Near a graffiti wall, a woman with neon green hair leaned back, cigarette in one hand, gaze sharp beneath heavy liner. Her leather jacket clung to her like history. Across the street, a man in a tailored suit thumbed through punk band tees, his polished shoes catching flecks of grit with every step.

Cassandra hesitated, then stepped closer to the woman. "I'm writing a piece for Vanguard Publishing. Would you mind answering a few questions?"

The woman arched a perfectly sculpted eyebrow, then shrugged. "Vanguard? Fancy. Go on."

They spoke for a few minutes, voices low beneath the churn of the market. Her answers were sharp, dry, and threaded with humour.

"It's about standing out, not showing off," she said, exhaling smoke in a slow ribbon. "London's contradictions are what make it interesting. You have to wear them, not fight them." Cassandra smiled, thanked her, and slipped back into the flow of the crowd.

The market pressed in, louder now. People and stories tumbled over one another like Autumn leaves caught in the wind. A boy with safety pins in his collar shouted over the music, his voice raw with something too old for his age. An older woman in velvet gloves bent to examine earrings made from old clock parts, her reflection flickering in the display glass. Every detail seemed to whisper with intention. Every face carried a history.

Eventually, drawn more by instinct than direction, Cassandra turned down a narrow side street tucked behind the main stalls. The sound fell away, as if the city had paused to let her pass. The air shifted, cooler here. Still.

She stopped in front of a shop with a deep green frame. The paint had cracked softly along the edges, like lines around an old eye. Gold letters gleamed above the door.

The Veiled Quill.

The sign was faded but elegant. A soft light glowed behind the window, casting long shadows across the threshold. Something in her chest stirred. A quiet shift, like memory rising before thought. She stepped inside.

The air changed. It was warm and still, laced with dust and the faint scent of paper and smoke. The space was dim, lit only by lamps and narrow windows that filtered the day into golden threads.

Books towered in every direction, some stacked haphazardly, others arranged with reverence. A few were marked with unfamiliar symbols. Most looked untouched for decades.

Cassandra walked slowly, trailing her fingers across the spines. The textures whispered beneath her touch. Worn leather. Cracked cloth. The occasional smooth gloss of something newer.

One book sat alone on a wooden stand near the back. Small and leather-bound, its cover was embossed with a swirling pattern that shimmered faintly when the light caught it. She reached for it. The weight surprised her. It felt solid. Intentional.

As she turned the pages, uneven and handwritten and filled with intricate symbols, a slip of parchment fluttered free and landed at her feet. She bent to pick it up. The edges were brittle. The ink, dark and slightly blurred.

The path to truth is always shadowed.

A quiet shiver passed through her. The air felt different again. Thicker. Still.

"An interesting choice," a voice said.

She turned.

A man stood behind the counter. She hadn't heard him arrive. Tall, composed, with a kind of stillness that seemed to shift the shape of the room. He wasn't old, but his presence felt older. His eyes were smoke-grey. Unreadable.

Cassandra didn't speak at first.

"I was just looking," she said finally. "I didn't mean to disturb anything."

He stepped forward. His movements made no sound. He wore a black waistcoat over a white shirt, the sleeves neatly rolled. A pendant hung at his throat, silver and unfamiliar, marked with a symbol she did not recognise.

"That one isn't for sale," he said.

Cassandra placed the book gently back on its stand, then turned and held up the parchment between her fingers.

"This slipped out while I was reading."

He didn't take it. His gaze rested on the words.

"The path to truth is always shadowed," he repeated, as if recalling something once known.

"What does it mean?" she asked.

He studied her. Not with curiosity. With recognition. "That depends on what you're willing to uncover."

She shifted her weight. The silence pressed close. The scent of old wood and ink folded around her like a held breath.

"Is this some kind of riddle?"

He almost smiled. "Most truths begin that way."

She looked down at the parchment again. The words pulsed softly, as if seen through water. Something stirred deep in her. Not fear. Not understanding. Just the ache of something hidden beginning to move.

"This feels like it was meant for me."

"Perhaps it was," he said. "The Veiled Quill doesn't draw just anyone."

A long silence settled between them. And within it, something flickered. Not memory. Not déjà vu. Just the quiet sense that she had been seen before she had fully arrived.

"Do people come here looking for answers?"

"Sometimes," he said. "But more often, they arrive because something has already begun. They are not seeking. They are remembering."

Before she could speak again, the bell above the door rang.

Two people stepped inside, their laughter sudden and bright against the stillness. The man's eyes shifted toward them.

Cassandra took it as her moment to leave.

She stepped out into the open air. Light struck her eyes, sharp and colourless after the dim interior. Her fingers closed around the parchment now tucked deep in her pocket.

Her heartbeat stayed steady, but her thoughts did not.

She moved with the rhythm of the market once more, but something had shifted. The scent of old pages still clung to her. So did the ache of recognition, quiet and persistent.

She did not look back.

The sky had begun to soften by the time Cassandra returned to Camden. Evening light filtered through the narrow streets, catching on windows, puddles, and the slick edges of stone. She walked more slowly now.

Her notebook held pages full of names, sketches, and half-formed thoughts. The parchment remained in her coat pocket, exactly where she had placed it after leaving the shop.

By the time she reached Miranda's building, the ache in her shoulders had settled in. The market's noise still rang faintly in her ears, like the echo of a song she couldn't quite forget. She climbed the stairs one step at a time, each footfall measured, deliberate.

Miranda was curled on the couch when Cassandra stepped through the door. She wore a loose jumper and held a half-empty mug of tea. The television flickered silently in the background. She looked up and smiled.

"I was starting to think you got swallowed by Camden," she said. "Or maybe wandered into a back alley and ended up in Prague."

Cassandra let out a quiet breath and closed the door behind her. "I nearly did."

She dropped her bag beside the armchair and kicked off her boots. Her body ached with the kind of fatigue that came not just from walking too far, but from thinking too much.

Miranda sat up a little straighter. "So? How did it go? Did you get what you needed?"

Cassandra nodded slowly. "More than I expected." She crossed the room and sank into the armchair. The warmth of the flat settled around her like a blanket.

"Camden is wild. But in a beautiful way. People were open. Generous. Their fashion choices are incredible. Strange and brave, and full of personality."

Miranda studied her for a moment. "But something else happened."

Cassandra hesitated. Then, slowly, she reached into her coat pocket and drew out the folded parchment. She held it out without unfolding it.

"I found a bookshop. Or maybe it found me. I have no idea how I ended up there. It was tucked between two vintage stores, down a side street I don't even remember turning onto."

Miranda's gaze dropped to the paper in her hand. "What was it called?"

"The Veiled Quill."

Something flickered across Miranda's face. A small shift. Too quick to name. It was gone before Cassandra could hold onto it.

"That place is still around?" Miranda asked. Her voice was casual, but not quite light.

"You know it?"

Miranda leaned back and cradled her mug. "I've been once. A long time ago. Most people don't notice it unless they're meant to."

Cassandra unfolded the parchment. The single line stood out, the ink darker than the rest.

The path to truth is always shadowed.

Miranda read it, then looked up. "That is very much the sort of thing you would find there."

"It felt personal," Cassandra said. "The man behind the counter... he said things that made it feel like I was supposed to be there. And the way he looked at me. It was like he already knew something I didn't."

"Did he give you anything else?"

Cassandra shook her head. "Just the words. And the feeling that it wasn't the end of something. It was the beginning."

Miranda's voice softened. "It usually is."

Cassandra leaned forward. "You've really been there? What was it like for you?"

Miranda didn't answer right away. She stood, crossed to the kitchen, and poured a second cup of tea without asking. When she returned, she handed it over with a quiet clink of ceramic, then sank back into the couch.

"It was different," she said. "But similar. The place is always the same, but never quite. And the man... I remember him, though I doubt he remembers me."

"You think it's the same man?"

"I think whoever is there is always who needs to be." Miranda looked down at her mug. "He told me something, too. Something that didn't make sense until much later."

"What was it?"

Miranda smiled, but it was a careful kind of smile. The kind that holds more than it reveals. "That's a story for another night."

Cassandra glanced at the parchment. Its edges were worn, and the ink looked as though it might never fade. The words rested in her palm as if they had been waiting there all along.

"I'm not sure what it means yet."

"You're not supposed to be," Miranda said. "Not yet."

They sat in silence for a while. The television flickered softly in the background. Outside, the city murmured beneath the gathering dark. Cassandra sipped her tea, but her thoughts remained with the bookshop.

She kept hearing the man's voice. Not the words, but the feeling of being known. The sense that none of it had been random. She didn't say it aloud. She barely admitted it to herself.

Instead, she folded the parchment and placed it gently on the coffee table. It rested there like something sacred.

Then Miranda stood, sudden and certain. "All right. Enough tea and cryptic life lessons. We're going out."

Cassandra blinked. "What?"

"You've seen Camden by day. Now it's time for the night version."

Miranda placed her mug on the table and vanished down the hallway. A wardrobe creaked open. Fabric rustled like breath. "There's a place I want to show you," she called.

"I'm not sure I'm up for more today," Cassandra called back, her voice barely audible over the music.

"You will be. Trust me. This is the kind of place that reveals who you really are."

Cassandra leaned back, her eyes drifting to the folded parchment. Her body ached, but something quieter had already begun to stir again.

Miranda reappeared, holding a dress aloft.

It was black, with sheer panels that shimmered in the lamplight.

The fabric moved in her hands like smoke. She turned it slightly. "This will do nicely."

Cassandra raised an eyebrow. "That sounds ominous."

Miranda gave a slow smile. "It is. In the best possible way."

Cassandra took the dress from her. It was lighter than it looked, cool against her skin. She held it up, studying the delicate cut, the way light passed through the sheer edges. It was elegant, but something in its shape felt like a question. "I'm not sure this is me."

"That's exactly why it works."

Cassandra glanced at the window. Her reflection hovered in the glass, shadowed and expectant. Without another word, she turned and walked to the bathroom. The door clicked shut behind her.

Inside, the air felt still. She changed slowly, each movement deliberate. When she turned to face the mirror, a different version of herself looked back.

The dress clung modestly but revealed just enough. The sheer panels at the arms and hem whispered of boldness. Her hair, still tousled from the day, softened her edges. Her eyes looked darker. More aware.

She placed one hand on the sink. Her breath moved in and out with care. "I can do this," she said.

When she stepped into the lounge, Miranda's face lit up.

"Now that," she said, "is something else."

Cassandra gave a soft, uncertain laugh. "You're sure I don't look ridiculous?"

"You look like someone who's ready for the night to offer her something real."

Cassandra zipped her boots. The heels gave her an extra inch. Just enough to feel grounded. Just enough to feel changed.

Miranda picked up her coat and her keys. "You ready?"

Cassandra glanced one last time at the coffee table. The parchment lay folded where she had left it, undisturbed. Waiting.

She did not reach for it.

She just looked.

Her instinct was to say no. To stay in the warmth of the flat. But something in her had already begun to say yes.

Then she nodded. "Sure, let's go."

2
THE DOOR BETWEEN

The cab ride through Camden was brief, but it felt suspended in time. Rain streaked the windows, turning the city outside into a blur of lights and shadows. The driver said little. Miranda gave the address with practised ease, her tone confident, her posture relaxed.

Cassandra sat beside her, hands folded in her lap, eyes fixed on the passing world. Her thoughts swam in slow motion, as if submerged beneath something vast. The dress clung with intent, not constricting, but present in a way that made her feel seen. She felt different in it. Not hidden. Not disguised. Revealed.

They turned off the main road and down a narrow lane. The buildings leaned in closer. Streetlights flickered with a tired buzz. Puddles gathered in uneven patches along the cobblestones, catching the golden glow and breaking it into pieces.

The cab pulled to a stop at the mouth of a narrow alley, its brick walls dark with rain. Miranda leaned forward and handed over the fare.

Cassandra stepped into the damp air. Her boots met slick stone with a muted sound. The scent of wet stone and something faintly metallic filled her lungs.

Ahead, a heavy wooden door waited beneath a wrought-iron sign. The letters above it curled like whispered spells, each one elegant and strange. *The Hollow.*

No music spilled out. No voices. Only a vibration lingered in the walls, as if the building itself were listening.

Cassandra stepped closer. Her eyes followed the carvings etched into the door, all twisting vines and claw-like marks that seemed too deep to be decorative. Above them, the lantern flickered once, then steadied.

"It doesn't exactly scream welcome," she murmured.

Miranda stepped beside her, calm as ever. "It's not meant to. But it's always waiting for the right people."

Cassandra glanced at her. "Are we the right people?"

Miranda's gaze stayed fixed on the door. "We're here, aren't we?"

Cassandra exhaled, slow and quiet.

The rain had softened to a mist. Somewhere in the distance, a train passed, its sound more felt than heard. Behind them, the alley was hushed, as if the world itself had paused.

Miranda reached for the handle.

"Ready?" she asked, her voice even.

Cassandra gave a small nod. "As I'll ever be."

The door opened with a deep creak, and warm air swept out to meet them, rich and layered with something ancient. They stepped inside.

The pressure shifted.

When the door closed behind them, the world re-formed in silence.

Inside, the warmth deepened. The air was dense with scent and sound, thick enough to feel. Fine trails of incense curled from iron bowls suspended overhead, their tendrils weaving between candlelight. The flames moved like breath, casting shadows that swayed along the stone.

Cassandra paused just inside the threshold, letting her eyes adjust. The lighting was low, but not dark. It pulsed softly, drawn from sources that seemed to glow rather than shine.

The walls were stone, not bare but etched. Symbols had been carved directly into them, curling lines that looped and folded through one another in layered patterns. Some had been filled with paint. Others looked burned in.

The room opened out in unexpected directions. What first appeared to be a single chamber revealed itself to be many: a series of alcoves, arches, and half-rooms that broke apart the crowd without separating it. Every corner offered something different.

A bar stood along one wall, lit from beneath by flickering crimson. At a nearby table, someone sketched with black ink on torn pages. Across the room, a woman in long silver earrings moved her hands through the air in time with music only she could hear.

A ripple passed through Cassandra. Not fear. Not unease. Just awareness, the sense of stepping into a place where something was being lived, not performed. The energy here was not meant to be seen. It was unfolding in real time.

Miranda touched her arm lightly and leaned close. "Come on. Let's find somewhere to sit."

They moved along the edge of the room. People passed them in slow, deliberate patterns. No one rushed. No one looked lost. It was as though everyone already knew their place.

They settled into a small alcove near the back. The seating was velvet, worn smooth with time. A low table sat in the centre, scarred with candle wax and faint burn marks that told stories without words.

A server appeared without a sound, dressed entirely in black. Miranda ordered two glasses of red wine without glancing at a menu. The server vanished just as quietly.

Cassandra rested her hands in her lap, watching. Across the room, a violinist played near the hearth. The sound was raw and haunting, each note pulling through the space like a thread. It was not a performance. It was a conversation with the silence between the sounds.

She leaned in. "You've been here before?"

Miranda nodded slowly. "A few times."

"What is this place?"

Miranda paused. "It's a space between. Between the surface and what lies beneath it."

Cassandra looked around again. The people were beautiful in their strangeness. Lace and leather. Velvet and bare skin. No one dressed the same, yet everything belonged. Every gesture felt chosen. Every presence, deliberate.

The server returned, setting two glasses on the table. Cassandra took hers with both hands. The wine was warm and dark. It tasted like mulled secrets.

"This is surreal," she said softly.

Miranda smiled. "It's not surreal. It's just hidden. Most people don't know how to see it."

A woman passed their table, her gown made of layered sheer fabric that rippled with light, as if woven from shadow and flame. Her hair was pinned with dark feathers. As she walked by, she met Cassandra's eyes. Just for a moment. Then she continued. Something in the glance lingered. Not curiosity. Not challenge. Just recognition.

Cassandra felt the shape of her own breath in her chest. Her fingertips brushed the rim of her glass. The room asked nothing of her. It simply waited.

Miranda lifted her drink. "You'll get used to it. Or maybe you won't. That's not really the point."

"What is the point?"

"To feel something."

Cassandra leaned back into the velvet. The fabric was cool against the dress. Flickering light traced her arms. The violin sang a slow lament, weaving through the room like something ancient returning home.

Her thoughts moved gently through the dim glow, brushing against fragments of the day: the soft light of morning, the scent of the market, Miranda's knowing smile. All of it flowed through her like a current beneath still water.

She closed her eyes and let it press in. The warmth. The music. The weight of unspoken things.

For the first time since arriving in London, something within her began to loosen.

And she did not resist it.

Time passed without markers. There were no clocks in The Hollow. No announcements. No sense of what the hour demanded. The room tilted instead. Music faded, then returned in new forms. Faces appeared and vanished without goodbye. The crowd breathed as one, folding and unfolding itself with a patient rhythm.

Cassandra spoke little. She let Miranda guide the conversation, drifting through topics without urgency. They shared glances and small, knowing laughter. Around them, people moved with intention, weaving through candlelight and shadow as if they belonged to both.

She drank the rest of her wine slowly, letting the warmth settle deep.

Her skin hummed with the closeness of the room, the scent of wax and spice, the flickering light that softened everything, even thought.

Miranda leaned close, her voice a hush. "There's more to this place than you see at first. It knows when to wait."

Cassandra nodded once, asking nothing. The truth of it was already taking root, quiet and steady. A knowing, not yet spoken but fully felt.

Later, when they stepped outside, the air touched her like a memory. Cool and damp, it clung to her skin as if trying to pull her back into itself. Mist hovered low across the alley, unmoving, like breath held in the quiet before morning. The streets stretched out empty ahead of them, slick with rain light. Night no longer felt new. It felt ancient.

They walked slowly, neither rushing nor wandering. Miranda said little now. The silence between them was whole, filled with everything they had seen and everything they had chosen not to name.

Back at the flat, Cassandra peeled off her boots by the door and slipped out of the dress with reverence, laying it across the back of a chair as if it might remember something. She moved through the space without turning on the overhead lights. Her hands were quiet. Her steps made no sound.

In the bathroom mirror, she studied her reflection. The woman staring back looked almost unchanged, but something behind the eyes had shifted. Not in expression. In depth. In alignment.

She washed her face, each motion measured, then brushed her hair slowly, as if combing through hours instead of strands. When she stepped into the bedroom, the silence welcomed her.

The parchment lay on the bedside table. She had carried it in without thinking, tucked between her fingers like a thread. Her hand brushed it gently as she passed. She did not open it. She didn't need to. The words were already moving inside her.

She pulled the blanket up to her chin and settled into stillness. The glow of her phone rested on the nightstand, black-screened and untouched. Behind her eyelids, the flicker of candlelight still danced. Velvet pressed against the backs of her thoughts. Music coiled softly around her spine, not a song, but something closer to a vow.

Sleep waited. It did not rush her. It hovered at the edge, watchful and old. And when it came, it brought no answers. Only a pull. Slow. Certain. Ancient. A drifting down through shadow and silk and sound. She was no longer in the room.

There was no sense of waking or falling. Only a quiet shift, like a breath turning over in the dark. The world around her had changed without movement. She stood in a place without edges, where light had not yet decided to exist, and sound had not been invited to speak.

Mist curled around her ankles, denser than fog, softer than cloth. It pressed in gently, not suffocating, but present, like breath against bare skin. The ground beneath her felt cool, but not cold. Smooth, but not stone. She could not guess its texture, only the certainty that it held her without weight.

Cassandra turned her head, though she no longer knew what direction meant here. Everything was still, but not empty. Something stirred at the edges. A rhythm beneath silence. The low thrum of an unseen tide.

She reached out. Her fingers moved slowly, expecting resistance, a thickening of the air, or some invisible boundary. But the mist gave way, gentle and warm, as if it had always been waiting to be touched.

Then, from somewhere ahead, a sound emerged.

Not music exactly, but its echo. A tone that shimmered at the edge of hearing, threaded with something like longing. It held no melody, yet it shaped the air around her. The mist responded, shifting in waves, drawn forward in spirals like smoke following breath.

A figure appeared.

It did not walk forward. It simply became visible, like a shape surfacing from deep water. Tall. Still. Cloaked in a presence that unsettled without threatening. She could not see its face. Its outline was clear, but never complete. The darkness of its form did not absorb the light. It existed without needing it.

Cassandra's heart beat once, then again. Slower. As if her body were listening to something her mind had not yet remembered.

It raised its hand.

The movement was fluid and deliberate. Not a greeting. Not a command. An invitation. As though it asked her not to approach, but to remember.

She stepped forward.

The air thickened. Each breath carried scents she could not place, rain falling on ancient stone, ash from a long-cooled fire, the inside of a book never opened. Her fingers tingled. Her spine lengthened. Something moved within her, not from fear, but from a knowing that ran deeper than memory.

Candles flickered into existence in a circle at the figure's feet. Their flames rose together, as if exhaling after a long-held breath. The light did not reach far, but it touched her in places her hands could not.

Symbols had been etched into the floor within the ring. They pulsed faintly in the glow. Some curved like vines. Others were angular, sharp and precise, like bone or blade. She could not read them, but they felt familiar, like a forgotten alphabet once whispered in dreams.

She did not speak.

The figure lowered its hand and stepped aside. Behind it, the mist grew denser. Then, with slow precision, it parted to reveal a door.

The door did not rise or swing into place. It simply was. Solid and still. Carved from dark wood that glimmered faintly, its surface marked with the same shifting symbols that circled the floor. There was no handle. No hinges. Only a soft pulse of light at its centre, steady and alive, like breath beneath skin.

Cassandra drew closer. The mist behind her stirred again. It did not warn her. It reminded her. She did not need to turn to understand. If she walked away, the moment would dissolve. But if she stepped forward, something within her would shift. Something long buried would begin to return.

She raised her hand. When her fingers touched the centre of the door, warmth bloomed.

It was not heat. It was recognition, a pulse of knowing that moved through her palm and into her chest, curling upward along her spine. It was like remembering a touch she had never known.

Her breath caught.

The carved symbols brightened. Light stirred across the surface of the wood, slow and steady, as if responding to her presence.

Then, with a silence that felt sacred, the door began to open. The light did not pour through. It unfurled.

Soft. Alive. Endless.

It was not the light of day, or of flame, or of any lamp. It was the light of memory, the kind that waits beneath the skin and rises only when called.

It moved like water over her form, brushing the edges of her being without claiming them. It revealed, but did not expose.

On the other side, there was no room. No corridor. No sky. Only space.

It stretched wide and unending, yet it was not empty. The space pulsed softly, rhythmically, like breath. If there were walls, they did not behave like any she had known. They shimmered with the same impossible script she had seen before.

Symbols drifted in and out of view, rising and falling like tide, alive with intent. The space itself seemed to breathe in time with her.

A sound stirred within the quiet. Low at first. Steady. Distant. It was not a voice, but something near to it. Not spoken, yet rich with meaning. She could not translate the words, but she knew they belonged to her.

She stepped forward, drawn deeper into the light.

The figure did not follow. It remained at the threshold, a presence without form, its edges dissolved into air. Though it made no move, she knew it was still watching. Not as a guardian. Not as a guide. But as witness.

She walked until her body no longer felt like her own. The weight of it slipped away, leaving only sensation. Only thought. Only awareness.

Then the light swung. Something moved at the centre of it, quiet and slow.

A kitchen table appeared. The old one from home. The wood was worn smooth at the corners where Ethan used to tap his rings without realising. A half-empty coffee cup. A bowl of mandarins. Light spilling through the window in quiet golden slants, striping the floorboards with warmth.

She could hear the soft clink of a spoon inside the mug. Smell the toast. See his shoes waiting by the door.

The longing struck without warning. It opened inside her, sudden and full. Her breath stilled. Her fingers twitched toward the image, aching to reach across the space and touch something solid. Something known. Something safe.

But there was nothing to hold. It was more than memory. It was the silent pull of something real. Something loved. Something just out of reach.

The image began to fade. She opened her mouth to call it back, but no sound came. Slowly at first, then all at once, the table, the window, and the light dissolved.

Only the glow remained. Not harsh. Not cold. But final.

And then she woke.

Her eyes opened slowly, adjusting to the light. The ceiling above her was pale with morning, a soft glow easing the edges of the room. She did not move. The stillness of the dream lingered, like breath held in the chest. Heavy, but not unpleasant.

Cassandra lay there a while, the blankets warm against her skin. Her body felt distant. Her thoughts, further still. The ache had not faded. It curled beneath her ribs, gentle but insistent, like a name she had not spoken aloud in too long.

When she finally sat up, the room met her with silence.

Her phone rested on the nightstand. One new message. She picked it up, already knowing who it would be.

Good morning, Cass. Your messages about London sound wild. Everyone misses you, and so do I.

She let the words settle. They should have made her smile. Maybe they did. But the warmth they stirred did not lift the weight the dream had left behind.

Her fingers hovered over the screen.

Morning. I miss you, too. London's been… something else. I'll tell you more soon.

She hit send. Then turned the phone over and placed it face down.

The dream pressed in again, whole and vivid. The light. The figure. The glimpse of Ethan, so real it ached.

She rose slowly, wrapped herself in the cardigan draped over the chair, and padded barefoot into the kitchen.

Miranda stood at the stove, barefoot in leggings and a faded jumper, stirring something in a small pan. She didn't look up.

"You okay?" she asked softly.

Cassandra leaned against the counter. "I don't know."

Miranda turned, her gaze steady but kind. "You look like someone who saw something they can't unsee."

"I think I did."

Miranda slid the pan off the heat and poured the oats into two bowls. She passed one to Cassandra, then nodded toward the table.

They sat in silence for a few spoonfuls. Outside, the city moved quietly behind the glass.

"I had a dream," Cassandra said at last. "One of those dreams that doesn't feel like one. The kind that stays with you."

"There was light," she continued. "And a door. It felt like it led somewhere

I wasn't meant to reach just yet. But I stepped through anyway."

Miranda stilled. Her fingers rested loosely around her mug, but she didn't lift it.

"Sometimes that's what changes everything," she said softly. "Not the place we go, but the moment we decide to cross."

Cassandra didn't answer right away. The kitchen felt smaller than it had a moment ago. Not closed in, but closer. More real.

"It wasn't what I expected," she said. "On the other side… it wasn't strange. It wasn't even unfamiliar. It was home."

Miranda's eyes met hers, calm and quiet.

"My kitchen," Cassandra added, her voice lower now. "Back in Melbourne. Ethan's coffee cup was still on the table. The light through the window. The bowl of mandarins. I could hear the spoon clink. I could smell the toast. His shoes were by the door, just like always."

"And how did it feel?" Miranda asked.

"Like being given something, just to remember what it was like to lose it." The words hovered between them. Cassandra swallowed hard. "Like memory wrapped in grief."

Miranda didn't speak for a long moment. Then she reached across the table and rested her hand lightly on Cassandra's. "Sometimes our dreams give us what we can't say out loud," she said. "Not to haunt us. Just to remind us of what shaped us."

Cassandra looked down at their hands. Miranda's was warm. Steady. Honest. "I don't want to forget him," she whispered.

"You don't have to." Miranda hesitated. When she spoke again, her voice was quiet. "Do you still love him?"

Cassandra's eyes flickered. "I think so," she sighed. "But it's like remembering a song you used to hum without thinking. The words are still there. The melody too. But the sound of it feels far away."

Miranda's gaze didn't waver.

"I miss who we were," Cassandra added. "But I don't know if I miss who I was with him. That version of me… she felt smaller. Softer. And in the dream, standing there in that kitchen, I knew I couldn't stay."

Miranda nodded once. "Then let her rest."

Cassandra looked up. Her eyes were glassy but calm. "That door didn't just lead away from home. It led away from who I thought I was."

"And maybe toward who you're becoming."

They sat like that for a while, hands touching across the table, the morning light creeping higher across the windowpane. Outside, London stirred. But inside, something deeper had begun to move.

When the kettle whistled, Miranda rose and walked quietly to the stove. Cassandra stayed at the table, tracing the rim of her bowl with her fingertip.

"I think I need to go back," she said softly.

Miranda paused. "To the dream?"

Cassandra looked up. "To Camden. To the market. The Hollow. Whatever this is. I need to be in it."

Miranda poured the water slowly. The scent of mint and chamomile curled into the air.

"Then that's what we'll do."

She passed Cassandra a mug and leaned against the bench. They didn't speak for a while. The tea cooled between their palms.

Outside, the clouds had begun to thin, and the pale light slipping through the window had softened.

Cassandra changed slowly. A charcoal knit dress. Her boots. A coat that still carried the scent of lavender from Miranda's cupboard. She tied her hair back loosely, then paused at the window for a breath. The sky outside was clearing. The city stirred beneath it with its usual rhythm.

Miranda waited by the door, scarf in hand, already humming something low and familiar. When Cassandra stepped out, Miranda gave her a quick once-over and grinned.

"You look like someone about to fall in love with a street poet."

Cassandra rolled her eyes. "You say that like it hasn't already happened."

They laughed, the sound easy and unforced.

No one rushed them. Camden opened slowly, street by street, like a story told in glimpses. The air held the scent of rain and warm bread. A saxophonist lingered near the tube station, his notes soft and slow, curling into the edges of the street.

They wandered past rows of market stalls, the path marked in velvet, smoke, and metal glinting in the light. Cloth shimmered beneath their hands. A table of leather-bound journals drew Cassandra in. Another offered incense, rich with the scent of places she had never been yet imagined enough to believe she had.

Miranda tugged her toward a rack of scarves, each one dyed in deep, moody tones. She ran her fingers along them thoughtfully, but instead of choosing one, she unwound the scarf from her own neck. It was deep red, the colour of old wine, soft from wear.

She looped it gently around Cassandra's neck without asking.

"That's it," she said, stepping back. "You're an art critic who once ran away with a sculptor and still writes him letters."

Cassandra blinked. "You're just giving it to me?"

Miranda shrugged. "I'll steal it back if you don't wear it well," she replied with a wink.

Cassandra grinned. "Too late. I've already named it. She's mine now."

They kept walking. A dog trotted past them in a tartan coat, its paws clicking against the damp pavement. A vendor near the kerb called out about hand-poured soy candles and healing crystals, his voice edged with theatrics and incense smoke.

The air around the stall was thick with scent. Lavender. Patchouli. Burnt vanilla. It tangled with the sharper smells of frying oil and cold metal from a nearby food cart.

Miranda stopped and picked up a candle labelled *Forest Moon*. She lifted it to her nose and inhaled deeply, her eyes narrowing in contemplation.

"This one smells like secrets," she said.

She tested another. "And this one is pure witchy heartbreak."

Cassandra leaned against the edge of the stall and watched her with quiet affection. Her arms were crossed. Her chin tucked into her scarf. The wind carried bursts of music from somewhere deeper in the market.

An acoustic guitar. Off-tempo clapping. Someone laughing too loud.

A stall nearby spilled over with second-hand coats, the kind with satin linings and broken buttons. Their collars hung heavy with memory.

A child ran past, trailing a balloon shaped like a fox. The scent of cinnamon sugar floated from a churro stand two stalls down. It clashed sweetly with the tang of roasted chestnuts drifting from a vendor further up the path.

Cassandra's senses buzzed. It was too much and not enough. A blur of textures and colours and sound, all stitched together with the strange rhythm of London itself. She didn't want to leave, yet part of her still hovered on the edge, unsure if she was meant to stay.

It had been a long time since she had felt this. A kind of safety that was not stillness. A kind of joy that did not ask her to shrink.

They turned a corner and passed a narrow record store with no sign, only a gold treble clef etched into the glass. From inside, music drifted. Not loud. Not attention-seeking. Just present.

A voice she did not recognise, soulful and deep, floated through the air. It moved through her before she had time to brace.

She stopped.

Miranda turned to her. "You okay?"

"I remember this song," Cassandra said, her voice quiet, unsure. "We were kids. On the floor in the old loungeroom. That night we stayed up late, and Mum put a record on."

Miranda's brow furrowed, then softened. "The one she called a soul cry?"

Cassandra nodded. "She left the room. Just let it play. We didn't say a word. Not then, not after. It wasn't this version, but it was this song."

They didn't go into the store. The music followed them down the lane anyway.

They lingered beneath an awning while a brief spell of rain passed, the kind that looked soft but soaked everything in minutes. From there, they watched the market breathe.

A boy with gold hoops in both ears spun fire sticks without flame. At the edge of a stall, a woman turned slowly, her long coat trailing behind her. The bells at her hem chimed with a sound that felt more ritual than performance. Someone sold beetroot brownies and told fortunes with a brass pendulum.

Cassandra stood close to Miranda beneath the shelter, the mist curling around them like a living thing.

When the rain eased, they moved again. They ducked behind the cheese vendor and into a narrow lane barely wide enough for two. The air changed, quieter now, the hum of the market fading behind them.

"Look at these," Miranda said, pointing.

A small stand had been tucked into the bend of the lane. A man sat behind it sketching in charcoal, surrounded by black books and narrow portraits. He worked in silence, his coat damp from the air, a single curl falling over his brow as he shaded in the curve of a doorway.

His drawings were all of entrances. Not faces. Not landscapes. Just doors.

Some were plain and wooden, sketched with blunt strokes and smudges of charcoal. Others arched like cathedrals, carved with intricate symbols that made Cassandra's breath still in her chest. One of them stood out immediately.

It looked exactly like the one from her dream.

She froze. Every sound around her dulled to a low murmur. The stall, the voices, the music. All of it faded into a kind of held breath.

Miranda followed her gaze and stepped closer. "What is it?"

Cassandra moved half a step forward. "That door," she said quietly. "It looks like the one from my dream. The one with the symbols and the light at the centre."

Miranda blinked, then looked again at the drawing. "Are you sure?"

"I could draw it myself," Cassandra murmured. "But I don't need to. That's it."

The artist did not look up. His hand moved steadily across a fresh page, pencil gliding in practiced strokes.

Cassandra inched closer. She didn't reach out, but something in the sketch reached for her. Not visibly. Not with movement. But with a quiet insistence that tugged at her chest the way gravity draws a tide.

"Do you sell them?" she asked, her voice barely louder than the wind.

The man gave a small nod.

Miranda glanced between them, eyes narrowing slightly. "How much for that one?" she asked, pointing toward the door.

The artist paused. His eyes lifted, but not to Miranda. He looked only at Cassandra.

"That one's already claimed," he said. Each word landed with slow certainty.

Cassandra's mouth went dry. Her stomach turned as if she had been told something important in a language she could not yet understand.

She stepped back slowly. The noise of the market returned in waves. A guitar strummed behind her. A dog barked. The scent of fried dough drifted past on the breeze.

Still, the sketch held her. Its lines. Its weight. The door. It lingered like the afterimage of a flame, burned softly behind her eyelids.

She turned away, each step carrying her further from a presence older than words. And still, it followed. A shape. A knowing. A thread pulled taut just beneath the surface.

Miranda didn't press. She only glanced sideways, her expression unreadable, and walked with her in silence.

They passed a vintage stall full of clocks. Some ticked. Others were silent. One had a cracked face and hands that spun backward.

"It's giving haunted attic vibes," Miranda muttered, leaning in for a better look.

Cassandra glanced down at the tray near the register. Most of the rings were rusted or oversized, dulled by time and touched by too many hands. But one stood out. A simple silver band, smooth and unadorned, with a small hollow circle carved into its centre. No stone. No shine. Just space.

She slid it onto her finger. It settled as if it had always belonged.

Miranda tilted her head slightly. "That suits you," she said.

Cassandra turned her hand in the light, watching the metal catch and hold the soft gleam from a nearby lantern. It did not glitter. It did not demand. But it felt certain.

She reached into her coat pocket and pulled out a few folded notes, placing them quietly on the counter. She did not speak. The gesture felt final, as if words might undo it.

No one moved to collect the money, and no one needed to. The exchange was already complete.

She looked down again at the ring. Still and unobtrusive, it grounded her. A small answer to a question she had not yet learned how to ask.

Miranda said nothing, but the curve of her mouth held a quiet satisfaction, the kind that came from witnessing something unfold exactly as it was meant to.

Cassandra left the market with the ring still on her hand, the metal cool against her skin, as though it belonged there and always had.

They wandered until they found a café tucked between a florist and a tattoo parlour. The window was fogged with warmth from within. On the glass, soft curling script read simply: *Homeground*.

They stepped into the smell of roasted coffee, cardamom, and something sugary just out of the oven. The space was small but full of light. Wicker lampshades hung from the ceiling. Books were stacked along the back wall. A black cat dozed on a windowsill like it belonged to no one and everyone.

They settled into a corner booth near the window, where condensation blurred the world outside into shifting shapes and softened edges. Miranda shrugged off her coat and draped it beside her, the fabric still damp and carrying the faint, earthy scent of the afternoon.

Cassandra curled her hands around the mug the barista had just placed in front of her. The warmth from the ceramic grounded her with quiet insistence.

Without ceremony, Miranda tore into a raspberry pastry, flaking sugar across the table with every bite. "Remind me why anyone ever leaves Camden," she said through a mouthful of pastry, her voice warm and easy.

Cassandra lifted her cup. The aroma rose with gentle comfort. "Because some of us are still getting used to the idea of being here at all."

Miranda grinned and reached for a napkin. "Give it a week. You'll be hexing landlords and naming your plants after dead poets like the rest of us."

Cassandra laughed softly, her body loosening from the weight of the day. "Maybe I'll just start with the plants."

"That's how it begins," Miranda said, licking sugar from her thumb with a knowing look that carried more truth than teasing.

Cassandra took a sip of her drink and felt the warmth settle deep in her chest. "I keep thinking it's all going to wear off. That I'll wake up one morning and the Hollow, the dream, the book, everything, will feel distant. Like something imagined after too much wine and not enough sleep."

"But it doesn't," Miranda said, her tone shifting with the weight of recognition.

Cassandra shook her head. "No. It feels closer. Like it's following me home."

Miranda wiped her hands and leaned forward, her gaze steady. "It's not just your mind catching up. Something is moving, Cass. Something in you."

Cassandra looked down at the swirling milk in her mug. The spiral held its shape for a moment, then slowly faded into stillness. "I think I saw something," she murmured. "Something I didn't know belonged to me."

"The door?"

Cassandra nodded. "I think I've been standing in front of it my whole life. I just didn't recognise it until now."

Miranda reached across the table and placed her hand over Cassandra's, steady and warm. The gesture held no urgency. Only presence.

"You don't have to open it today."

Cassandra's throat tightened. Her voice caught before finding shape. "But it's already started, hasn't it? I've already stepped toward it."

Miranda held her gaze. "And I'm still here."

They sat in quiet understanding as the café pulsed gently around them. A man near the counter laughed into his phone. The barista dimmed the lights and wiped down the machine. The cat stretched across a low shelf, yawned, and blinked into the half-light as if the world moved at its own quiet rhythm.

"I'm not ready," Cassandra whispered, her fingers tightening slightly around the mug.

"You don't have to be," Miranda said, her voice sure and steady.

A smile found Cassandra's lips. Small, but real. "You always know what to say."

Miranda leaned back and reached for the last bite of pastry. "That's because

I've already said all the wrong things."

They laughed together, and this time it wasn't weighted with doubt. It was light. Shared. Real.

When they stepped outside, the light had altered. The market was folding in on itself. Tables covered. Stalls packed. The last of the music trailing off.

They didn't speak much on the walk home, but it wasn't silence born of distance. Miranda's scarf still rested around Cassandra's neck, soft and faded, carrying something unspoken between them.

Miranda reached out and touched the edge of the fabric where it fell against Cassandra's collarbone. Her fingers were light but lingering. Not to adjust it. Just to feel it there on someone else for the first time.

"I used to wear this the first year I went to the Hollow," she said softly. "Before I understood what it meant."

Cassandra nodded. "Thank you."

Miranda smiled, the quiet kind of smile that comes from having once stood in the same place.

By the time they reached the flat, the windows were fogged and the hallway smelled faintly of cinnamon and sleep. Miranda unlocked the door. She kicked off her boots with a sigh.

"That scarf suits you," she said, unwrapping her own and tossing it over the back of a chair. "Like it was always yours."

Cassandra smiled faintly and loosened the scarf around her neck. She folded it with care and laid it on the edge of her bed before stepping softly into the living room.

The light in the flat had grown dim. Without switching on the overheads, she lit one of the small candles from the windowsill. Its glow brushed the walls, catching the edges of her notebooks and the corner of a framed photograph from Melbourne she had not yet found a place for.

Miranda disappeared down the hallway without a word, her bare feet silent against the floorboards. A door clicked shut.

Cassandra stood for a moment near the couch, her hand resting lightly on the back of it. The dream still lived somewhere inside her, just beneath the ribs, like a breath not fully released.

She opened her notebook. Not to write a story. Not even about the dream. She wrote a question.

What part of me has always known?

She left the page open. Then gently closed the book and returned it to the shelf.

Outside, the wind picked up, brushing against the glass. The candle's flame swayed once and held.

Cassandra curled into the corner of the couch, pulled a blanket over her legs, and rested her head against the cushion.

She did not feel finished.

But she felt awake.

And somewhere beyond the candle's glow, beyond the softened hush of the room, the city waited.

3
SOMETHING IN ME WATCHED

The flat was quiet, but not silent. When Cassandra sat up, the blanket slipped into her lap. Her shoulders ached. Her hair was tangled at the nape of her neck.

The light had changed. It no longer poured in like it had the day before. Now it moved softly across the curtains in pale grey ribbons, cool and uncertain, as though the morning was not yet ready to begin.

She rose slowly and padded toward the kitchen, pulled more by instinct than thought. The scent of steeping tea lingered in the air, mingled with the faint whistle of the kettle as it clicked into stillness.

Miranda stood at the counter, barefoot in an oversized jumper, her hair swept into a loose knot. The room seemed to fold around her, quiet and complete.

She turned and met Cassandra's eyes with a small nod, then went back to pouring water into two mismatched mugs.

"Did you get any sleep?" Cassandra asked. Her voice felt rough, touched by the weight of the night.

Miranda stirred a spoon through one of the mugs. The sound was soft, measured. "A little," she said. "You?"

"Not really. Just… fragments."

Miranda slid one of the mugs across the counter. Cassandra caught it before it could slide too far, then wrapped both hands around the warmth. She stood still, letting the steam rise and meet her face. It softened the tightness in her cheeks.

They lingered in the hush together, the kind of quiet that didn't ask anything from either of them. Outside, the rain had started again. It tapped gently at the windows, a steady rhythm that sounded like memory.

The kettle had gone still. The flat seemed to settle with it, each corner folding back into place as if the space were breathing again.

"I need to head out for a while," Miranda said eventually. Her voice held a soft certainty, the kind that didn't require explanation.

Cassandra looked up from her tea. "Where are you going?"

Miranda placed her mug down and watched the surface settle. "Just a shift at the gallery. There's a new installation coming in. I said I'd help with the setup."

For a moment, the words didn't register. Cassandra blinked. She had almost forgotten that Miranda had a life beyond these walls. Outside this strange, warm cocoon they had been inhabiting together.

"Oh," she said quietly. "I didn't realise you still worked there."

Miranda gave a small shrug. "Only a few days a week. It keeps me tethered." She reached for the sleeve of her jumper and smoothed it down her arm.

The movement was quiet, almost absent. But it caught Cassandra's attention. There was something in the gesture that felt instinctive, almost ritual.

Cassandra hesitated. "Do you want me to come with you?"

Miranda smiled. Not evasive. Not quite inviting. Just steady. "No. I think you need some time to yourself."

Cassandra nodded, though she wasn't sure she agreed. Alone no longer felt like something she knew how to be.

Miranda rinsed her mug and reached for her coat and bag. Cassandra watched from the doorway, hands curled loosely around her own. There had always been something quietly otherworldly about Miranda. In the way she moved. In the way she knew things without asking. But in this moment, she seemed different.

Not distant. Not mysterious. Just grounded.

Separate.

As though she belonged to a world that had nothing to do with Cassandra at all.

"Try to work on your piece," Miranda said as she wrapped her scarf once around her neck. Her voice was gentle, but there was something behind it. "It might help."

Then she left, and the door clicked shut behind her with a soft finality.

Cassandra stood in the kitchen a while longer, listening to the stillness that followed. The sound of Miranda's departure faded quickly, leaving behind something thinner. Not quite silence, but absence.

The flat felt changed. Not darker. Not colder. Just… altered.

She walked back through the hallway, her steps quiet against the worn floorboards. In the bedroom, the laptop waited on the desk. Its screen glowed faintly in the dim light, the cursor blinking in a slow, steady rhythm like a breath held too long.

She sat down. Her legs folded under the chair. The warmth from the tea had already begun to fade.

The working title hovered at the top of the blank page.

Layered Lives: Camden's Winter Fashion on the Streets

Lydia had loved the concept. Cassandra could still hear her voice, half-text, half-command. *Fresh eyes. Authentic voice. Make it yours.*

She stared at the screen for a while, then placed her fingers gently on the keys. A sentence came. Then another.

Camden does not follow fashion.

It folds it. Stitches it. Leaves the seams exposed.

She paused. The second line lingered awkwardly, too clever, too written.

She deleted it. The blinking cursor returned.

Her phone vibrated softly on the edge of the desk.

Lydia.

Hi Cass. Just a gentle nudge. Is there any chance I could see your first draft this week? Love the energy you are capturing in your notes. Let me know if you need anything.

Cassandra read the message once. Then again.

She tapped out a reply, her thumbs moving slowly over the screen.

Hey Lydia, yes, I'm working on it today. Just trying to find the right angle.

Cassandra set the phone aside and turned back to the laptop, but her focus had already slipped. Her fingers hovered above the keys, unmoving. After a long moment, she closed the lid without a sound.

The flat had grown quieter again. Not silent, but thick with the kind of stillness that wrapped around the edges of thought.

In the kitchen, she made another cup of tea, more from habit than desire. The kettle hissed and clicked, the steam curling upward like breath.

Mug in hand, she drifted back to the living room, but the tea sat untouched beside her on the windowsill.

A book lay on the arm of the couch. She picked it up and turned a few pages slowly. Nothing held. Nothing stayed. The words passed through her like water.

The cover closed with a quiet press of her hand. She set it down with precision, the motion giving her something to complete.

Her movements began to take on their own rhythm. A slow loop through the flat. From the window to the hallway and back again. The day passed in quiet stretches that had no edges.

Time went unchecked. No words were spoken.

The scarf Miranda had given her now hung by the door. Its colour caught the light in deep, shifting tones. Red, almost black. It seemed darker than she remembered, though she knew that could not be true.

Only silk. A gift. Soft and simple.

And yet it felt heavier now, as if it had absorbed something unseen. Something that lingered in the air without form.

Back in the kitchen, the kettle stood cool. The mugs had been rinsed and stacked neatly. A spoon rested beside the sink, a faint water ring beneath it like a quiet echo.

The flat did not feel empty.

It felt paused.

Cassandra leaned against the counter and looked out at the street below.

The city moved with a quiet rhythm. Umbrellas bloomed and folded in careful repetition. Car tyres whispered against the wet pavement. From somewhere beyond the rooftops, a child's laugh rang out, light and sudden, before vanishing. A siren drifted past in the distance. Its wail rose, softened, and faded into nothing.

Deeper in the building, a door opened and closed. The sound was muffled, but it moved through her like the breath of something waking.

She remained at the counter, unmoving. Thoughtless. Her fingers curled gently around the edge of the bench, palms resting flat against the cool surface.

Then, softly, the sound of a key turned in the lock.

The door eased open, and Miranda stepped inside, brushing droplets of rain from her sleeves. Her cheeks were pink with cold, her breath still caught the edge of the air.

Cassandra remained where she was, hands resting on the counter. "How was your day?" she asked softly.

Miranda shrugged as she slipped off her coat. "Strange," she said. "One of the new sculptures had already been installed when I arrived. I wasn't expecting it."

She hung the coat carefully and loosened her scarf. Damp threads clung to the collar of her jumper. "It looked like someone I used to know," she added. "Not exactly, but close enough to make it uncomfortable."

Cassandra tilted her head. "Who installed it?"

"The sculptor wasn't there. No name on the piece either."

Miranda moved into the hallway, speaking over her shoulder as she passed. "It just appeared. On the manifest, yes. But no artist bio. No label. Just the piece."

Cassandra watched her go, the quiet returning in Miranda's absence. A faint crease formed between her brows.

"That's so odd," she said eventually.

Miranda did not respond right away. She disappeared into the shadows of the hallway, the sound of her footsteps soft against the floorboards.

Then her voice came back, low but clear. "Come with me tonight."

Cassandra turned.

Miranda had returned from the hallway and was now standing by the mirror, smoothing the edge of her scarf. Her expression was calm, but unreadable.

"Where?" Cassandra asked, though part of her already knew.

A small smile flickered across Miranda's lips. Barely there. "You'll see."

That evening, they dressed without ceremony.

Miranda wore black, as she always seemed to when the night asked for more than ordinary hours. Her sleeves were fitted, her silhouette fluid. She moved with the same quiet certainty she carried everywhere, as if the night was already shaped around her.

Cassandra reached for her coat, then paused. Her fingers brushed the scarf from Camden where it hung near the door. She held it for a moment, thumb sliding across the softened silk. Then she wrapped it loosely around her neck. Its weight was light, but grounding.

This time they left the flat without calling a cab. Miranda had said the night air would help clear their heads. They did not speak much on the walk.

Cassandra stayed close to Miranda, expecting to feel lost, but each turn tugged at her like a half-remembered melody. Landmarks that had flashed past the cab window on her first visit surfaced now in full shape. Somehow her feet knew when to cross, when to slip between wrought-iron gates, when to follow the curve of a narrow lane.

She could not have mapped the path if asked, yet her body moved with a certainty her mind could not explain.

The Hollow appeared suddenly, just as it had before, as though it chose when and to whom it revealed itself. The door was exactly as she remembered. Worn wood, black iron hinges, and that faint symbol near the handle, the one that looked more like a breath than a mark.

Miranda knocked once, then pushed the door open.

Inside, the hush returned.

Candlelight flickered along the corridor, its glow bending around stone and smoke. The scent of clove lingered in the air, threaded with something older, something harder to name.

Cassandra stepped through. The threshold felt different this time. Heavier.

Not with dread, but with weight. A presence. As though she were wading into velvet shadows, thick and soft and slow.

Miranda glanced at her, eyes steady, but said nothing.

She turned and walked ahead, each step confident and known.

Cassandra followed.

The main room still held its moody warmth. A low thrum of music moved beneath the quiet, more sensation than sound. Worn velvet chairs gathered in corners. Shadows parted just enough to make her wonder what they might be hiding.

It wasn't crowded. But it wasn't empty either.

Near the back, where the curve of the room bent into another space, Miranda paused. She looked over her shoulder, her voice low.

"This part's quieter. For talking. For listening."

Cassandra nodded. She wasn't sure what she was being led toward, but she followed without hesitation.

Miranda reached for a set of heavy curtains and parted them with care. The fabric was faded but soft, the colour lost to candlelight and time.

They stepped through.

The space beyond felt different. Quieter, yes, but more alive.

A few people sat in low armchairs gathered around a scarred wooden table. Cut-glass tumblers caught the flicker of the flames, each one reflecting a different hue.

As Cassandra entered, a few heads turned. Faces lifted. No one smiled, but no one turned away either. The expressions were calm, unreadable. Curious, perhaps. Not unkind.

Miranda gave a simple nod. "This is Cassandra."

No one spoke at first.

Then a tall man leaned forward, his eyes thoughtful beneath the soft play of candlelight. He extended a hand.

"James," he said. His voice was smooth but grounded, like a violin played close to the chest. "Welcome."

Cassandra reached out and took his hand. The steadiness of it surprised her.

It was warm, assured, without demand.

Next was a woman with pale features and long, ink-dark hair. She didn't smile, but her gaze held something quiet and measured, as if already weighing what had not yet been said.

"Sophia."

Beside her sat a third figure, younger and lean, his frame wiry, his energy restless. His hands moved slightly on the arms of his chair, but his eyes stayed fixed. Watching. Studying. Not unkind, but cautious.

"Victor," he said. He didn't offer his hand. Just a nod. Slow. Deliberate.

"You've come back."

Cassandra didn't answer. The words didn't feel like a question. Something in the way he had said them did not require a reply.

They made space for her on a velvet chair patched at the seams. The fabric was worn smooth where others had sat before her, but it felt steady beneath her. Miranda settled beside her, close but not shielding. Her presence was calm. Known.

Cassandra realised, with a quiet pulse of awareness, that she wasn't afraid. Not exactly. Just present.

Sophia's voice broke the hush. "Drink?"

Cassandra nodded.

A deep red liquid shimmered in the glass tumblers on a carved wooden tray. The surface caught the candlelight, rich with spice and something darker she could not name.

Sophia passed one to her without a word.

The glass was warm before it even touched her lips. The heat travelled through her fingers in a quiet pulse, as though the warmth itself was alive. The first sip burned gently. The sensation was sharp at first, but not unpleasant. It grounded her. Something inside her chest loosened, the tension giving way to a slow, steady release.

The conversation that followed was not what she had expected. No one asked direct questions, and no one pressed for answers.

Thoughts drifted between them like smoke. Each one was a fragment, a small offering placed into the quiet.

Someone spoke about the way candlelight flickered differently depending on who lit it, as if intention could shape the flame. Another described dreams remembered only after walking beneath certain trees. Someone whispered about ivy that grew where no sun had ever touched, its roots drinking from secrets buried deep in the earth.

Cassandra listened, not to understand, but to absorb. Each voice felt like a thread, weaving something unseen.

James leaned back in his chair, eyes still on her. "Do you always wear silver?" he asked, nodding toward her hand.

She looked down. The ring caught the light in a soft circle of reflection. She hadn't realised it was visible beneath her sleeve. "Not always," she said. "But I bought this recently."

Victor tilted his head as he studied her. "Was it already your size?" he asked.

"Yes," she answered slowly. "It fit perfectly."

A faint smile touched his lips. "Of course it did."

Cassandra glanced toward Miranda. She said nothing, only sipped quietly from her glass.

Sophia set her own drink down with care. "Do you know what you're looking for?" she asked.

"I'm not sure," Cassandra replied, her voice low, thinking it was an odd question to ask.

Sophia nodded once. "Good," she said. "That's the right place to begin."

There was no shift in the room. No single turning point.

But something inside her had begun to settle.

Not like dust.

Like a shape taking form.

Someone lit incense. The air thickened. The room grew denser, layered with the scent of myrrh and something deeper beneath it. Cassandra closed her eyes and let the moment find her.

When she opened them again, someone new had entered.

He stood in the archway between rooms. His presence was quiet but unwavering. The candlelight curled around him like mist, as if it had always known where to gather. His face was calm. Not soft. Not severe. Steady. Something inside her responded before she understood why.

Sophia turned her head slightly and announced to the group, "Lucas is here."

Miranda rose from her seat and stepped forward. Her voice was gentle, but clear. "Lucas, I'd like you to meet someone. This is Cassandra. She's from Melbourne."

Sophia's mouth curved faintly. "Careful. The Aussies tend to shake things up."

Victor let out a low chuckle. "If they don't disappear first."

Lucas stepped into the room. The movement was quiet, unforced.

He studied Cassandra for a moment, not with scrutiny, but with something closer to recognition. Then he extended his hand.

She reached for it without thinking.

The moment their palms met, something moved through her. It was not electricity. Not shock.

It was older. Felt rather than understood. Her fingers closed gently around his, and she forgot to breathe.

Lucas held her hand a second longer than was necessary. "It's good to meet you, Cassandra," he said.

His voice was steady and clear. It did not press through the room, but it reached her. Fully.

He released her hand and took a seat beside the others. A hush followed, not awkward, but thick with something unspoken.

Then he asked, almost casually, "Have you ever stood still long enough to hear the ivy grow?"

Cassandra blinked. For a moment, she wasn't sure if she had heard him correctly. Her reply rose without hesitation. "I don't think I've ever been still enough."

Lucas looked at her. His gaze was quiet but precise. "You will be."

The answer settled like a stone dropped in water. It didn't echo. It sank.

Cassandra glanced toward Miranda, as if to check for explanation, but Miranda only sipped from her glass and gave nothing away.

All evening, the others had spoken in fragments. About candlelight and trees. About memory. About silver and flame. And now ivy.

She felt as though she had stepped into a world made entirely of questions, none of them the kind she had been trained to answer.

Lucas's gaze lingered a moment longer before he rose from his chair. He did not hurry. The room seemed to quiet with him. "I'll leave you to your evening," he said.

The words were spoken to the group, but Cassandra felt them settle on her alone.

"We'll speak again soon."

He turned and stepped through the curtains, his silhouette folding back into shadow as easily as it had appeared.

Victor leaned back and let out a low breath. "That was the most I've heard from him all week."

Sophia smiled faintly, her gaze still fixed on the space Lucas had left behind. "You made an impression."

"Is he always like that?" Cassandra asked. She wasn't sure why the question felt strange in her mouth.

James tilted his head slightly. "Lucas is precise. He says what needs to be said. Nothing more."

"And always just when you think he won't," Victor added. "He has a way of turning silence into the loudest thing in the room."

Cassandra looked down at her glass, swirling the dark liquid slowly. The surface caught the light, fracturing it into soft amber. "He said we would speak again."

Sophia lifted her chin. "He will," she said. "If you keep listening."

The energy in the room began to shift again.

The sharpness of Lucas's presence gave way to something softer. The group eased into a gentler rhythm. The questions turned toward Cassandra, but none of them pressed.

They asked what she thought of the city. Whether the Underground still felt like a maze. If she had tried the local bakeries, or if she still missed Melbourne coffee.

She answered what she could. Sometimes in full sentences. Sometimes with a nod. They didn't seem to mind. There was space here for half-spoken truths.

Victor studied her with a kind of amused detachment. "You've stepped further than most do their first time here."

James gave a low chuckle. "Some of us barely made it through the front door."

Sophia leaned forward slightly, the candlelight catching the sharp line of her jaw. "But you walked in like you were expected."

Cassandra hesitated. "I didn't feel like I had a choice."

"That's the illusion," Sophia said. "You always do."

Victor smirked. "But some choices are louder than others."

Their voices wrapped around her, soft and drifting, as if testing the air before landing.

They did not press her with too many questions, but they watched her closely.

Cassandra could feel it. She was being read in ways she did not yet understand.

Miranda had not spoken since Lucas left. She sat quietly, watching. Not with distance, but with intention. Something thoughtful. Something measured.

James rose first. He drained the last of his drink and let out a quiet breath. "I should go before I talk myself in circles," he said. "Some of us still pretend to have jobs."

Sophia stood with fluid ease. She gathered her coat over one arm, then looked to Cassandra with the same unreadable expression she had worn all night. "We'll see each other again," she said. "It happens that way."

Victor lingered a little longer. He leaned forward, his elbows resting on his knees. His eyes found hers and held. "Some nights begin quietly and leave you changed," he said. "This was one of them."

Then, after a pause, he added, "Try not to overthink it." He rose and left with no further words.

The room felt larger once they were gone. The candles still flickered. The velvet chairs still held the warmth of bodies recently moved.

But something in the space had changed.

Miranda stood and reached for her coat. Her movements were calm, unhurried. "There's something I want to show you," she said. "If you are willing."

A knot formed in Cassandra's stomach. Not fear. Not hesitation. But weight. She rose without answering, grabbed her coat, and followed.

They stepped back through the curtain and into the corridor. The air cooled quickly. Behind them, the low music of the room faded into silence. Only the soft sound of their footsteps remained.

Miranda walked ahead without speaking.

They turned down a narrow hallway, one Cassandra had not noticed before.

The stone here felt older, the shadows deeper.

They stopped in front of a door. It was unlike the others. Shorter. Wider. Built from wood so worn it gleamed in the centre, polished smooth by time and touch. There was no handle. Only the subtle indentation where many hands had once reached without knowing why.

Miranda turned to her. She raised a finger to her lips. A silent request. Cassandra nodded, though her heart had begun to beat harder.

Her palms were damp. She could not explain why.

Miranda pressed her palm against the door. It opened with barely a sound.

The room beyond was circular, low-ceilinged, and carved entirely from stone. The walls curved inward like the ribs of something ancient. Candles burned in the corners, their flames steady and low.

At the centre stood a pedestal. Wide and flat, it rose from the floor in pale marble steps, each one worn at the edges as though many feet had once climbed them.

Cassandra's breath caught.

A young woman stood barefoot at the top.

Her skin was pale, bare to the shoulders. She wore a sleeveless black slip that clung to her body, unadorned.

Her hair was twisted and pinned. Her chin was lifted slightly. Her eyes remained closed. She looked as though she could have been Cassandra's age, not exactly, but close enough to feel familiar.

Five cloaked figures surrounded her. They wore long dark robes, their hoods pulled low to cast their faces in shadow. None of them moved. None of them spoke. They stood spaced evenly around the pedestal, not touching, not swaying, not reacting. They waited with the kind of stillness that did not feel human.

Cassandra turned slightly, her shoulder brushing the edge of the doorway. The air felt heavier here. The scent of smoke and something older clung to the stone.

The candlelight in this room flickered with less confidence. She leaned closer, careful not to make a sound.

The woman did not move.

Her hands rested lightly at her sides, her fingers relaxed. But there was something in her posture, a quiet tension that suggested she had been there for some time.

Not waiting.

Enduring.

One of the cloaked figures stepped forward. The movement was slow, almost too fluid to be real. In his hands, he held a strip of red silk.

He climbed the steps and tied the fabric around the woman's left wrist. His motions were careful. Precise. He did not tug. He did not speak.

When the knot was secured, his hands hovered just above her skin, as if reluctant to break contact. Then they lowered, and he stepped back into place.

Another figure moved next. A woman, judging by the shape beneath her robes. She carried a small glass vessel. Inside, something gold shimmered and caught the light.

She knelt at the base of the pedestal. With deliberate care, she poured the contents over the woman's bare feet.

The liquid moved like oil. It glistened as it touched skin, then slid across the marble in slow, deliberate threads.

Cassandra's eyes moved between them, quick and searching, but nothing made sense. Her breath had begun to quicken, shallow and uneven. Thoughts pressed against the inside of her skull, too many to hold at once. What was this? Why was she seeing it?

The questions came fast, layered over one another, none with room to settle.

She felt cold despite the warmth of the room. Not on the surface of her skin, but beneath it, as though something deep inside her had drawn back in retreat. Her fingers were damp. Her pulse skipped and stuttered. Though she stood perfectly still, every part of her felt braced, not for danger, but for something unspoken. Something she had no language for.

The remaining cloaked figures lifted their arms. They did not move forward, nor did they speak. Their hands rose slowly, palms open, fingers spread wide. The gesture formed a loose, triangular frame around the woman's body, but no one reached out. No one touched her.

Candlelight trembled against the dark folds of their sleeves. For a moment, Cassandra thought she heard the soft rustle of fabric, but the sound faded before she could be sure it had ever been real. The air between the figures and the pedestal felt altered, denser somehow, as if it held a charge. The space itself seemed to pulse, invisible yet unmistakable, and she could feel it pushing gently against her chest.

She stared, unblinking. Her lips had parted without her noticing. Though the room was silent, something pressed against her ears, a sensation like deep water or a distant buzz. The woman on the pedestal still had not moved. Her chest rose and fell in slow, shallow breaths. Her eyes remained closed.

Then the flames rose higher. Just once. A flicker, too tall to be natural. The light jumped, then stilled.

The woman's eyes opened.

Cassandra flinched. The movement was so small, so quiet, and yet it broke something in the room. She felt it in her stomach. A shift. Not violent. But irreversible.

The cloaked figures lowered their arms. One of them stepped forward.

With slow, deliberate care, he reached out and tucked a loose strand of hair behind the woman's ear. His touch was reverent, almost ceremonial.

Then, as if responding to a cue no one had spoken, the figures stepped down from the pedestal and walked toward the back of the chamber. Their movements remained soundless, their bodies calm and composed.

The woman lingered for only a moment. She did not look at Cassandra. She did not look at Miranda. She stared at the flame. Then, without hesitation or ceremony, she descended the steps and followed.

Miranda reached for the door and closed it behind them. The click of wood against stone was soft, but final.

They stood together in the darkness of the corridor.

Cassandra stared at the closed door as if she could still see through it, as if the firelight might still be flickering on the other side. Her breath came shallow. Her mouth was dry. The echo of her own pulse pulsed in her throat like a second heart.

"What was that?" she whispered.

Miranda did not speak at first.

The silence between them stretched, not heavy, but full. When she finally answered, her voice was low and steady.

"You saw what it means to be watched," she said. "And to be willing."

Cassandra turned away. She did not reply. But the sensation had not left her. Her skin still burned where the firelight had touched it, even though the room was gone.

The main room had dimmed. The candles burned low now, small pools of gold surrounded by thickening shadow. The space no longer pulsed with conversation or breath. It felt hollow, not abandoned, but exhaled. The warmth had folded inward, as if waiting for the next gathering to begin.

Outside, the air had veered again. The rain had softened into a fine mist that kissed their skin without weight. The pavement shimmered with reflected streetlight, every puddle a mirror. The buildings glistened. Steam curled from vents in gentle waves.

The city was quieter than before. Not asleep, but listening.

They walked side by side through the narrow streets, coats drawn close, steps unhurried. Neither of them spoke at first.

Cassandra kept her eyes forward, though her mind was still somewhere else. Her coat collar brushed against her cheek, but she barely felt it. The cold registered only at the edges of her awareness.

The noise of London had grown distant. Faded. The drone of cars, the occasional burst of laughter from a doorway, the soft echo of footfalls behind them, all of it sounded as if it came through a veil.

It felt as though she were still behind that door. Still quietly peering into that room. The silence of the ritual space had not stayed behind. It had followed her.

The woman on the pedestal. The red silk tied so deliberately around her wrist. The circle of cloaked figures, their movements slow and exact, as if choreographed by something older than time.

Her thoughts did not follow a straight line. They looped and turned in on themselves. She tried to hold onto them, to find sense in them, but they would not sit still.

"I wasn't supposed to see that," she said at last.

Miranda did not respond right away. Her pace did not change. Her breath did not hitch. Only after a few quiet steps did she reply.

"But you did."

Cassandra nodded, though it didn't settle anything inside her. She tightened the scarf around her neck. It still held a trace of warmth, but tonight even that felt foreign.

"It felt like I was interrupting something," she said. "Like I was watching something sacred and didn't deserve to."

Miranda glanced at her but didn't stop walking.

"There's a difference between interruption and invitation," she said. "And you weren't stopped, were you?"

Cassandra swallowed. "No," she said. "But I don't understand why."

Miranda looked ahead. The traffic light at the end of the street changed from green to orange, casting a faint glow across the wet street.

"Not everything reveals its reason straight away," she said. "Sometimes you're shown things because a part of you is ready, even if the rest of you hasn't caught up."

They crossed the street. A car passed behind them, its tyres hissing along the slick bitumen.

Cassandra's steps slowed.

"Why that?" she asked. "Why show me that? The cloaks… the silk… She just stood there. Still. They did not speak. They tied her like she belonged to something. And the candles, the oil… it felt like a ritual. Like she was being offered. But why? What does that mean?"

Miranda finally stopped. She turned to face her. "It wasn't about her," she said quietly. "It was about you."

Cassandra blinked. "I don't understand."

"You were shown a threshold," Miranda said. "What you felt watching it was more important than what you saw."

Cassandra's voice dropped. "I felt like I should leave."

"But you didn't."

"I couldn't."

Miranda nodded slowly. "Exactly."

They walked on. The rhythm slower now. The world around them moved like a background that no longer required focus.

Cassandra hugged her arms around her chest. "She looked so calm," she said. "Not blank. Not passive. Just… like she had surrendered to something."

Miranda's voice was soft. "That's not always weakness."

"I didn't say it was."

"I know. But it's something we've been taught to fear."

Cassandra stared at the wet ground as they walked. The slick pavement mirrored her steps, catching her reflection in broken pieces of light. She barely recognised the way her body moved now, slower, more deliberate, as if something inside her had altered the rhythm.

There was a weight behind her ribs that hadn't been there before. Not pain exactly. Something quieter. Something deeper.

When they reached the flat, she paused on the step. Her fingers curled around the edge of her coat, and she turned slightly toward Miranda. "I feel like something changed in me tonight," she said.

Miranda's reply was simple. "It did."

"I don't know what it means."

"You don't need to."

Miranda unlocked the door and stepped inside, leaving it open behind her. Cassandra followed. The familiar warmth of the flat wrapped around her, but she didn't remove her coat.

Instead, she moved slowly to the lounge and lowered herself onto the edge of the couch near the window.

The glass pane was fogged in places, the city beyond softened into suggestion. A car passed with a hush of wet tyres. Streetlights cast their gold onto the pavement, and beyond that, darkness swallowed the edges of things.

In the kitchen, Miranda moved without turning on the lights. Only the ambient glow from the hallway spilled across the floor, illuminating the gentle outline of her movements. She filled a glass and set it on the coffee table before sinking into the armchair across from Cassandra.

Cassandra reached for the water but did not drink.

Her fingers rested against the cool surface as she watched the way the light shimmered inside it, how it caught and bent with every breath she took.

"It felt quiet," she said finally, her voice low and unsure. "But not empty. Like something was moving through the room. Not seen, just… present. As though it knew I was there."

Miranda's expression didn't shift.

"Rituals rarely announce themselves," she said. "They change the air, not the volume."

"She didn't speak," Cassandra added, her voice tightening slightly. "None of them did."

"They didn't need to."

Cassandra leaned forward, resting her elbows on her knees, hands wrapped around the glass now as if it might anchor her. She stared at the rippling surface, watching the light move across it in subtle lines.

"I keep asking myself why you brought me there," she said. "Why now."

Miranda didn't answer immediately. She met Cassandra's gaze, her expression unreadable, as though weighing something unspoken. When she did speak, her voice was soft but steady.

"I didn't bring you to understand it," she said. "I brought you to feel it."

Cassandra exhaled slowly. The breath left her as though she had been holding it for longer than she realised.

"I still don't know if I should have been there," she said.

Miranda's voice came gently, without challenge.

"Then why did you stay?"

Cassandra didn't answer. The silence between them was not empty, but full of truths she had never spoken aloud.

"You stayed," Miranda continued, "because some part of you was drawn to it."

Cassandra turned her head slightly, as if to shift the weight of the words. The air seemed to still around them. *Drawn.* The word lingered in the space between her and the window. It echoed in a part of her that had not yet found language. She did not know what to do with it.

"Drawn to what?" she asked. Her voice was barely above a whisper. "I didn't even know what it was."

Miranda did not reply. She only looked at her, quiet and steady, as though the stillness itself was the answer.

Cassandra leaned back into the couch and tucked her knees beneath her, folding into the silence without resisting it. The city lights outside blinked in slow patterns. Nothing hurried. Nothing demanded.

Miranda stood then, her silhouette soft in the low hallway light. She moved without urgency, pausing only once before turning away.

"Sleep if you can," she said. "But don't worry if you can't. Sometimes you carry a night with you for a while before it sets down."

Then she disappeared into the quiet shadows of the flat.

Cassandra remained where she was, unmoving. The room seemed suspended, the sounds of the outside world distant and dulled. She did not cry. She did not reach for her notebook, or the blanket draped nearby. She simply sat, watching the window until her reflection dissolved and the glass turned to black.

The image returned without invitation. The woman standing barefoot on the pedestal. The red silk around her wrist. The moment her eyes had opened, not startled but certain.

Cassandra pulled the scarf closer around her neck. Its scent had changed. There was incense in it now, faint and clinging. She had not touched anything inside that room. She had not spoken. Had not moved. And still, something had moved within her.

Something had changed. She did not know what came next. But she knew she had already stepped toward it.

The flat had gone quiet.

Cassandra remained on the lounge long after Miranda's footsteps faded into the back room. The silence around her felt full, not empty. Outside, the rain had softened to a fine mist that blurred the edges of the streetlamps. The pavement shimmered, catching the light in shallow pools. Everything looked washed clean. And yet nothing felt resolved.

She pulled the throw around her shoulders, its weight a small comfort, and reached for her notebook on the coffee table. It was still open to a blank page. She had placed it there earlier, hoping for clarity, for rhythm, but she had not written a single word. Not since everything had begun to shift beneath her.

For a long time, she simply stared at the page. Her fingers hovered above it, unmoving. Part of her resisted the impulse. Naming it might give it shape. And once it had shape, it would have weight.

Then, slowly, she lowered the pen.

At first, there was nothing. Only the hush of the flat and the soft, steady rhythm of the rain beyond the glass. Then the memory returned, and the words followed.

She did not speak.

She stood still.

She chose not to resist.

Cassandra paused. The image rose again. The woman on the pedestal. Her silence. Her stillness. The way she had filled the space with nothing but her presence, and somehow, it had spoken more than words could.

And something in me watched, as if it understood what I could not.

Her fingers trembled slightly, but she kept writing.

What am I stepping into, and what part of me already knows?

She closed the notebook gently and set it beside her. Her hand lingered on the cover. The warmth of the moment had not quite faded.

Then she felt it. A faint sensation at her left wrist. Not pain. Not pressure. Just warmth. Subtle. Lingering. As if fabric had rested there too long.

She turned her hand over, slowly, as though something might be revealed. But the skin was unmarked. There was nothing to see.

The air turned.

On the coffee table, her phone lit up. The screen glowed with a single name. Ethan.

She stared at it without moving. The room around her remained still, the kind of stillness that held its breath.

The message read: *Hey Cass. Just thinking of you. Miss you.*

A tightness pressed behind her ribs. It was not pain exactly, but something familiar trying to reach her.

She didn't reply.

Not yet.

It wasn't that she didn't want to. She did. The familiarity of his name, the warmth of his message, wrapped around something tender in her chest. A part of her still ached for that kind of simplicity, for a world where softness was enough.

But how could she explain it?

She had no words for what she had witnessed. Not even for herself. What had happened tonight belonged to another world. A place without maps. A place where language bent and slipped, where meaning lived in silence and smoke and the weight of breath.

She let the screen fade to black.

In the silence that followed, the blanket's weight remained around her, grounding her in a way she did not fully understand. It clung to her shoulders like something remembered. Not quite comfort. Not quite closure. But real.

Outside, the rain began to fall again, steadier now. The soft drumming against the glass blurred the last traces of the city.

Cassandra leaned back into the cushions. She closed her eyes. The image of the pedestal lingered. The silk. The hands. The stillness that had spoken through a body, without words.

Whatever she had entered, it was not finished.

And neither, she realised, was she.

4
THE WEIGHT OF READINESS

The couch still held the warmth of sleep, but it was the kind that lingers after restless hours, not rest. Cassandra stirred slowly, her breath catching in the quiet. The blanket had twisted around her legs during the night, and her neck ached from the angle she had collapsed into, somewhere between dreaming and not. For a long moment, she didn't move.

The light beyond the window was a diluted grey, the in-between colour that comes before dawn claims the sky, when the world outside hasn't yet decided whether to begin again or remain suspended.

There was a hush in the flat that didn't feel like silence. It pressed softly against the corners of the room, the kind of stillness that settles after something has moved beneath the surface. Not final. Not loud. Just present.

Cassandra sat up carefully, every motion deliberate. The throw slipped to the floor in a whisper of fabric. Her limbs felt heavier than they should have. Not with pain, but with the pull of something unspoken. A dream, perhaps, or the echo of one. Whatever sleep she had managed was not the kind that restored her. It had left its imprint in the ache behind her eyes, in the shallow drift of her thoughts.

She rubbed her eyes with the heel of her hand, then rose. Her bare feet touched the floor, grounding her for a moment in the cool stillness beneath.

The hallway was short, but it felt longer somehow, stretched by the quiet. Her bedroom door stood slightly open. She blinked at it. She didn't remember leaving it ajar. The thought drifted through her mind without urgency, like something noted and filed away for later.

She stepped into the room. The curtains had not been drawn aside, but light crept in around the edges in a thin, hesitant line.

It traced the shape of her desk, the soft drape of clothing over the back of the chair, the outline of the bed still unmade from the days before.

Her gaze caught on something unfamiliar. A single detail that didn't belong to yesterday.

She stopped.

At the foot of her bed, placed with quiet intention, lay a robe.

It had been folded with care. The fabric gleamed faintly, dark and luminous in the grey light. She stepped closer without speaking. Her breath shallowed, the air thinner now, though she couldn't say why.

The robe appeared black at first, but as she moved, the light shifted across its surface and revealed something more complex. Colours emerged that were not colours at all, shades only glimpsed in the space between one breath and the next. Midnight blue, edged with a suggestion of something deeper. A whisper of burgundy, almost wine-dark, woven so subtly it seemed to come from within the fabric itself.

The lining was silk. Crimson. Not bright, not glossy, but rich and soft, like the inside of a velvet theatre curtain, touched by decades of hands and candlelight. The fold where it parted held a memory of warmth. It shimmered faintly, not with light, but with presence.

Cassandra reached out. She didn't touch it yet. Only let her hand hover above the fabric. The air above the robe was still, but something in her skin responded. A flicker. A hush lingered. As though the robe was not just a garment, but an invitation.

Next to it, placed with equal precision, lay a book. The same leather-bound volume she had seen before, the one from the Veiled Quill. Its cover bore the same symbol, embossed in fine detail across the surface, elegant, curling, and now familiar in a way that made her stomach shift with something close to recognition, or dread.

A quiet shiver moved along her spine, not from cold, but from the sense that she was being seen. Not in the usual way, but in a deeper, more deliberate way. As though someone had been watching her, not just yesterday, but longer. As though she had been chosen.

Between the robe and the book, a note had been placed. Small and unobtrusive, but impossible to ignore.

Cassandra picked it up carefully, her fingers brushing the smooth parchment. There was no envelope. No seal. Just a folded square of thick paper, soft at the edges, the texture dense and almost warm to the touch. The ink was dark, the handwriting clean and fluid, like the curve of something drawn with absolute certainty.

The Hollow at midnight.

Lucas.

She read the words once. Then again.

Her mouth felt dry.

It wasn't a surprise. Not entirely. But it landed with force. The name alone carried something inside it, something that unfolded the memory of the way he had looked at her, the stillness of his voice, the sensation that had moved through her the moment their hands touched. He had said very little. He had not asked anything of her. And yet, even now, it felt as though part of her had been altered simply by being near him.

She exhaled slowly and let her gaze shift across the room, as if someone might be there, just beyond the reach of the early light. A shadow in the corner. A presence waiting to be named. But there was nothing. She was alone. Still, the air held a density she couldn't explain, a quiet that did not feel empty so much as expectant.

Cassandra lowered herself to the edge of the bed. The robe remained beside her, undisturbed. The note stayed open in her lap. She stared at it without reading it again. The words had already imprinted themselves. They pulsed just beneath the surface of her skin.

She hadn't seen Miranda since they had returned. There had been no sound of the door. No footsteps in the hallway. No movement in the kitchen. And yet here it was, the robe, the book, the note.

She ran a hand through her hair and tried to follow a straight path through her thoughts, but nothing came cleanly. Had Miranda left them? Was that the answer? Or had someone else entered while she slept? The idea should have unsettled her more than it did. But the discomfort wasn't about intrusion. It wasn't about the flat at all.

It was about herself.

About the part of her that had accepted it. The part that had not bolted upright in alarm, that had not questioned the robe's presence with fear or outrage.

The part that had known.

Her gaze returned to the book. She reached for it, but did not open it. Instead, she let her fingers drift slowly across the cover. The embossed symbol did not glow, and it did not shift. It made no sound. But it felt alive beneath her palm. As though, if she listened long enough, she might hear something breathing inside.

She folded the note with care and placed it on the bedside table, setting it beside the untouched glass of water she had meant to drink nights before. The water caught a sliver of light from the window, still and cold.

Then she lay back on the bed. The robe remained beside her, its fabric uncreased, untouched, but present in a way that felt louder than speech. Her gaze moved to the ceiling, where faint lines of shadow curved and softened in the pale light.

Her pulse had returned to normal, slow and even, but the quiet inside her had not. Something beneath the stillness bristled. Not in warning, exactly, and not in fear. It was something more elusive, a recognition she could not yet name.

She didn't know what this night would bring. She didn't know whether the robe was an invitation, a test, or something she herself had called into being without realising.

But whatever it was, something in her had already answered.

She sat up again, slower this time, and reached for the robe. The fabric slipped between her fingers like water, cool and supple, the texture finer than it had any right to be. When the fabric's lining brushed the inside of her wrist, she inhaled sharply without meaning to.

For a long moment, she held it in her lap. The folds rested heavily across her legs, not burdensome, but laden in a way that suggested intention. Putting it on did not feel like getting dressed. It felt like stepping over a line. A decision that could not be easily undone.

Still, she moved. Slowly, deliberately.

Her arms slipped through the sleeves, and the silk lining met her skin like a second breath. It did not cling. It did not resist. It draped around her body with quiet certainty, as if it had always known the shape it was meant to hold.

She rose to her feet and turned toward the mirror.

The woman who looked back at her did not appear older. Her features had not sharpened or changed, and yet something had moved. She stood taller, not in posture, but in presence. The difference was subtle, but undeniable. Her eyes held questions now, ones she had not yet spoken aloud, and beneath those questions, something shimmered just out of reach. A knowing. A waiting.

She did not fully recognise herself.

Not yet.

The robe swayed gently with her movement. There was nothing excessive about it. Nothing ornamental. It was simple. Measured. But it held meaning, and that meaning felt layered with something ancient and unnamed. She could feel it against her skin, both exposing and shielding her. She was no longer dressed in the way she had been before. She was wrapped in something else.

She crossed the room with measured steps and returned to the bed. The book, still resting where she had left it, seemed to call to her with a different tone now. Not louder. Not desperate. Just closer.

She picked it up with both hands and leaned back against the pillows. The robe gathered around her, soft and silent, and she opened the book.

The first page was no longer what it had been.

She was certain of it.

The line she remembered, something about beginnings, had disappeared. In its place, new words had formed, as though the page had rewritten itself not to reflect her, but to receive her.

And the line that met her eyes felt unfamiliar, but entirely true.

You saw her because the moment had been waiting for you.

Her breath caught in her throat.

She flipped the page, expecting the next line to follow.

The following page was blank. So was the one after that. She turned another, then another. Each one was empty. A smooth field of paper without mark or meaning.

Only the first page held any writing. She returned to it and let her eyes scan the line again. The ink looked fresh, almost wet, as if it had only just been written. But when she touched the words with the tip of her finger, there was no smear. No sign that anything had changed at all.

A quiet unease crept into her chest, low and steady. This was the same book. She was sure of it. The same weight in her hands, the same leather-bound cover, the same one she had held in the shop. The same book with the torn parchment that had slipped loose and the shopkeeper who had told her it was not for sale.

But something had changed. Either it had never been complete, or it had been waiting for her to return.

She ran her hand slowly along the edge of the page, letting her palm slide down the margin. A corner lifted, just slightly, as if moved by breath or thought. The fibres turned beneath her touch. There was a suggestion of movement, but no message. No hidden mark. No revelation.

Only the sensation that something had passed between them. Something quiet. Something withheld.

She could not tell whether she had missed something vital, or if the book was choosing to remain silent.

Or if it was simply waiting.

Cassandra closed it with care. The cover met itself without sound. She held it in her hands for a long moment before setting it gently aside. It had grounded her while it was open, but now, with its pages sealed, she felt strangely untethered.

She looked down at her hands. The robe had shifted as she moved and now draped softly over her wrists. The fabric caught the light in quiet ripples. It was the same silk she had seen the night before. The same that had engulfed the woman in the ritual. The same deep red. The same impossible softness.

Was it a symbol? A calling? Or merely a mirror of something that had already begun to unfold within her?

She didn't feel ready. Not in any way she could explain, and yet, part of her already belonged to whatever this was.

She reached for the note again. Her fingertips found its edge and traced the lines she now knew by heart.

The Hollow at midnight.

If this was a dream, then it had grown too intricate to escape without consequence. If it was real, then the night ahead would change everything.

She placed the book gently on her bedside table and folded the robe across the foot of the bed. The fabric held its shape for a moment, then relaxed, as though it understood it was being watched.

Then she lay back on the mattress, arms loose at her sides, eyes open to the slow dance of light and shadow across the ceiling. The morning had not begun, not truly. But something already had.

Her limbs felt heavy, and her thoughts pressed at the edges of her mind, too full to hold. Sleep came before she could resist it. Not the deep kind that restores or settles the body, but the thinner kind, the kind that drifts just above the surface of waking. It moved through her like mist, light and insubstantial, filled with half-formed impressions that vanished the moment she tried to touch them.

When she stirred again, the light in the room had changed. The grey of pre-dawn had softened into morning, and pale gold filtered through the curtains, drawing long shapes across the wall like slow-moving shadows.

A knock sounded at the door. Not loud. Not rushed. Soft. Measured.

Cassandra sat up slowly. Her mouth was dry. Her thoughts lagged behind the sound. For a moment, she didn't speak.

Then came the word, barely more than breath.

"Yes?"

The door eased open with the sound of hinges that had grown used to silence. Miranda stood in the hallway holding two mugs, each one trailing steam into the stillness of the room. Her hair was loosely tied, a few strands framing her face. She wore a thick cardigan and leggings, familiar and unassuming, but her eyes were alert. Steady. Watching.

"I made tea," she said. Her voice was careful, not hesitant, but offered with consideration. "Thought you might want one."

Cassandra nodded and moved over slightly as Miranda stepped inside. The robe and the book were still in full view. Cassandra made no move to hide them. Instead, she picked up the book and placed it on the quilt between them, her gaze drifting to Miranda's face, waiting to see what it might reveal.

Miranda's eyes flicked to the book. She didn't reach for it. Didn't speak. Only looked at it for a breath too long before handing Cassandra the mug and sitting gently on the edge of the bed.

They sat in silence. It stretched between them, unforced, carrying a weight that did not feel heavy. It filled the room with all the things neither of them knew how to say.

Cassandra took a sip. The tea was mint. Warm. Calming. It steadied her.

She stared down at the cup in her hands before her voice emerged.

"They were already here when I came to bed," she said. "Sometime after I woke on the couch. Sometime in the early hours."

Miranda said nothing.

Cassandra looked toward her, waiting. "The robe. The book. The note."

Still, Miranda didn't answer. She held her gaze, calm and unreadable.

Cassandra hesitated, then added, more softly, "The Hollow. Midnight. From Lucas?"

She glanced back toward the book, then to Miranda again. "What does Lucas have to do with all of this?"

Miranda's expression didn't change, but something in her eyes drifted. A faint softening. A breath of quiet understanding. "He is a part of it," she said. "Just as you are."

"That's not an answer."

"No," Miranda said, her voice lower now. "It isn't. But it is the only one I can give you right now."

The silence returned. It was not the same silence from earlier. Not empty. Not cold. It was filled with hesitation, but also with something else. A closeness. A beginning.

Cassandra looked down at the book again. Her fingers rested lightly on the cover, as if some part of her hoped it might shift beneath her hand, offer another message, reveal another clue. But it didn't move. It didn't change. It only waited.

"I don't know what I'm meant to do," she said quietly.

"You're not meant to know," Miranda replied. "Not yet. But the book chose you. That much is clear."

Cassandra glanced sideways at her. "Did you leave it?"

Miranda's eyes dropped to her own mug. She turned it slightly between her hands, watching the way the steam curled and faded.

"I brought it in, yes."

Cassandra exhaled, not quite in relief. "When?"

"While you were sleeping," Miranda said. "You looked so peaceful. I didn't want to wake you."

So, it had been her. Miranda had placed them there. The robe, the book, the note. But still, a question pressed against the inside of Cassandra's chest.

"Why then?" she asked. "Why not earlier?"

She set her cup down on the bedside table, the ceramic clicking softly against the wood.

"You could've told me." she said. "You could have said something last night."

"You weren't ready then," Miranda said simply.

Cassandra turned her gaze away. Her jaw tightened. The robe still lay folded at the foot of the bed, its fabric catching the slant of morning light in a way that seemed almost intentional. As though it was waiting for her to ask the right question. Or accept the answer.

"I don't understand what this is," she said. Her voice held more tension now. "Any of it. The book. The dreams. The robe. That ritual."

Miranda was silent for a moment. Then she looked up and met Cassandra's eyes with quiet clarity.

"You're not meant to understand it all at once."

"That's not comforting."

"I know, I'm sorry. That's all I can tell you now, you need to discover this on your own and... when the time is right."

Cassandra leaned forward, her elbows resting on her knees, her fingers laced in front of her. Her shoulders curled in slightly, not in weakness, but in thought.

"The book changed," she said slowly. "I swear it did. When I opened it this morning, the words were different. There was only one line, and the rest of the pages were blank."

Miranda's voice came gently. "What did it say?"

Cassandra hesitated, the line echoing back to her with more weight than she expected.

"You saw her because you were meant to."

Miranda said nothing. Her eyes flicked toward the book, but she remained still.

Cassandra watched her. "Who is she?" she asked. "The woman on the pedestal. The one they tied with silk. The one who just stood there and let it happen."

Miranda's lips parted, but no words came at first. She sat still for a moment, as though weighing her answer against something only she could feel.

"She was part of the ritual," she said at last. Her voice was soft, but steady. "Just like the figures around her. Just like you will be..." She hesitated, then continued, her tone gentle but certain. "...if you choose."

Cassandra blinked. The words struck something inside her, and her breath caught. She swallowed the sudden heat that rose in her throat and pressed her palms together, searching for some sense of grounding.

"I don't know if I can do that," she said. Her voice sounded quieter than she intended. "Whatever 'that' was. I don't know if I can just stand there while people bind me and pour things over my feet. I don't even know what it means."

"It doesn't mean submission," Miranda said, and there was something warm beneath her words, something that didn't try to persuade, only to clarify. "It means presence. It means choosing to remain in a moment that asks something of you. It means stepping into something without running from it."

"And the robe?" Cassandra asked. Her voice thinned, stretched taut with uncertainty.

Miranda looked down at her lap. "It is a symbol," she said. "Of readiness. Of being seen."

Cassandra leaned back slightly. As she moved, the edge of the robe brushed her leg, and the sensation startled her. It felt too deliberate, too aware. She flinched without meaning to.

"I didn't ask to be seen," she said, her gaze fixed on the far corner of the room.

"No," Miranda replied softly. "But you were seen anyway."

A long silence settled between them. The light that filtered through the curtains continued to move across the wall, golden and patient, as though waiting for them to catch up.

Cassandra reached for the book again. She held it in both hands and ran her fingers along the edge of the cover, tracing the grain of the leather as if it might answer her.

"It came from the Veiled Quill," she said, not as a question, but as a truth that had finally taken shape. "Didn't it?"

Miranda nodded once, her expression unreadable.

"You knew I would end up there," Cassandra said.

"I suspected," Miranda replied. Her voice was calm, steady. "The Book finds those who are already asking the right questions. Sometimes even before they realise, they are asking them."

Cassandra shook her head, her fingers tightening slightly on the edge of the book. "But I didn't do anything.

I wasn't searching for symbols or signs. I wasn't trying to find meaning. I just wandered in."

Miranda tilted her head, a faint smile at the corner of her mouth. "That was all it took."

Cassandra's eyes stung, sudden and sharp. She didn't understand why it hit her in that moment. Perhaps it was the burden of not knowing. Perhaps it was the robe draped beside her, or the book in her lap. Perhaps it was the note on her table, quiet and final in its invitation. Or maybe it was the creeping realisation that nothing in her life felt entirely her own anymore.

She wiped the corner of her eye with the back of her hand and whispered, "Why me?"

Miranda's voice was steady, without hesitation. "Because something in you has always known. And now it is waking."

Cassandra looked at her. Not just a glance, but a real, searching look. The woman sitting on her bed didn't seem enigmatic or distant. She looked familiar. Human. Even tired. But behind her eyes, something stirred. Something that did not belong to sleep or tea or soft cardigans. Something older. Something that would never be spoken outright.

"What happens if I say no?"

"Then you say no," Miranda said. "And we go to the market. And we eat pastries. And nothing changes. Not on the surface."

Cassandra drew in a breath, and it caught halfway through. "But something would change," she said.

Miranda nodded once, slowly. "You would feel it. Even if you never said it out loud."

The robe shimmered faintly beside her, catching a sliver of morning light that turned as if the fabric breathed. The book rested in her lap, its presence no heavier than it had been before, but suddenly filled with meaning.

Cassandra closed her eyes. She didn't answer. She didn't move. She simply let herself feel the hush of the moment, the tension that existed between now and whatever came next.

Outside, the morning continued. The light thickened. A bird called out from the rooftop across the street. A car passed, slow and steady, and faded into distance.

But beneath it all, something waited.

It waited not with urgency, but with certainty.

And somewhere inside her, part of her was already listening.

5
THE EDGE OF SURRENDER

The light had shifted since she first opened her eyes. It had stretched from a muted grey to something gentler, warmer, spilling through the curtains in thin ribbons that moved as the morning passed. Cassandra sat on the edge of the bed, cradling the last of her tea. The warmth had dulled, though she still held the mug close, as if its comfort depended more on familiarity than heat.

Miranda lingered in the doorway, her presence quiet but watchful. She had not said much since placing the cup in Cassandra's hands, and she had not asked for more. The silence between them was not strained, only full, as though everything that could be said was still finding its shape.

"I was thinking," Miranda said gently, "we could go out for breakfast. Just something simple."

Cassandra looked up at her. The suggestion was soft, without urgency, but it offered something she did not know she had been waiting for. She nodded once, her movements slow and deliberate, then set the mug aside.

"All right."

Cassandra dressed without speaking, choosing a cream jumper and jeans, her heaviest boots, something that felt like a tether. She braided her hair to keep it out of her face, needing the small routine.

As she reached for her coat, her eyes landed on the robe still sitting at the foot of the bed. Its silk surface caught the light in a way that felt deliberate, as though it was watching her too. She left it there.

They did not speak much as they gathered their things. Miranda moved easily, slipping into her coat and scarf, brushing a stray hair from her eyes with a gesture so familiar it made Cassandra's chest ache with a weight she did not fully understand. It was not fear, not exactly, but something close to it.

Outside, the cold air met them like a breath held too long. It wrapped around Cassandra's neck and cheeks, bracing but not unpleasant. It cleared her head, just a little, though her thoughts remained unsettled.

The streets were quiet in that peculiar way London could be when the day had started but not fully arrived. Camden's usual rhythm was still asleep, its noise muted beneath the hush of early footsteps and shuttered shopfronts. They walked without a destination, following the curve of the footpath as it wound past old brick terraces and narrow lanes that led to nowhere in particular.

The market was in sight but untouched by movement. It waited at a distance, known yet distant in the hush of the hour.

Cassandra breathed in the scent of warming stone and faint traffic, of a city just beginning to wake. She did not speak, but her mind wandered. The thought of midnight pressed gently at the edges of her thoughts, not loud but constant.

Would tonight be like before, or would the ritual change now that she had been seen?

Would she be drawn closer, or asked to stand still while unseen hands wove something around her? She had seen others watching. She had felt Lucas watching. And though she did not understand the meaning, something in her had not looked away.

She glanced at Miranda beside her, who walked with easy familiarity, as though this were just another day. There was no sign in her face of what they had shared. No mention of the robe or the book or the strange sense that something had changed forever. That, more than anything, unsettled Cassandra. She did not know whether to be grateful or afraid.

They passed a florist arranging buckets of daffodils and lilies outside a shop window. A woman stood nearby wiping down the glass with slow circular strokes. There was no music. No calls from stallholders. Only the city breathing, quietly and without rush.

Cassandra wondered, not for the first time, how many others passed through days like this with the weight of unseen things pressing on their skin. How many others carried questions without names, or memories that did not feel entirely theirs.

She almost asked Miranda then. She almost reached for her arm and said, tell me what I am becoming. But the words stayed in her throat.

They continued walking. The narrow lane turned toward a wider street, one lined with small shops and quiet cafés still setting up for the morning.

Bicycles leaned against poles. A pigeon fluttered down near the curb, pecking at a discarded chip wrapper before lifting away again into the grey-blue sky. Cassandra watched it absently, her breath fogging in the cold.

"Do you think it ever stops feeling strange?" she asked, her voice low enough that Miranda might have missed it if they were not walking so close.

Miranda looked over. "What do you mean?"

Cassandra let her gaze drift over the quiet storefronts. "This feeling that I have stepped sideways. Like I am here, but not quite in the same world everyone else is walking through."

Miranda's expression softened. She tucked a strand of hair behind her ear, considering the question. "I don't think it stops feeling strange," she said after a moment. "But it does stop feeling unfamiliar."

Cassandra let that settle. The distinction was subtle but clear. She nodded, then looked down at the footpath, watching the way her boots disturbed small puddles left from a light overnight rain.

They walked past a boarded-up shop where faded posters curled at the edges in the window. One of them bore a slogan she could no longer read, but the image caught her. It showed a black silhouette of a woman standing before a swirling doorway.

She paused, the figure snagging at something inside her. The way the door curled inward, it was not only familiar, it was known. When she looked away, the tension in her chest had grown slightly heavier.

They reached a quiet intersection, and Cassandra recognised the diner they had passed once before, tucked between a record store and an art gallery. It was the kind of place she would not have noticed before coming to London, but something about it now felt safe, grounded in its smallness. She followed Miranda inside.

The interior was warm and smelled of toast, coffee, and something faintly sweet. A radio played quietly in the corner. It sounded like an old jazz tune, muted by static. The floor was tiled in black and white, the tables wooden and slightly worn, and the server behind the counter greeted them with a nod before returning to arranging a tray of spoons.

The girls chose a table near the window. Miranda shrugged off her coat and set it on the back of the chair, her eyes flicking toward the glass as if watching for something unspoken. Cassandra did the same, then sat with her hands curled in her lap. The warmth of the space clung to her slowly, like sunlight through glass.

They ordered simple things. Toast with marmalade. Porridge with brown sugar. One tea and one coffee, both served in mismatched mugs. When the plates arrived, the smell made Cassandra's stomach stir, but her appetite remained elusive.

She picked at the toast, turning it over in her fingers. The butter had melted unevenly, leaving pale streaks along the crust. She studied it longer than it deserved.

"I feel like something's waiting," she said quietly, not quite looking up. "Something I can't see. But it's not new. It's been there a long time."

Miranda stirred her coffee. "It has," she said. "But it waited because you weren't ready. Now it senses you are."

Cassandra frowned slightly. "But I don't feel ready. I feel... pulled."

Miranda sipped before answering. "That's how it begins. Readiness is rarely a feeling. It's a recognition. You don't always notice it until after the step has been taken."

Cassandra finally looked up, meeting her gaze. "And what if I don't want to take the step?"

"Then you won't," Miranda said calmly. "But you're here. That says something."

They sat in silence for a while after that. Cassandra took a few bites of her porridge. It was too sweet, too warm, but she kept eating as if the act itself might anchor her. She watched the steam rising from her tea, swirling in small, ghostly ribbons that disappeared before reaching the edge of her cup.

Outside, the street had begun to stir. A man passed by, walking a dog in a pink puffer coat. A cyclist zipped past with a basket full of apples. The gallery across the road flicked on its lights, illuminating a display of abstract paintings, all crimson and gold. The city was beginning to remember itself again.

Cassandra wrapped her hands around her mug and drew in a long breath.

"Sometimes I think if I close my eyes, I'll open them somewhere else. Somewhere older. Or deeper."

Miranda's voice was soft, but certain. "That place already lives in you."

The words settled somewhere low in Cassandra's chest. She looked down at her tea again and whispered, "Then maybe that's what unsettles me."

Miranda didn't answer this time. She only placed a hand lightly on the table between them. Not quite a touch, but an offering. A friendly presence.

And in that still moment, Cassandra realised it wasn't the unknown that frightened her most. It was the sense that she might already belong to it.

They walked home slowly. The breakfast had settled in her stomach like something symbolic rather than nourishing, a gesture that hinted at normalcy while the rest of the day held its breath. Cassandra noticed things she might have missed another morning.

The way the pavement glittered faintly where the sun touched leftover rain, the smell of warm stone mingling with distant cigarette smoke, the hollow clang of a gate closing somewhere nearby.

Each sound and scent felt sharper, more specific, as if the world had narrowed its focus on her alone.

Miranda kept pace beside her, their silence companionable but tinged with something else. Cassandra sensed the space between them filling with questions neither had yet asked. Not because they couldn't, but because the answers might pull them further in.

Back in the flat, the door clicked shut behind them with a softness that made the rooms feel larger than they were. Cassandra slipped off her coat and boots, letting them rest in a quiet heap by the door. Miranda moved into the kitchen, wordlessly beginning to tidy a few things left from the night before. The faint clink of a spoon against a glass echoed softly.

Cassandra stood for a moment in the middle of the lounge, unsure of what she needed. Her gaze drifted to the table where she had moved the book. It remained closed, its leather cover unmarked by dust or fingerprints, but heavy with implication. She didn't touch it. Instead, she walked past it and into her room, where her laptop sat untouched on the desk.

She sat slowly. The chair creaked under her, familiar and unforgiving. The article she had begun earlier in the week still sat open, the blinking cursor waiting like a question.

Her notes for the fashion piece, Winter Trends in Camden, lay beside it. Scrawled phrases about layered textures, sustainable fabrics, and colour palettes felt alien now, like a language she had once known but could no longer speak fluently.

She placed her fingers on the keyboard. Typed a single sentence.

Winter has arrived like a whisper instead of a scream, softening even the sharpest corners of the city.

She paused. Read it twice. Then deleted it.

Another attempt followed. She listed what she had seen over the past week. Coats made from repurposed denim. Velvet scarves dyed in bruised lilac. Boots with upturned toes and metal studs. She tried to describe the energy of the streets, the layered choices people made between function and flair. But everything she wrote felt disconnected, hollow.

Her thoughts circled back to midnight. The robe. Lucas. The silence that seemed to gather around them. And the sense that something would shift the instant she stepped inside. The robe was not just a costume. It had felt like a threshold in cloth form. What did it all mean?

Her hands trembled slightly, and she lowered them from the keys.

In the quiet, the sound of Miranda boiling the kettle reached her. A door creaked open, then closed again. The world outside continued to move, but Cassandra's thoughts remained stuck, pinned beneath a weight she couldn't yet name.

She stood and walked back into the lounge. The light had changed again, this time more golden, slanting across the carpet in long, broken stripes. The book still waited. Its presence was no less powerful for being silent.

Miranda appeared a moment later, holding two fresh mugs of tea. She offered one to Cassandra without a word, then sank into the armchair by the window.

Cassandra took the drink but didn't sit. "I tried to work," she said softly.

Miranda looked at her, her gaze unreadable but steady.

"I couldn't write. I couldn't even focus. I kept thinking about last night. And what happens tonight? And I'm trying to be calm, but I feel like I'm split in two. Like part of me is standing in this room, and the other part is already back there, waiting."

Miranda nodded once. "It's normal to feel that way."

Cassandra swallowed. "You've done this before."

"Yes."

"So... what is it, really? What happens there?" She sat down slowly, curling one leg beneath her. "And how did I end up being the one chosen?"

Miranda held her tea close to her chest. "Some things I can explain. Some I can't. And some... are not mine to explain at all."

"But you knew this would happen to me."

Miranda didn't answer at first. Her eyes drifted toward the book on the table, then returned to Cassandra's face.

"I suspected," she said quietly. "But I didn't know for sure until last night."

Cassandra followed her gaze. The Book. The robe. The memory of that moment flickered in her chest.

"You left them for me," she said softly. "You knew what they would mean."

Miranda nodded, her expression unreadable. "Because that was the moment you were ready to see them."

Cassandra stared at her, the tea cooling quickly in her hands. She wasn't sure whether the answer calmed her or disturbed her more.

Miranda leaned forward, setting her mug down on the table. "You don't have to go tonight. Nothing will force you."

"But you think I should?"

Miranda met her gaze, her voice soft. "I think you've already decided."

The hours passed slowly, though Cassandra couldn't have said how many. Time seemed to loosen its grip as the sky shifted from pale gold to deeper grey, the softness of morning giving way to a muted hush.

The tea remained unfinished beside her. Miranda had returned to the kitchen at one point, murmuring something about needing to prep a few things for work the next day. Cassandra let her go. She needed the quiet.

She sat curled in the corner of the lounge, a blanket drawn across her legs. The book still rested on the table in front of her. She hadn't opened it again. There was something too final about what it might reveal, and she wasn't ready to let it speak just yet. Its presence, though silent, had begun to feel like a companion, a watcher. It was no longer just an object but part of the rhythm of her days now.

Outside, the light dimmed further. The walls of the flat seemed to lean inward as the shadows grew, not ominously but with a quiet understanding. This was the shape of things now: the waiting, the not-knowing, the sense of being called even when no words were spoken.

Back in her room, the robe remained at the end of the bed. She hadn't touched it again. Its presence was enough.

Eventually, the sound of Miranda's footsteps returned. She entered the lounge with two bowls of soup, placing one gently in front of Cassandra without comment. The warmth of the meal cut through the heaviness, grounding them both in the present.

Cassandra had questions, so many that they crowded her throat, each one heavier than the last. But she feared the shape of the answers, feared what they might confirm about the path she was already walking.

They ate in near silence, the only sounds the scrape of spoon against ceramic and the soft murmur of the city shifting beyond the windows.

Afterwards, Miranda gathered the bowls and stepped away, but returned a few minutes later, this time not with food or tea, but with a small silver ring. She held it out to Cassandra.

"You left this by the basin," she said simply.

Cassandra took it, surprised by how cold it felt. She slipped it back onto her finger and nodded her thanks.

Then the moment settled again.

Evening fell quietly, without fanfare. The city didn't dim so much as turn inward, its noise softening, its movements slower and more deliberate. Cassandra stood by the door, the robe wrapped around her now like something inevitable.

When the moment came, she had reached for it without hesitation. The material's lining brushed her skin like a whisper she was already beginning to understand.

As she turned, her chest tightened.

Miranda stood beside her, the robe gathered around her shoulders in folds of black and deep crimson. Its fabric gleamed faintly in the dim light, nearly identical to Cassandra's own. The sight stirred something deep and unsettled in Cassandra's chest.

A thousand questions rose, but only one made it past her lips.

"You too?" she murmured, the words catching at the edge of her voice.

Miranda's eyes held hers for a moment. Then, with a soft, knowing smile, she said quietly, "Some things are only understood on the other side."

There was no further conversation. No instructions. No reassurances. Only the uncertainty of what waited in the darkness.

They left the flat without ceremony. Outside, the street welcomed them with a hush that felt rehearsed. Streetlamps glowed in amber halos above their heads. A car passed, distant and slow, slipping into the quiet as if the night itself had absorbed it. Cassandra's boots struck the pavement with a steady rhythm, the robe moving around her legs with a grace she hadn't expected.

Moving through the quieter edges of Camden, they passed old buildings and shuttered shops, following the alley that curved just far enough from the main road to feel hidden. Somewhere behind them, life continued: music from a rooftop bar, a laugh from a passing couple, the murmur of someone on a phone.

Then, from far off, the cathedral bells began to chime. Just once. Low and deliberate. Eleven-thirty.

The sound pressed against her thoughts like a reminder. Midnight was no longer far away.

A few minutes later, at the mouth of the alley, stood The Hollow. The door was open. A thin line of candlelight spilled onto the street, cutting a clean edge between the known and the unknown.

Cassandra paused. Her hand hovered just inside the entrance. The robe felt heavier now, as though it had absorbed everything unspoken.

Miranda stepped closer.

"You don't have to go in alone," she said softly.

But Cassandra didn't move.

Miranda's hand slid away, her fingers brushing the sleeve of Cassandra's robe in a final touch.

"Only you can walk through," she said. "But I'll walk beside you, until the moment you must choose."

The words lingered between them, quiet and absolute.

Cassandra held her gaze for a long moment. Then she stepped forward into the dim corridor beyond.

The door closed behind them with a heavy click that echoed down the narrow passage. Candlelight flickered along the stone walls, each flame enclosed in shallow glass sconces that threw long, uneven shadows. The air held a faint chill, threaded with the scent of wax and something older, an earthy sharpness, like damp stone warmed by time.

Miranda walked a few steps ahead. Her movements were measured, unhurried, the hem of her robe brushing the floor in a slow rhythm. Cassandra followed without speaking, her own robe whispering around her ankles. Each step seemed to draw them further away from the city above and deeper into something ancient and waiting.

They passed through two more archways, their curves etched with the same delicate symbols Cassandra had seen before. She didn't pause to study them this time. It wasn't that she wasn't curious, but that she no longer felt separate from what they represented. It was as though the symbols had moved inside her, whispering their meaning in a language she hadn't yet learned to understand.

Eventually, they reached a heavy wooden door at the end of the corridor. It stood slightly ajar. The candlelight within was warmer than the rest, casting a golden glow onto the flagstones beneath their feet.

Miranda turned to her. For a moment, neither spoke. Then, gently, she reached out and touched Cassandra's shoulder, a quiet grounding gesture. Not possessive, but steady.

"From here, I'll wait," she said softly. "This space belongs to you now."

Cassandra opened her mouth, but no question formed. Miranda's face held no fear, only a quiet knowing that made her chest ache with something close to longing.

With a final glance, Miranda stepped aside, and Cassandra crossed the threshold.

The chamber beyond was larger than she had remembered. The ceiling arched high above, lost in shadow. Stone walls curved inward, forming a circle that seemed to hold the air in place. At the centre stood the figures, hooded and still, arranged in a ring around a low pedestal that bore a single lit candle and a silver chalice.

Her chest tightened. The candle's flame didn't waver. It stood impossibly steady, as though the room itself refused to move.

Lucas stood just behind the pedestal. His robe was like the others, black with crimson lining, but his presence cut through the stillness with quiet force. His silver-grey eyes lifted as Cassandra entered, and the space between them seemed to contract. She felt it like a current drawing her forward, not violently, but with inevitability.

The others remained motionless, their heads bowed. The vibration of a chant hadn't yet begun, but it lingered at the edges of her awareness, like something waiting to return.

She hesitated at the edge of the chamber. The soft crunch of her boots against the stone sounded too loud in the vastness. She saw the way Lucas's eyes never left her, and the flicker of recognition there sent her pulse quickening.

"Cassandra," he said. His voice was low, velvet-smooth, and filled the space without effort. "Step forward."

Her gaze darted to the doorway. Miranda was gone from sight, but Cassandra felt her presence still, like a thread that hadn't been fully cut. With her heart hammering, she stepped forward.

Each footfall seemed to echo longer than it should have. The candlelight touched her face, caught the edge of her collar, warmed her wrists where the robe parted slightly. When she reached the glowing symbols that circled the pedestal, she stopped.

Lucas did not move. "Do you know why you're here?" he asked.

She shook her head. Her voice was there, caught inside her, but it didn't rise.

"You've entered a space few ever reach," he said, his tone measured. "A space that reflects. That reveals. That waits for no one and asks nothing but willingness."

Cassandra swallowed. The words pressed into her chest. "What made it me?" she asked, her voice barely more than a whisper.

Lucas's lips curved faintly, but not into a smile. "Because the shadows stirred when you arrived. And because... I've been waiting too."

The pause stretched before he added, "Because you heard something others ignored. And you followed it."

She stared at him, trying to understand. Her fingers trembled where they clutched the fabric at her sides. The symbols beneath her feet glowed faintly, their light steady and alive.

Lucas extended a hand. "Step inside," he said.

The distance between them was only a few feet, but it felt vast. Her limbs were heavy, her body rooted to the floor by a thousand unspoken questions. And yet, she moved.

One step. Then another.

The moment she crossed the circle, something altered. The temperature dropped, not in discomfort, but with the sudden clarity of still water. The others didn't move. Lucas watched her.

He reached for the chalice and held it out. "Drink," he commanded.

Cassandra looked down. The liquid inside was dark, with a faint shimmer that caught the candlelight like scattered stars. Her hands moved before her thoughts caught up, lifting the silver rim to her lips.

It was cool. Metallic. Bitter, but not unpleasant. As it touched her tongue, the hum returned, deep and steady, running through her bones like a forgotten rhythm. Her vision blurred. The room disappeared.

And in its place came fragments, memories, glimpses of something larger than thought. A flash of Ethan's smile. A candlelit street she had never walked. The whisper of silk against skin. Her childhood bedroom. A garden filled with ivy and lavender. A voice that might have been her own, saying, *I'm ready.*

Her knees gave way, but Lucas's hand found her elbow. His touch was firm, grounding, impossibly warm.

"Stay with me," he whispered, his voice cutting through the tide of images.

She clung to that voice, to the steadiness of his presence, until the chamber returned. The floor was solid beneath her. The candle still burned. The figures remained unmoved.

Lucas stepped closer. "You're no longer standing on the edge," he said.

She couldn't speak.

"Now," he continued, his hand brushing her jaw with impossible gentleness, "you must decide what to surrender."

Her chest tightened beneath his touch. His fingers rested just long enough for her skin to register their warmth before he withdrew them, leaving behind a silence that felt like a question. She blinked, steadying herself, though the undercurrent inside her hadn't eased. If anything, it had grown denser, circling inward as if seeking its core. If anything, it had deepened, thickened, turned inward.

Her gaze lowered to the glowing circle around them. The symbols etched into the stone floor pulsed faintly beneath her feet, as though responding to the beat of her own heart. Every line and curve seemed to shimmer with hidden language. She didn't know what they meant, but she felt their age, their purpose.

"What am I surrendering?" she asked quietly, her voice thin with uncertainty.

Lucas didn't answer at once. Instead, he moved to stand beside her, facing the circle with her, his hands folded loosely in front of him. His presence was calm, almost reverent.

"Not a piece of yourself," he said at last. "Only the illusion of control."

The words struck something inside her. They landed with the force of truth, though she had no way to name why. Cassandra's throat tightened. She had clung to control every day since arriving in London. Through her writing. Through routine. Through the quiet belief that what she did still mattered in a world that had begun to feel unreal.

And now, all of it. The stories. The rules. Even her name. It all felt fragile, as though she were made of paper and someone had breathed too hard.

Lucas stepped toward the pedestal once more. The chalice remained where she had placed it, a dark mirror within the flame's reflection.

"It doesn't happen all at once," he said softly. "Surrender is not a single act. It's a choice repeated."

The figures surrounding them began to move. Slowly, like mist stirred by wind, they raised their arms in unison. Their sleeves fell back to reveal hands, pale and still. Their fingers curled toward the centre, open but not reaching.

The chant began. Not loud. Not rushed. But with the rhythm of breath, rising like smoke, curling between the candle flames, weaving itself into the stone.

Cassandra closed her eyes as the sound filled her head, her chest, her limbs. It didn't ask for understanding. It didn't demand belief. It simply was, and it was enough to carry her inward.

Images returned. Not visions now, but sensations. The feeling of the robe when she first unfolded it. The sound of Miranda's voice, low and careful. The look in Lucas's eyes when he first saw her. The way the book had refused to stay still on the page. It all came back, as though the chant were a key unlocking memory in fragments.

She opened her eyes.

Lucas had turned to face her again. The figures remained in place, their chant steady, their heads bowed.

"Are you ready?" he asked.

Her voice wasn't certain. It wasn't strong. But it didn't tremble when she said, "I think so."

Lucas extended his hand again. Not as a command this time, but an invitation.

Cassandra placed her palm in his.

He led her further in, and when she reached the heart of the circle, the chant responded. A new note rose, higher and more delicate, like a thread of silver winding through shadow.

She felt it run through her skin, brushing against something deep inside her that had no name. The air was different here, thicker, charged, as if the very space inside the circle breathed with memory.

The others stood still. Their eyes weren't on her, yet she felt seen. Not watched. Witnessed.

Lucas said nothing. He simply stepped back, his presence lingering just behind her like gravity.

He turned to her, his face close. He didn't release her hand. His other hand rose, fingertips hovering just above her heart.

"Whatever weighs you down," he said, "offer it here."

Cassandra's chest rose and fell beneath his hand. The pressure of the moment wrapped around her ribs like a band.

She thought of Ethan. Of Melbourne. Of everything she had left behind and not yet named. She thought of how far she had come just to reach this place where nothing required explanation.

And slowly, without quite understanding how, she let it go.

It left her like an exhale. She released it, eyes fluttering shut, and something heavy unlatched inside her. The ache didn't vanish, but it loosened.

Lucas stepped back.

The chant ended.

For a moment, the chamber was still. The figures lowered their hands. The candle's flame wavered once, then steadied. The quiet that followed felt earned.

Cassandra stood in the centre of it, her robe whispering against her ankles, her hands loose at her sides.

She looked at Lucas.

He gave a small nod, almost imperceptible, then turned toward the outer circle. The others began to move, their motions quiet, respectful. One by one, they turned away, vanishing into the shadows that lined the chamber's edge. No words were spoken. No instructions given. Only departure.

Cassandra remained where she was. Her body hummed with something new. Not quite power. Not quite peace. But presence. As though she had, for the first time in weeks, come back into herself.

Lucas approached once more, his voice low. "You may leave when you are ready," he said. "Or stay, if you need to."

She nodded, her eyes not leaving his. "What happens next?"

His expression softened, though no smile formed. "Whatever you choose."

And then he turned, the folds of his robe trailing behind him, and disappeared into the dark beyond the candles.

Cassandra stood alone in the centre of the circle, the warmth of Lucas's touch fading from her skin like mist. The stillness that followed was not hollow. It was whole. It filled the room like water fills a glass, slow and complete. She listened to it.

The steady rhythm of her own breathing. The flicker of candlelight. The subtle shift of fabric as her robe settled against her body.

She turned slightly, taking in the chamber that only moments before had felt so vast, so unfamiliar. Now it seemed different. Not smaller, but less foreboding. The shadows remained, the symbols still glowed beneath her feet, but something in her had changed. Or perhaps something that had always been there had finally stirred.

Her eyes lifted to the pedestal once more. The chalice sat quiet in its place, untouched now, but no longer just an object. It held memory. Meaning. A before and after.

Her fingers grazed the cup's edge. The metal was smooth and cool beneath her touch. Not to claim it, not to drink again, but to say goodbye to the moment it had held.

Cassandra let her hand fall to her side. She turned slightly, her gaze drifting toward the chamber's edge. The glow beneath her faded just enough to acknowledge a shift, but she didn't cross it.

The corridor was waiting. Beyond it, the city. The flat. Miranda. The robe that clung still to her shoulders, familiar now. And something else, nameless, moving through her blood like a quiet resonance.

She stayed where she was, feeling the resonance settle deep inside her, not as a question but as a truth that no longer needed to be spoken.

This was not an ending. It was a crossing.

And the night was not over yet.

Outside, the air was cool. The night had deepened into a darker hour, one that carried less of the world's noise and more of its listening. The street was empty, the city attentive.

Miranda walked beside her, saying nothing. There was no need.

Each step brought a small return of weight, but it no longer settled in her the way it once had. Her thoughts were her own, but they moved differently now. She could feel the night pressing softly around her, not threatening, only reminding her that something had awakened.

By the time they reached the flat, the sky showed the first signs of softening. Not morning yet, but something like it. Cassandra entered without turning on the lights. She placed the robe on the back of the chair and walked barefoot to the lounge. The book still rested on the table.

She let it be. She only looked at it for a long moment before sitting beside it. The quiet was gentle. Her body, though tired, didn't ache. Her mind, though full, didn't overflow.

She reached for her notebook and pen. The pages whispered as she opened them. She didn't know what she would write, only that something inside her needed to speak now.

What have I become a part of?

Why does it feel like the ritual didn't change me, but revealed something I had always carried?

And why did I walk through the door, knowing I would never return the same?

She paused. The pen hovered.

Then came different words.

Not everything needs answers. Some things only need presence.

The notebook closed with a soft thud, and she set it gently on the table. Beyond the window, the city began to shift. Light edged along rooftops. Shadows withdrew from the streets.

The robe remained draped over the chair. The book rested where it had been placed. A hush lingered, filled not with emptiness, but with meaning.

She sat in the stillness. Not finished. Not certain. But no longer afraid.

No longer afraid of shadows.

No longer afraid of questions without answers.

And not afraid of the path unfolding beneath her feet.

Whatever waited beyond this night no longer felt like a test.

It felt like invitation.

Something was beginning again. Quietly. Just beyond the edge of surrender.

6
CLOSER THAN MOST

T he light was thin when Cassandra stirred. Not the hush of true morning, but something quieter, paler, as though the world had exhaled and not yet breathed back in. The night was gone, but it hadn't left her. She lay still beneath the blanket, her limbs heavy, her breath shallow, her mind struggling to separate memory from dream.

There was a tenderness in her chest that hadn't been there before. Not a bruise, not quite pain, but a kind of imprint, the afterglow of something deep and invisible, as though the ritual had left a presence behind that still moved with her breath. The hum lingered low and steady, not intrusive, only there, like the faint pressure of a name waiting to be remembered.

She sat up slowly, the blanket slipping from her shoulders in a soft collapse. Her muscles ached in unexpected places, in the curve of her ribs, along the tops of her thighs, the base of her neck. It wasn't the kind of ache that asked for stillness, but the kind that suggested something had moved just beneath the surface of her skin, and that it would take time to understand what had been re-shaped.

She reached for the tea mug she had abandoned the night before. The ceramic was cold against her palm. She held it for a moment, remembering the warmth it had once carried, and then set it back down without drinking. The thought of tea felt hollow now, too much like a routine that belonged to someone else.

The flat was quiet in a different way. Not just empty, but altered. The silence held a weight to it, a slight pressure in the air that made each room feel like it was listening. She crossed the hallway barefoot, moving with a kind of reverence, as though anything louder than breath might disturb something delicate still settling into place.

In the mirror above the dresser, her reflection returned her gaze with a cautious recognition. The same face. The same loose hair falling around her shoulders. But the eyes were different. Still dark with sleep, still quiet. Yet no longer asking the same questions.

In the kitchen, she hovered for a moment, her hand resting lightly above the kettle. Then she let it drop back to her side.

Instead, she stood at the window and watched the city. London moved below her, indifferent and alive. A van reversed slowly into a narrow lane. A woman in a navy coat passed beneath a crooked streetlamp, adjusting her beanie without breaking stride. Somewhere nearby, a dog barked once and was answered by another, farther off. And yet all of it felt strangely distant, as if she were watching a life that no longer belonged to her.

Her phone buzzed against the counter. The sound was too loud for the moment, sharp and ordinary. It broke the stillness like a dropped glass. She crossed the floor and turned it over.

One message.

Hey, Cass. Been a while. Hope you're alright. Call me when you can. Miss you.
Ethan.

His words landed gently, but they carried weight. Familiar. Steady. Still capable of reaching something in her that hadn't been entirely lost. Her chest tightened. Not with regret, but with a kind of longing she no longer had a name for.

She read the message twice. Then typed a reply.

I'm okay. Things have just been… a lot. Miss you too.

It wasn't a lie. Not really. But it felt like the kind of truth spoken through glass, distant and slightly warped. A truth from the girl she had been a few days ago, or maybe longer than that.

She placed the phone face down on the counter and exhaled.

From the lounge, something caught her eye, a flicker of crimson silk bathed in the morning light. The robe had not moved from where she had left it, still draped over the back of the armchair, yet something in its stillness felt aware, as if it had not merely remained, but waited.

Slowly, she approached the chair, her fingers reaching out almost without thought. The fabric yielded softly beneath her touch. When she brushed the lining, something within her responded, the low hum rising again, not with urgency, but with recognition. It wasn't painful. Only aware.

The book sat quietly on the table nearby, untouched, its presence no less weighted for its silence. Cassandra looked at it for a long time, uncertain whether she was waiting for something to change or merely to feel ready. Then she reached out and opened it.

The pages whispered beneath her fingers as she turned them, slow and steady, until one stilled of its own accord. There, across the centre of the page, text had formed in delicate ink that seemed to shift slightly in the light. Her pulse quickened.

The closer you are to the fire, the darker the shadow you cast.

The words held for a moment, as if waiting to be read again, then began to fade. She reached instinctively, fingertips brushing the parchment, as though she could hold them in place with her touch. But they dissolved beneath her skin, vanishing into blankness.

Cassandra remained motionless, her breath light and thin. The book had spoken. And now it had taken the message back.

A second buzz cut through the stillness. Her phone. Another message. She rose and crossed the room.

Not Ethan.

We are going even deeper tomorrow night, if you are willing.
Lucas.

Her chest tightened for a different reason. She read the message twice, then a third, each word gaining weight as it settled.

Even deeper.

The phrase moved through her like a ripple, brushing against something still tender from the night before. She wasn't sure if it was meant as a warning or a promise.

It felt like both.

Her fingers hovered above the screen. She could have closed the message. Could have walked away, let the words dissolve into the day like they had never arrived. But the silence that followed felt deliberate, not empty but expectant, like a breath held just long enough to be noticed.

She swallowed, uncertain. Was she truly willing to go further? To offer more of herself to something she still didn't fully understand.

The answer didn't come as a thought, but as something quieter, something rooted in the place beneath doubt and reason.

"I think I am," she whispered.

The words barely stirred the air, but it was enough. Something in the room responded, subtle and immediate, as though a current had passed through the quiet. Not a sound. Not a shape. Only a shift in presence.

By midday, the city had grown louder. Cars grumbled through narrow streets. A motorbike shrieked past with too much urgency. Somewhere, a street performer shouted into the cold.

Cassandra moved through it all like smoke. Present, but ungraspable. Her coat clung to her damp skin, and the sky hung low with heavy cloud, the kind that made the day feel longer than it was.

She didn't flinch at the sound of a horn. Didn't react when a stranger brushed her arm too closely. The city pressed in, indifferent and alive, but she moved untouched, as if her edges no longer belonged to the same world.

People moved past on either side. Conversations rose, drifted, and faded like vapour. The familiar sounds of London reached her ears but failed to register.

Her body kept moving. Something deeper lagged behind.

The only thing tethering her to the day was her appointment with Lydia.

Vanguard's polished world felt impossibly far now. All pale glass and quiet ambition. Once, the thought of it had grounded her. Given shape to her purpose. Now it felt like stepping into someone else's memory. Familiar, but no longer hers.

Still, she owed Lydia a visit. A check-in. Proof that she hadn't disappeared completely.

She boarded the train without thought. The carriage was packed, thick with motion and noise. Bodies pressed too close. The stale scent of rain-damp coats and too-warm breath filled the air. She stood with one hand wrapped around the nearest pole, her knuckles pale against the metal.

Posters drifted in and out of focus above her. A smiling woman sold insurance. A theatre production promised transformation. Cassandra's gaze dropped to the window, to the blur of tunnel walls flying past, and stayed there.

She wondered if anyone else could feel it. The hum beneath her ribs. The thing she had carried home from the night before.

Would it ever leave her? Or had she taken something inside that could not be given back?

When she reached the building, the sudden brightness felt almost hostile.

Inside Vanguard, the lights buzzed faintly overhead, far too white, and the space echoed with soft keyboard taps and filtered air. The reception desk was still neat, still unmoved by time. Cassandra walked across the pale wood floor with careful steps, her boots sounding louder than she remembered.

The receptionist offered a polite smile.

Cassandra returned it, though it didn't land. It felt like a borrowed smile, just enough to get her through the door.

Lydia was waiting in a small conference room at the end of the corridor. Her notebook was open beside her, a black pen tucked into the fold. She looked up and rose immediately, her arms extending in effortless welcome.

"Cass," she said warmly. "There you are."

Cassandra let herself be pulled into a brief embrace. Lydia smelled of cedarwood and coffee, something grounded and clean, as if her presence alone might offer stability. Cassandra closed her eyes for half a breath, inhaling it as if steadiness could be taken in and held.

But the comfort didn't last.

"You look… tired," Lydia said gently, her voice quiet but not without concern.

"I didn't sleep well."

Cassandra sat across from her, smoothing the sleeves of her coat with absent fingers. The movement was habitual, something her body remembered even if her mind was elsewhere. The room felt foreign now. Too defined. Too precise. It was as though her edges no longer fit within the clean lines of the furniture, or her breath moved slower than the steady tick of the wall clock.

Lydia observed her closely, not intrusively, but with the clarity of someone accustomed to reading beneath the surface. "Let's take a look at what you've been working on."

Cassandra opened her notebook. The pages were filled with scattered observations, textures, and half-formed thoughts that no longer felt connected to her. Even her handwriting looked strange, as though it belonged to a different version of herself, someone who hadn't walked into a ritual and emerged altered.

She spoke quickly, hoping speed would make up for the lack of conviction. Layers, tonal shifts, Camden's winter vintage, the blend of sustainability and nostalgia. The words came out in order, but they landed without heaviness. They felt borrowed from the person she had been last week, someone who still believed surface could be separated from depth.

Lydia nodded where appropriate, though her gaze never left Cassandra's face for long. She was listening, but not only to the words.

When the explanation ended, Lydia stood. "I'll make you a coffee. Something strong."

Cassandra didn't argue. She nodded, then let herself sink a little further into the chair, as if the cushions might hold what she couldn't.

The lights above hummed with low electricity. Voices passed softly in the hallway beyond the glass, blurred fragments of conversation that rose and fell without clarity. Cassandra pressed her fingertips to her temples. Her head pulsed in quiet beats, each one carrying traces of what she wasn't ready to revisit.

Lucas's message returned, curling at the edge of her awareness.

Even deeper.

The words lingered behind her eyes, not as memory, but as something still unfolding.

Lydia returned a few minutes later with two mugs. She set one gently in front of Cassandra before taking her seat again. Her expression was composed, but watchful.

The scent of coffee rose between them, sharp and earthy, grounding but not enough to settle the tremor beneath Cassandra's skin.

"You can tell me if something's wrong," Lydia said at last. Her voice was calm, anchored. "You seem a little… elsewhere today."

Cassandra wrapped her hands around the mug. The heat spread across her skin in slow increments, but it took longer to settle beneath the surface.

"I'm all right," she said softly. "Just been in my head, I suppose."

Lydia studied her in silence, reading more than the words allowed. Then she nodded once, not pushing. "If you need time, you've got it. But let's aim for the end of the week, if that still feels manageable?"

There was a pause before Cassandra nodded. "Yes. I think so."

"Good. I have something else in mind for you after that."

She didn't elaborate, and Cassandra didn't ask. Some part of her registered the words, but already her thoughts were drifting.

She took a sip of the coffee. It was strong and bitter, grounding in the way only something tangible could be. She let it linger on her tongue longer than usual, as if hoping it might anchor her fully back into the moment.

But her mind was already slipping away. Back to the feel of the robe against her skin. The presence of the book in her lap, solid and waiting. The message that had appeared and vanished as if pulled from some unseen place. This world, this office, these glass walls felt increasingly like a version of life she had only imagined belonging to.

And somewhere beneath the quiet responses and steady nods, a question stirred. Not loud. Not urgent. Just present.

What would tomorrow night bring?

And where would it lead her?

They spoke a little longer. Lydia filled the space with quiet updates, news from the editorial team, a handful of names Cassandra recognised but no longer felt connected to. She nodded when she should, murmured brief replies, but the distance grew with every moment.

Each breath inside the room felt thinner than the last, as though she were inhabiting her body only in outline, watching herself move and speak from just beyond the glass.

When she finally rose to leave, Lydia stood with her and walked her to the door.

"Take care of yourself, Cass," she said, resting a hand lightly on Cassandra's arm. "And remember, if it all starts to feel like too much... I'm always around."

Cassandra met her eyes. There was kindness there, familiar and sincere. She offered a tired smile, one that didn't quite settle.

"I know. Thank you."

She stepped out into the corridor, the lights overhead too bright, the hum of conversation from the other rooms oddly far away.

Outside, the sky had softened into its usual overcast hush. The street was a tangle of umbrellas and headlights, the air damp with a promise of rain. Cassandra walked without hurry, coat wrapped close, the city's noise slipping past her like mist.

She didn't look back.

Whatever she was returning to, it wasn't the same place she had left that morning.

By the time she reached the flat, the light had changed again. A quiet glow filtered in from the streetlamps, casting soft shapes against the walls. She locked the door behind her, slipped off her boots, and stood for a moment in the stillness.

The silence inside was not empty. It carried a presence, soft and attentive, as though the flat had been waiting for her return.

The front door opened just after ten. Miranda stepped inside, hair windblown, eyes tired. She paused in the doorway, taking in Cassandra and the hush of the room.

"You're still up," she said softly.

"I couldn't sleep."

Miranda removed her coat without answering. She poured two glasses of wine, her movements quiet and practiced. When she handed Cassandra hers, she finally met her gaze.

Cassandra stared into the glass. "Do you remember the first time you saw the book?"

Miranda sat beside her. "Not the exact moment. It doesn't always come like that. But I remember the feeling. Like something was shifting underneath everything I thought I knew."

Cassandra glanced toward the table, then back at Miranda. "It feels like it's always known me."

Miranda nodded slowly. "It probably has."

The silence that followed was not hollow, but full of the things they didn't say. Outside, a siren rose and fell in the distance, fading into the quiet like a memory released.

"You could have warned me," Cassandra said at last.

"I know," Miranda replied gently. "But would you have listened?"

Cassandra didn't answer. The wine sat heavy on her tongue, darker than memory, deeper than comfort. She swallowed, then spoke again, her voice thin at the edges.

"I didn't choose this."

Miranda's eyes stayed on hers. "You didn't have to. It chose you."

They drank in silence. The flat held its breath around them. Shadows stretched across the walls, long and soft, as if listening. Cassandra's gaze drifted toward the table. Her fingers tightened slightly around the stem of her glass.

"It showed me something today," she said at last. "A line. Then it vanished."

Miranda's tone was calm but weighted. "It only reveals what you're ready to see."

Cassandra pressed her palm to the centre of her chest. The hum beneath it stirred again, sharper now, not loud but undeniable. It pulsed in quiet rhythm, as if it had heard them speaking. As if it understood.

"It said, the closer you are to the fire, the darker the shadow you cast."

Her voice was barely above a whisper, but it carried more than the words themselves.

"What does that mean?"

Miranda's expression changed, not in surprise but with recognition.

"It means you're close now," she said. "Closer than most ever get."

Cassandra's chest tightened. Her hand lowered, and with it, the glass came to rest in her lap.

"And Lucas?" she asked, the name catching in her throat. "He messaged and said we're going deeper tomorrow night."

Miranda's fingers tightened slightly around her own glass. One brow lifted, but she stayed silent for a beat longer, her gaze dimming as though something in her had drawn back.

"Then you are," she said finally. "Whatever you experienced before… that was only the surface."

Something moved through Cassandra at those words. Not fear exactly, and not hope. Something older. Something she couldn't name.

"And what if I'm not ready?"

Miranda stayed silent. Rain began to thread through the quiet, each drop tapping gently against the windows with insistent rhythm.

At last, she spoke.

"The shadows don't wait."

The hum rose again in response. Not pain. Not discomfort. Just presence.

Just truth.

Cassandra leaned forward, elbows resting on her knees, the glass balanced carefully between her hands.

"What was it like for you?" she asked. "When you started going deeper."

Miranda didn't answer straight away. She stared into her glass as though something inside it might rise and speak for her. The pause carried weight, not reluctance but history.

"I fought it," she said eventually. "For a long time. I thought I could take the pieces I wanted and leave the rest behind. But that isn't how this works."

"What happened?" Cassandra asked, quieter now.

Miranda's gaze lifted but didn't quite reach her. In the fading light, she looked older. Not in her skin or posture, but in the way memory moved behind her eyes.

"I got lost," she said. "Or maybe I found something and couldn't come back from it. There's a cost, Cass. Not everyone sees it right away, but it's there. In the things you start to give up. The parts of yourself that stop fitting in the daylight."

The words settled between them. Cassandra felt them drop into her chest like stones sinking through deep water.

"Did it change you?" she asked.

Miranda gave a small, sad smile, the kind that needed no explanation.

"No. It revealed me."

The pause that followed lasted longer this time. Not emptiness, but a fullness too dense to name. Cassandra lowered her gaze to her hands. Everything around her seemed charged with a quiet expectancy, as though the room itself was waiting.

"I don't know if I can go through with it," she whispered.

Miranda's voice softened but held steady. "Then don't. Not yet. Not until you know."

"Was there someone for you?" Cassandra asked gently. "Someone like Lucas?"

Miranda blinked. The question landed with more intimacy than either of them had expected.

"There was someone," she said slowly. "But not like him. Lucas is different. He doesn't lead you. He waits. If you follow, it's because you chose to."

Cassandra turned toward the window. The rain had eased, but the city beyond remained glazed in reflection, its streets slick with residue, the air still taut with quiet tension.

"I'm scared," she admitted.

Miranda didn't speak right away. When she did, her tone was steady, almost kind.

"Good. That means you haven't lost yourself yet."

Neither of them moved. The stillness that followed wasn't heavy, only present. It opened slowly, like space being made between two breaths.

"Do you remember that summer we went to Mornington?" Cassandra asked.

Miranda's mouth curved. "The caravan park. You tried to convince me the sea had secrets."

"It does," Cassandra murmured. "We just weren't listening properly."

"You made us collect stones," Miranda said, a faint thread of amusement in her voice. "Said they would protect us."

Cassandra felt the edge of a smile. "I still have mine."

"I don't," Miranda said. "I think I lost it the year I moved to London."

The smile slipped from Cassandra's face. "Maybe I should've stayed home."

Miranda didn't respond at first. She reached forward, set her empty glass carefully on the table, then folded her hands in her lap with quiet deliberation. "Would you really be happier there?" she asked, her voice low and steady.

"I don't know," Cassandra said. "But it was simpler. Before all this. Before Lucas. Before the robe. Before the book started whispering to me when I closed my eyes."

Miranda tilted her head slightly. "Was it really simpler? Or just quieter?"

Cassandra stared down at her fingers, curling slightly against her jeans. "Ethan was there," she said. "That mattered."

A slow nod passed between them, Miranda's expression unreadable in the dimness. "He still is. In some way."

The ache rose without warning, sharp beneath Cassandra's ribs. She closed her eyes and let it crest. "He would hate this," she whispered. "He would tell me to run."

"And would you?"

"I used to."

Miranda reached out, her touch light against Cassandra's wrist. "He was part of who you were," she said gently. "But that doesn't mean he's all of who you are."

Cassandra opened her eyes again. The room had softened around them. Only the amber glow of a single lamp lit the space, stretching light into the corners, flickering against the rim of her nearly empty glass.

"I do miss him," she said.

"I know," Miranda replied.

They sat together in quiet memory, their thoughts rising like old photographs held too long in the sun. Cassandra could almost smell the salt air again, feel the warm grit of sand between her toes, hear Ethan's laugh carrying across the water like something half-remembered. She had written whole pieces about that summer. None of them had ever felt finished.

"Do you think he would recognise me now?" she asked.

Miranda tilted her head. "I think he'd see the same heart. Just in a different skin."

Cassandra drew in a slow breath and released it. Her hands rested in her lap, drifting lightly across the fabric of her jeans. The motion was small, grounding, something to hold while the rest of her kept shifting.

"I don't know where this ends," she said.

"No," Miranda said softly. "But you're not there yet."

A gust of wind stirred against the windowpane. Outside, the city blurred beneath the steady draw of rain, its outlines softened, unreachable.

"Tell me something," Cassandra said after a pause.

Miranda turned toward her. "What kind of something?"

"Something true. Something that helped you stay."

The air turned again. Miranda's gaze drifted to the glass, as though the answer lived somewhere just beyond it.

"I stopped asking whether it was real," she said finally. "And started asking what it wanted to show me."

Cassandra nodded. The words didn't settle easily. They moved through her like water in a dark place, shaping themselves against edges she hadn't yet faced. Still, something in her recognised their shape.

She set her empty glass on the table and rose slowly, the cushions shifting behind her.

At the window, the streetlights burned through the rain, casting a gold haze across the blur of night. She placed her palm against the pane, flat and unmoving, as though trying to reach something waiting on the other side.

Behind her, Miranda stepped closer. "You should sleep," she said gently. "Tomorrow will find you soon enough."

Cassandra didn't answer at once. Her breath clouded faintly on the glass. Below, the city moved in flickers of light, unaware.

The silence stretched.

"I think part of me already knows I'll go," she said at last.

"I know."

When she finally turned, her expression was unreadable. "But not because I'm ready," she added.

Miranda nodded. "Because something in you is learning to listen."

They stood for a while longer, two outlines in the dim, caught in thoughts they didn't speak aloud, tethered by something unspoken between them.

Eventually, Miranda gave a small sigh. She touched Cassandra's arm as she passed. "I'm going to bed. Try to rest, even if you don't sleep."

Cassandra watched her disappear down the hallway. The soft click of the closing door settled over the room like a full stop.

She turned back, letting her gaze drift across the quiet space. Two glasses sat on the table, each holding only a trace of red, a quiet record of everything left unsaid.

Cassandra gathered them without thought and carried them to the kitchen. The water from the tap ran cold. She washed them slowly, the rhythm steadying. The faint scent of wine lingered on her fingers.

Back in the lounge, something had changed. The robe had moved slightly, only an inch from where it had been, but enough to catch her breath. She stood still, hands damp, staring at the dark fabric folded in its patient shape. The hum within her had settled there. Not gone. Only resting. Waiting.

She turned off the lights.

In the dark that followed, the city's glow brushed the windows, painting the walls in muted gold and grey. It felt less like illumination and more like a breath moving through the room.

Upstairs, the floor creaked once. Then silence.

She lingered, unmoving. A slow breath left her, and she stepped into the dark.

Sleep came gradually, but not unwillingly. Something in her had begun to yield. And though the pull beneath her skin never truly faded, she no longer feared it.

Closer than most.

And something in her had started to listen.

.

7
THE EDGE OF BECOMING

E vening had settled softly over the flat before she realised the day had gone. She had moved through the hours in fragments, and now the light outside had dimmed once more.

Cassandra sat at the desk in the corner of the lounge, her fingers hovering above the keyboard, unmoving. The glow of the screen cast a pale sheen across her hands, making them look colder than they felt. A single sentence blinked in the document before her, half-formed and unsure of itself.

She read it twice.

Then pressed delete.

The silence around her did not feel heavy, only watchful. As though the flat was waiting for her to speak aloud something she had not yet admitted to herself.

Outside, the city had fallen into dusk. Lights shimmered along the street below, softened by the mist that clung stubbornly to the rooftops. Somewhere in the distance, a siren rose and faded like a breath released too late.

The air inside the flat was still, but not restful. Time felt thick, as though it had paused just beyond her reach, each minute stretching longer than it should have. The robe remained folded on the arm of the couch. The book sat quietly beside it. Neither had moved since the night before, yet their presence filled the room. Charged. Waiting.

Her tea had gone cold long ago. She did not remember making it.

Every sound felt sharper. Every silence deeper. She told herself she would write, just to pass the hours, to steady her thoughts. But nothing settled. Her body remained at the desk, but her awareness drifted elsewhere.

Something in her already knew the night had begun.

When the knock came, it was soft.

Not urgent, but it found her like it had been waiting.

She stood slowly, a tightness gathering in her chest, somewhere between readiness and unease. She crossed the room, each step deliberate.

And opened the door.

A parcel rested on the mat, wrapped in brown paper and bound with black cord. Her name was written across the front in deep ink, the same careful hand that had marked the book. There was no return address, no note enclosed. Only a silence that seemed deliberate, as though it had chosen the moment to arrive.

She carried it inside, her bare feet soundless against the floorboards. The air shifted as she crossed the room, not quiet exactly, but suspended, as if the space itself were holding still.

Cassandra placed the parcel beside the book. Her hands moved without hesitation, though her chest tightened as she loosened the string. It slipped free with the softness of a whisper, and the paper opened like something long kept and only now revealed.

Inside was a key.

It was darker than brass, its surface aged in a way that suggested time but not use. Carvings spiralled along the shaft in a language she did not know yet somehow recognised.

The handle curled inward, forming an elegant loop, and where the teeth should have been sharp, they instead shaped a symbol she had already seen, embossed into the spine of the book.

She turned it slowly in her palm. The metal carried a quiet warmth, and when it caught the lamplight it shimmered faintly, casting a slender shadow across the table. She tilted it again. The shadow bent unnaturally, curling in a direction the light could not explain.

She set the key beside the book and lowered herself onto the rug, legs folded beneath her. The hush in the room thickened, carrying the sense of something leaning closer. Her fingertips hovered over the cover, then touched it lightly, the surface cool and steady beneath her skin.

The book opened without resistance.

The first pages were blank. Cassandra turned them slowly, one after the other, the paper soft at the edges. Her breathing shallowed.

Then the ink appeared.

It rose from the fibres gradually, as though pulled upward from the paper itself. Dark and deliberate, the words shaped themselves with careful grace, like memory returning from silence.

To unlock the truth, you must first unlock yourself.

Her pulse faltered. The message was simple, yet it carried a weight beyond its words, as if the answer to everything hovered close, formed but not yet spoken.

Her hand drifted toward the phone without thought, not to check for anything, but as though it might hold a response she had not yet found. She didn't unlock it. She only held it, the weight grounding her but not easing the unease beneath her ribs. Ethan's name rose in her mind, soft and insistent, a thread she had not let go of.

She saw him clearly. The slight furrow of his brow. The quiet crease between his eyes whenever something unsettled him. That was always his way, careful and measured, searching for shape before giving it a name.

The phone vibrated once in her hand. The suddenness startled her.

For an instant she thought it might be him.

But it wasn't.

It was Lucas.

Bring the key. I'll send for you shortly.

Her stomach tightened. The hum within her stirred in answer, no longer resting but rising again. It should have unnerved her, how easily the key had found its way to her. How certain it seemed that Lucas had always known this moment would arrive.

Behind her, a door eased open.

Miranda stepped into the lounge, the sleeve of her jumper pulled halfway down one hand, a tea mug cupped in the other. Her hair was gathered low at the nape of her neck, a few loose strands falling forward to frame her face. The light from the hallway softened behind her, casting her in the kind of quiet that only arrived late, when the city had stilled.

"Was that the door earlier?"

Cassandra nodded. "A key. From him."

Miranda's brow furrowed. "From who exactly?"

"Lucas. He sent a message too."

Miranda stepped closer, her gaze tightening. "What did it say?"

Cassandra hesitated, her fingers brushing the edge of the table. "He said… bring the key. That he would send for me shortly."

Miranda's eyes dropped to the key beside the book. The carved symbol shimmered faintly in the lamplight. Her expression changed, cautious, thoughtful.

"I've seen that symbol before," she said. "Not just on the book. A long time ago."

Cassandra waited, but Miranda didn't continue.

She moved in closer, mug held to her chest like a shield, though her voice stayed even, carrying a quiet warning.

"Lucas has a way of getting into your thoughts. He doesn't always knock first."

Cassandra met her eyes. The book sat near her elbow like a presence, still open to the page where the words had risen. Across the room, the robe lay folded neatly on the arm of the couch, unchanged but not forgotten. Everything in the space felt poised, caught in suspension.

"He always knows, Cass," Miranda continued, "and that's what makes it so easy to fall into him. And so hard to find your way back."

Cassandra didn't answer straight away. The hum beneath her ribs had stilled. It neither pulled nor pressed. It simply lingered.

Miranda tilted her head slightly, studying her. Steam rose from her cup in slow spirals, delicate and deliberate, as though it, too, was listening.

"Just be careful tonight," she said. "Not just with him. With yourself."

"Careful feels like something I've already stepped past."

Miranda held her gaze. "Then please… be sure."

She stepped forward and placed a hand on Cassandra's shoulder, her fingers curling just enough to anchor her for a moment. It felt more like memory than instruction.

Then she turned and disappeared down the hallway.

The door closed with a soft click.

Her phone buzzed again.

It's time.

Not a command. Not even a request. Just the flame at the edge of the wick, breathless before the burn.

Cassandra stood. The key slipped easily into her bag. The robe flowed, draped over her shoulders like a second skin. She moved through the flat with quiet precision. Lights off. Windows closed. No words spoken. Only the subtle creak of the floor and the soft tick of the hallway clock.

Outside, the city had darkened. Streetlamps flickered against the fog beginning to settle low across the road. A black car waited at the curb. Its engine barely made a sound.

The driver stepped out. Cap low. Hands gloved. He opened the rear door without a word.

Cassandra paused. Just for a moment. She thought of Ethan, the steady path once laid out in golden hours. The quiet certainty in his touch. Sunlight on their shoulders. Laughter carried by coastal winds. A life imagined in daylight, shaped by logic and love.

Then, she stepped into the car.

And the night took her.

♥

The car pulled away from the curb in silence. Cassandra sat still, the robe drawn close around her shoulders, its folds soft against her arms. Streetlights passed in steady intervals, each one swallowed by the dark until the glow of the city thinned into shadow.

She didn't speak. Neither did the driver.

The hum inside her had steadied, no longer pressing forward, only present. It matched the rhythm of the tyres, a soundless measure keeping time for something unnamed. She turned to the window. Her reflection floated across the glass, faint and translucent, layered over the shifting dark beyond.

They weren't going to The Hollow. She knew it without alarm, without reason offered. The knowledge settled quietly in her bones as the last edges of London receded.

No music bled from basement walls. No shimmer of Camden neon followed. Only a narrowing road ahead, lined by trees that leaned close, branches drawn together like interlaced fingers. Fog clung to the ground, pulled tight across the edges of the verge.

Her hand slipped toward the bag at her side. The key was still hidden, yet its weight pressed against her hip, steady and insistent.

The streetlamps ended. Forest replaced them.

The road thinned into a single lane, headlights slicing through mist to reveal tangles of bramble and bare limbs that arched overhead like the ceiling of a cathedral. Time blurred. Distance folded.

Then came gravel, a new rhythm beneath the tyres, each crunch a deliberate sound. The path curved gently until the gate appeared.

It rose from the fog, tall and spired, its surface veined with rust and climbing vine. The ironwork was intricate, patterned with shapes that hinted at meaning she could almost recall. Familiar without memory.

As the car approached, the gate opened. Not with protest, not with haste, but with the slow grace of something long prepared.

Beyond it, the house revealed itself in pieces, as though it had been waiting for the right moment to show its shape. First the silhouette, then the sweep of weathered stone. Then the faint glow of windows, light folded deep inside the façade, as if it had always burned there, beneath the surface.

Ivy clung tight along the walls. Symbols were carved into the stone, not hidden but displayed, etched like scars that spoke not of damage but of endurance.

The car slowed to a stop.

The driver stepped out and opened the rear door with a quiet gesture.

Cassandra emerged into the cold. The air here was heavier, shaped by soil, moss, and something more elusive. Beneath it lingered a faint sharpness, a scent like incense long since extinguished.

The robe drifted against her in the breeze. Her breath unfurled in a pale cloud and dissolved.

The house did not loom in threat, but in certainty. It stood as though it had always been here. As though she had always been meant to arrive.

It did not call her forward. It did not need to.

Her feet moved before her thoughts had followed.

The front doors opened as she approached. No figure waited behind them.

Warmth met her first. Not comfort, not invitation, but the warmth of something long-burning, lived in, layered with memory. The air inside pulsed faintly, as though the walls themselves remembered.

The entryway stretched wide, its vaulted ceiling held aloft by dark timber beams. A chandelier turned slowly above, scattering shifting patterns of light that moved across the walls. Every shadow seemed to carry its own intention, as if shapes were watching from the edges.

Recessed alcoves lined the hall. Each cradled a single object: masks, carved figures, relics beyond words yet drawing her closer.

They did not hang as decoration. They had been placed, chosen, held.

The staircase curved forward, broad and steady. Its railing bore symbols cut with deliberate precision, markings that caught the glow in quiet flashes. As Cassandra stepped nearer, the designs seemed to stir. Not in sight, not fully, but the hum within her chest deepened in reply.

Something in the house answered her.

A floorboard groaned.

Lucas stood at the base of the stairs.

He did not move at once, nor fill the air with words. He only watched her, the light tracing the edge of his coat, the line of his shoulders, the stillness in his stance. His gaze fixed on hers with quiet exactness, as though nothing else existed beyond their recognition of one another.

"Cassandra."

Her name travelled through the space like it had belonged there, waiting for its return. A single note restored to silence.

"You came."

His mouth tilted faintly. "I wasn't sure you would. But still, I left the door open."

She didn't answer straight away. The robe lay close against her frame. The book and the key pressed at her side. The message lingered somewhere beneath thought, unspoken but present. None of it explained why she was here, and yet none of it felt wrong.

"You knew I would."

Lucas's eyes lowered briefly to the bag at her hip. A flicker touched his expression, not surprise, not pride, but a quiet recognition, as though something in him understood before words could.

"Some things arrive before we do," he said.

She could have asked him how he knew. Whether the parcel had been sent by his hand. Whether the words that revealed themselves within the book had truly been meant for her. But the questions dissolved before they reached her lips. The answers did not seem concealed. Only biding their time.

Without another word, Lucas turned. He began to ascend the stairs, his footsteps absorbed by the timber beneath him. His pace was steady, deliberate, unhurried, like a man returning to familiar ground rather than guiding someone new, a path worn into him through countless passages before.

Behind her, the front doors closed with the weight of finality. There was no echo. No draft. Only the sense that something had folded inward, sealing the threshold behind her.

"Did you bring the key?" he asked.

Cassandra remained at the base of the stairs for a moment longer. Then her fingers slipped into her bag, brushing the cool edge of the object.

The metal was colder than she remembered. Her hand curved around its shape, the carvings etched deep into the surface catching the light in fractured flickers. As she drew it out, its weight seemed to alter the space between them.

Lucas glanced back. His gaze fell to the piece in her hand. A smile ghosted across his mouth, restrained and unreadable, belonging less to the present moment than to something older, something carried.

As if he was reading her mind and all of the unanswered questions that swirled within it he said in a calm voice, "There is little I do not know."

The silence that followed was not oppressive. It lingered, open, as though listening.

Cassandra held the key a moment longer, then began to climb.

The rustle of her robe mingled with the creak of timber beneath her steps. The sound dissolved into the house itself, absorbed as if the walls had been built to swallow such movements. A scent rose to meet her, cedar, aged leather, and something more elusive. Not cologne, not smoke. Presence. Him.

The staircase curved upward, opening onto a landing framed by tall arches. A hallway stretched ahead, elegant and hushed. Paintings lined the walls, their pigments muted by age and shadow. Though she could not make out every detail, the figures seemed almost in motion, their eyes fixed yet attentive, their half-lit faces holding expressions too intricate to dismiss.

Beneath the paintings, alcoves cradled statues poised mid-action. Marble and bronze limbs stretched outward, hands frozen in gestures of defiance, prayer, or sorrow. Their precision was flawless, yet something in them felt unsettled. Not lifeless, not at rest. Paused. As though the moment she turned away, they might continue what had been interrupted.

Between the alcoves, weapons gleamed against dark wood panels. They were not relics dulled by age, but artifacts cared for, sharpened, and ready. Swords with jewelled hilts, their blades narrow and keen. Daggers etched with curling script she could not decipher. An axe whose edge shimmered coldly beneath the low golden glow.

This was no ordinary building. It was not simply old. It was alive in a way that defied language, as though the walls themselves carried a slow awareness and watched her passing.

Cassandra's chest tightened. The air pressed differently here, weighted yet not stagnant. Her steps slowed. She glanced down at the key still resting in her hand. The metal was warmer now, as if the house had claimed it. The carvings no longer felt foreign. They seemed to thrum faintly beneath her touch, not glowing, not shifting, but alive with recognition. What once felt powerful now seemed to belong both to her and to this place.

She drew the robe closer across her collarbones. The fabric slid against her skin with a softness that carried its own intent, as though following an unseen current. Whatever force had drawn her this far still moved ahead, unspoken, invisible.

Lucas slowed at the landing and turned. The light touched one side of his face, sharpening the lines of his features. There was a composure to him that quieted the very space around him.

"You feel it, don't you?" His voice was low, carrying no surprise, as though the answer had already been given.

Something beneath his tone vibrated like a chord held taut before release. Cassandra stopped. A restless tension gathered in her chest, lifting high through her ribs, sharpening every nerve.

She swallowed and managed, "Feel what?"

"The house," he said. "It knows you are here."

The words unsettled her. Her gaze flicked to the edges of the corridor where the shadows seemed deeper, still but attentive. The house did not press with weight but with nearness, the way a hand hovers just above the skin. She could not tell if it meant to welcome her or to warn her.

Lucas stepped closer. The edge of his coat brushed the hem of her robe with a sound so slight it was almost imagined. He reached forward. His fingers touched her palm. The contact was brief, but it sparked, a quiet heat that travelled into her hand.

He did not take the key. He only acknowledged it, as though affirming something that already bound them.

"This is the moment it was meant for," he said, his words steady, carrying through the stillness. "Are you ready to accept it?"

Cassandra hesitated.

The sensation inside her climbed, a mounting pressure that filled her ears and blurred into the beat of her heart. For an instant, Ethan's voice cut through, calm and familiar, the sound of safety. She held on to it, then let it fade.

Her grip closed firmly around the key. "What is it for?"

Lucas did not answer at once. His eyes held hers briefly before shifting toward the darkness ahead.

"It doesn't just open a door," he said.

Her brow tightened. "Then what?"

"It opens you."

Cassandra said nothing. The words settled over her like velvet, soft and weighty. She looked down at the key again. It appeared unchanged, yet something in her had shifted. She was no longer only a participant. She was the crossing itself.

The key anchored her. Its weight pressed into her palm like a question she had not yet learned how to answer. The shadows around her stirred, not with sound, but with pull, with a gravity all their own.

"Yes," she said, the syllable quiet, escaping before she had even chosen it.

Lucas's smile deepened. It was not kind, nor cruel. It was knowing. Without another word, he turned and began to walk.

Cassandra followed. With every stride, her energy sharpened.

The corridor stretched long and hushed, its walls marked with symbols she could not decipher. The lines shimmered faintly as they passed, not with light, but with awareness.

They moved together, silent and steady, toward the source of a deeper sound.

The door at the end opened as they neared, not abruptly, but with a fluid, sentient grace, as if the house itself had chosen to grant passage. The shift of air carried through her, a vibration that spread low and deliberate, quickening her pulse not in fear but in recognition. It moved through her with the weight of something remembered.

The passage beyond stretched into dimness, more impression than architecture, its edges softened by shadow that seemed to shift with intent. Lucas moved without hesitation, his steps measured and exact, as though walking a path he had always known.

Cassandra tightened her hold on the key. The metal felt cool, firm, unwavering. It steadied her. The robe swept close as she walked, its folds catching stray glimmers of light from no visible source.

The air altered again. Every faint groan of timber, every subtle movement above, carried like a whisper just beyond comprehension. The space did not merely enclose. It observed.

"Where are we going?" she asked, her voice scarcely more than a murmur, dissolving into the quiet.

Lucas glanced back. His face remained unreadable, his eyes holding pale reflections in the dark. "To where the shadows have called us."

The reply curled through her like rising mist, cool and certain. A shiver touched her spine, but she did not falter. Unease stirred lightly, yet still she moved. Her name seemed to linger behind them, bound to the space where he had spoken it. The key warmed faintly against her hand, as though alive to his nearness.

Whatever this was, it kept drawing her onward.

She moved through the hush with the sense that the shift had already taken place. Not in the world around her. In herself.

Then, somewhere ahead, a lock turned.

The sound rose gently, like the first intake of air.

Quiet. Certain. Close.

The hallway narrowed. The walls pressed closer, etched with markings she couldn't decipher. As they descended a winding staircase, the air changed. The temperature dropped. The scent of damp earth deepened, layered with something older still. Each step creaked softly beneath her, while Lucas moved without sound, as if the house itself yielded to him.

The carvings pulled at her attention. Spirals. Eyes. Unfurling roots. Each line cut deeply into stone, worn smooth by countless passages. They seemed to respond to her gaze, a faint recognition rising from their surfaces. She couldn't read them, but she felt observed. Not threatened. Accepted.

The staircase turned again. The air grew thicker. A fine mist gathered, curling around her ankles. Cassandra drew the robe closer, its fabric holding warmth against the chill that coiled in the stairwell. The key warmed faintly in her palm, not insistent, only present.

She tried to form a thought, to name what stirred in her, but words dissolved before they found shape. This place moved beneath language. Beneath quiet. Beneath waking.

Lucas did not speak. His figure held steady ahead of her, outlined by the glow rising from below. A shimmer of light appeared, dim and flickering, alive in a way that revealed more than it showed.

Cassandra fixed her gaze on him. The line of his shoulders. The unbroken precision of each step. The way he moved through the dark as though it belonged to him.

And then, the staircase ended.

At its base, Lucas stopped before a door unlike any she had seen in waking life. It towered above them, carved from ancient wood so dark it was nearly black. Its surface rippled with patterns she recognised at once. Spirals. Lines. Symbols that shimmered faintly in the candlelight. The same markings embossed on the spine of the book from The Veiled Quill. The same shapes that had followed her through moments unnamed and dreams she had never escaped.

Something within her answered. The pressure inside her body bloomed outward, no longer subtle, and the key pulsed in her grasp as though it had found its purpose.

A shiver moved through her, not from cold, but from recognition. She had seen this door before.

Not here. Not like this. But in the dream, the first dream, where the world had tilted and time had slipped loose. She remembered its weight beneath her hand, how it had yielded to her touch, not as something new but something long known. Now it stood before her, carved and solid, no longer imagined but inevitable.

Her breath slowed, but her heart refused to follow.

She looked at Lucas. The flicker of light softened the edges of his face, but his presence was unchanged. Watchful. Still. Unshakeable. The faceless figure from her dream had never revealed itself, but the patience was the same. The pull.

Had it been him all along?

Before she could speak, he turned as though he had heard the question rise, and let it remain unspoken.

"This is where you decide," he said. His voice didn't echo. It didn't need to. Finality carried in the quiet between them. "Everything changes beyond this door."

Her fingers tightened around the key. It pulsed with steady rhythm, no longer silent. Not a suggestion. A summons. Something in her had already crossed, though her body remained still.

Doubt flared sharp and precise. What if she lost something vital on the other side? Some tether she could never reclaim.

Ethan's face rose in her mind. The way he had looked at her the night before she left. Steady. Hopeful. Real.

You don't have to do this, Cass.

The words arrived like an echo from another life. Not wrong. Not gone. Just distant.

She would always love him. But he belonged to the version of herself that had been. And this belonged to the part still becoming.

Her gaze lifted. Lucas had not moved. His expression gave nothing away, yet his presence wrapped around her like flame unlit, waiting to be touched.

He was not safety. He was change.

And beneath every hesitation, desire no longer lay hidden.

She wanted to step through. She wanted to be undone.

The key slid into the lock without resistance. A click followed, soft but final, and something unspoken released within her. The door creaked inward on its own, not urged by wind or force, only inevitability.

Candlelight stretched across the floor, revealing the edge of a vast chamber cloaked in shadow. The air carried the sharp tang of metal laced with sweetness, like perfume lingering in an emptied room.

She stepped forward. Mist curled at her feet, deliberate, as though it had lingered for this exact moment. The silence was complete, not hollow but listening.

Behind her, the door remained open. Lucas entered after her without a word.

Ahead, the chamber unfolded in slow, impossible layers. Candles burned in sconces carved from the stone itself. The ceiling arched high above, swallowed in dimness. At the centre rose a low circular platform veiled in silks that moved as if moved by unseen hands.

A pedestal waited at its heart. Cassandra felt its call. Not a demand. Not a pull. An invitation.

Each step forward felt like release, layers falling away until only the ache of becoming remained.

She didn't look back.

Whatever this chamber held, whatever the key had opened, was no longer something to fear. It was the part of her she had refused to face. The flame smouldering too long in silence.

Now it had been lit.

And she walked into it willingly, standing at the edge of becoming.

8
THE SHAPE OF SURRENDER

The chamber was a paradox, vast yet suffocating, intimate yet endless. Shelves stretched upward, stacked with books bound in leathers she could not place, their titles obscured, their presence heavy and silent. The air was dense, not hollow but watchful, as if every object in the room was caught in its own suspension.

At the centre, the circular dais seemed to pulse faintly. Symbols carved into its surface shimmered in rhythm with something deep within her, the same resonance that had first stirred when she touched the key, when she opened the book, when she stepped through the door she had always half-known was waiting.

She had expected something different. A dream repeated. Brightness without origin. Space without boundaries. But what opened before her was not a return. It was continuation. Not memory, but extension. And as she crossed its threshold, something within her adjusted, like a taut thread finally slackening.

Lucas moved ahead, his presence subtle yet magnetic, not pushing but drawing. He walked toward the dais with unhurried grace, his coat brushing the edges of silks that cascaded from the ceiling, their folds stirring faintly as he passed.

"We are alone tonight," he said, his words resonant more than spoken. "No interruptions. No expectations. Only truth."

Cassandra followed. Her steps were careful, deliberate, though steady enough to bring her forward. The floor beneath her seemed altered, less certain, as though something beneath it observed her passing. Her pulse rose with the intimacy of his voice, sharp and precise, cutting into her thoughts. The vibration inside her deepened, not urgent, but constant, attuned to the unseen energy that filled the room.

Behind her, the door remained open, yet it no longer felt like escape. Whatever waited beyond had blurred into memory. Ethan's voice, his steadiness, his face. Not gone, but softened, as though she were already too far to turn back.

It was Lucas who filled the space now.

His presence did not impose. It absorbed. The room seemed to shift with him, each step bending the air toward his gravity. When he reached the dais, he turned, his gaze steady, not demanding, but holding. Cassandra felt the robe stir faintly across her shoulders, though no breeze moved.

"You're still holding back," he said.

She didn't flinch, though the accuracy struck. His words were exact, like fingers pressing into places she had not admitted even to herself.

"I don't know what I'm supposed to be," she said. The honesty surprised her, though she realised it had lived in her for weeks, waiting to take shape.

Lucas descended from the dais and crossed the space between them, his gaze unwavering.

"You are not supposed to be anything," he said. "You already are. The only question is whether you'll allow it."

The silence that followed was thick but alive, the kind that leaned close to hear an answer.

Cassandra's gaze moved to the symbols on the platform. They glimmered faintly, alive in the way fire is alive before it catches. She did not know their meaning. She did not need to. Some part of her understood enough.

She stepped forward. Not to him, not yet, but to the dais.

Lucas did not move. He watched, his stillness its own command.

Her hand hovered over the carved stone. The surface trembled faintly beneath her fingertips, the same subtle vibration she had felt in the book, in the robe, in the key, and in the dreams that had shadowed her waking life.

"What happens here?" she asked.

"Whatever you choose," Lucas replied, his voice low, as though spoken into the marrow of the room.

Stillness settled through her, not absence but anchor, as if something had rooted itself deep inside. She thought of the thresholds already crossed: the night at The Hollow, the robe, the key, the silences that had never been empty.

She looked at him. Not for instruction. For alignment.

He gave a single nod.

Then she stepped onto the dais.

Lucas reached out. His fingertips brushed along her wrist, then traced the line of her palm, coaxing her hand to open. A chill followed, fleeting, and into that space he placed the chalice.

Its surface met her skin with unyielding cold, its weight anchoring her as her hands closed instinctively around the stem. She had held it once before, but now it felt altered. Denser. Awake. What had once been surrender now carried the edge of something sharper, something permanent.

"It has been waiting for you," Lucas said, his voice a quiet current that threaded through her. "Just as I have."

Her throat tightened. She didn't raise her eyes, but the echo of his words moved through her, subtle and insistent. The chalice shimmered faintly where symbols curved along its sides, the glow soft and inward, as though it rose from a depth she could not reach. Its presence sank into her like water into fabric, not demanding, only inevitable.

"Let go of everything else," he murmured, his breath warm against her ear. "There is only this moment."

Cassandra hesitated. Her heart hammered, each inhale uneven, shallow. Ethan's voice surfaced, low and pleading, spun from mornings they had once shared. She could still feel the steadiness of his presence, the familiar press of his hand at her back, the sound of his laugh breaking sunlight in a quiet kitchen.

This is your chance to turn back, the memory whispered.

But even as it spoke, its hold loosened. The air around her gathered into a pull she could not ignore. The charged quiet of the chamber, the calm certainty of Lucas, rose like a tide she had already stepped into. She did not need to answer. Her body had already chosen.

She closed her eyes.

The resonance inside her spread, no longer faint but coursing, threading through every limb. The chalice pulsed in her grasp, no longer just an object but a conduit. Heat flowed into her, eclipsing hesitation, searing and soft at once. It ran along her arms, into her spine, into the space behind her eyes, reordering what she thought was fixed.

Ethan's voice flickered once more, frayed and distant, a whisper she could not hold. She reached for it, but the sensation surged higher, overtaking thought, consuming every question until nothing else remained.

As the liquid passed her lips, fire unfurled beneath her skin. Not burning. Becoming. It spread outward in waves, reshaping the quiet between her bones, altering the space she carried within. The room turned too, its edges dissolving. Light seeped through stone, strange and fluid, revealing carvings across the chamber walls. They moved with slow intention, like something roused from centuries of sleep.

She was no longer a visitor. She was seen. Not as a figure standing apart, but as something summoned, recognised. Not judged. Not measured. Welcomed.

Lucas reached for the chalice, steadying it as her fingers slackened. His touch brushed hers, grounding and electric at once. He leaned closer, his mouth finding the edge of her temple. The kiss was brief, but it ignited a spark that travelled through her like recognition. Not desire. Not comfort. A truth without name, one that had always been there, waiting for her to step into it.

"Everything here has always known you," he said. "It was only waiting for you to know it too."

His words did not persuade. They named what had already changed.

"You only needed to cross."

Cassandra opened her eyes, the chamber bending around her as shadow and light folded together, the space reshaping itself as if silence had found a body. Energy shimmered in the air, not loud but absolute. For the first time, she was not falling. She was lifted, carried by something older than speech, held in a stillness vast enough to contain her.

The chamber seemed to move with her, its rhythm entwined with her own. Shadow, flame, silence, motion. Her heartbeat matched its cadence, each thud resonating through the stone beneath her feet. Lucas's fingers tightened around hers, his touch steady, carrying a current that rippled through her in waves.

They stood together at the heart of the dais. It no longer felt like a platform but the calm centre of a storm, the axis of something that had waited far too long to be acknowledged.

Beside them, draped over a carved stand, a length of silk shimmered in the candlelight. Deep crimson, rich as fire and blood. It caught the light in a way that made it seem to breathe, folds alive with promise. Something in its colour stirred her. Not memory. Not reason. Something deeper, elemental, a pull that was hunger and awe in equal measure.

Lucas reached for it with slow precision, his fingers brushing the edge of the fabric as though it might answer back.

"Trust me," he said.

His voice did not coax or soothe. It held, like the charge in the air before lightning strikes.

Cassandra nodded, unable to form words. Her gaze remained on his hands as he let the silk slide between his fingers, reverent, deliberate. The space between them seemed to narrow, the chamber dimming at its edges until there was only this: his nearness, the warmth radiating from his body, the quiet swell of meaning building between them.

"Close your eyes."

She obeyed. Darkness fell. A moment later, the silk brushed her face, soft, unhurried, and Lucas tied it at the back of her head with care. The blindfold settled against her skin like shadow made tangible, warm and seamless. In an instant, her world shifted.

Every sound sharpened. The flutter of flame. The faint creak of leather. The hush of the chamber as it leaned in to listen. Even her own inhale came louder, measured against the invisible rhythm that vibrated faintly in the air.

She stood still. The silk pressed lightly at her temples, and in losing sight, everything else awakened. She felt his nearness before his hands touched her. The scent of him lingered, clean but edged with something darker, something spiced. Warm air stirred against the curve of her neck, not quite contact, but enough to set every nerve on edge.

When his fingers traced her arms, a tremor coursed through her. He did not rush. His palms moved with slow intent, following the line of her forearms, pausing at her wrists before guiding them gently behind her back.

The silk slid once more across her skin, this time winding around her wrists. The knot he tied was firm but careful, the final pull certain. The fabric tightened just enough to remind her. It was not confinement. It was naming. A physical echo of a choice already made.

A shiver rose, not fear exactly, but something close, sharp and electric, as his fingers lingered against her pulse. He held there, memorising her rhythm, not as a map but as a vow.

"Do you feel it?" he whispered, his mouth close to her ear. "The power between us?"

"Yes," she breathed. The word slipped free before thought, carried on the tension that coiled between them, charged as static before a storm breaks.

His hands moved again, sliding from her shoulders down her arms, then along her sides in a motion both reverent and claiming. The robe she wore offered little shield. Her skin rose to meet the touch, alive, insistent, every part of her aware.

Still, memory flickered. Ethan's smile, clear as sunlight. The way he once looked at her as if she were the only certainty in the world. The image cut through the haze like a crack of light through a closed door. He would not understand this. He would not recognise her here. And a part of her was no longer sure she did either.

Do I even understand it? Or have I been unravelling all along?

Lucas's lips grazed the hollow at her collarbone, a fleeting touch that stole the thought away. Her body leaned into him without permission, into the certainty, into the fire.

His voice followed, low, taut with restraint, a tension trembling beneath its composure.

"You're radiant, Cassandra. You don't just belong to this. This belongs to you."

The words struck somewhere deep. Not flattery. Not even seduction. A truth she hadn't been ready to face until now.

The current inside her was more than longing. It was reckoning. Guilt twisted through her for a moment, pulling her back toward the edge of retreat, but the flame was stronger. The ache to feel, to cross, burned brighter.

Lucas's hands moved with intent. The robe parted beneath his touch, sliding from her shoulders like a veil drawn aside. The air rushed in cool against her skin, sharp and clear, and the contrast made her tremble. Not with fear, but with the undeniable certainty that something within her had awakened.

The space between them grew dense, tension winding tighter until it pressed through her, filling her thoughts. The room itself seemed to fold inward, as if nothing existed beyond this single axis of silence and closeness.

His body brushed hers, his chest against her back, his hands anchoring at her hips with a familiarity that felt both intimate and ancient. Their connection was primal, their movements guided by something older than language, older even than memory.

The vibration that had first stirred in her now rippled through her entire body, pulsing into her limbs, syncing with the symbols carved beneath their feet as though her very rhythm had found its echo in stone.

She slipped past the limits of herself, her senses stretched wide. The air shimmered with a resonance that rose and fell like a tide. When Lucas's hands travelled her, it was not simply touch. It was knowledge. It was recognition. It was her, unfolding.

Her vision blurred. Somewhere beyond the moment, she saw them together, entwined, radiant, their forms threaded with veins of gold. Shadows curled in slow spirals around them, not in menace, but in reverence, as though bearing witness to something sacred.

Cassandra moved in two worlds at once. Anchored and adrift. Immersed in sensation. Each trace of his hand, each kiss at her throat, sent a current rising higher and higher until she thought even the chamber itself was waiting, though for what she could not yet understand.

The atmosphere thickened, charged with a power poised on the edge of form. The carvings beneath her feet glowed faintly, their rhythm a silent drumbeat moving through her bones. Lucas's hand lifted to her jaw, tilting her face upward. His mouth met hers, and the kiss was not gentle. It was flame and gravity, a pull that rewrote her balance and drew her deeper into the vastness of something unknowable.

His heartbeat pressed against her spine, steady and insistent, until it was indistinguishable from her own.

And then, through the rush of sensation, came a whisper. Not sound. Not touch. Presence. Ethan. Distant, but certain.

This isn't you, Cass. Come back to me.

A chill rippled across her skin. The warmth of the chamber thinned, as if his voice had pulled something essential from the air. Guilt tore through the heat, sharp and sudden, a splinter too deep to ignore.

But Lucas's touch steadied her. His presence did not waver. He was not memory. He was here. Real.

"I see you," he breathed against her lips, each word reverent, as though she were not a woman, but truth revealed. "All of you."

The moment crested. The chamber burst into light and shadow, a storm of energy flooding outward from them both. Cassandra cried out, raw and unguarded, the sound torn from the deepest place within her. Power surged through her, unrelenting, ecstatic, filling every corner of her being until she was no longer certain where she ended and the chamber began.

As the glow receded and stillness settled again, Lucas's arms caught her. Her body slackened against him, her wrists loosening until the silk bindings slid free and fell soundlessly to the floor.

He kissed her temple, his voice a quiet vow. "You are extraordinary."

Cassandra could not answer. Her breath came shallow, her body alive with the lingering echo of what had just passed. She leaned into him, letting his silence hold her, and in that stillness she understood. She was no longer falling. She had become something else. Awakened into something at once terrifying and true.

Her gaze lowered to the dais beneath them. The symbols continued to glow with slow, deliberate rhythm. Ethan's face flashed in her thoughts. How he might look at her now. The guilt still cut at her, but it no longer held her captive. Something else had taken root, deeper. Not defiance. Not forgiveness. A knowing. That whatever path had brought her here, it had not been wrong.

The chamber exhaled. Her lungs filled in shallow rhythm. The air was laced with scent, ash and something older than flame, something she could not define.

Lucas steadied her as her vision wavered. And then, for an instant, she saw past the room itself. A horizon of fractured light. Figures moving far away. A chasm that burned with impossible brilliance. From its heart, a voice rose. Fierce. Familiar.

"You're not ready, Cassandra."

Her body went rigid. "Did you hear that?" she whispered.

Lucas's head tilted. His eyes narrowed, sharp with something unreadable. "What did you hear?"

She hesitated. The charge of his touch still held her, but something cold stirred inside. "A voice. It said I wasn't ready."

His mouth curved slowly, the shadows shifting in response. "Perhaps that's true. Or perhaps that's what they want you to believe."

Her chest tightened. She searched his face for something fixed, something solid, but found only mystery. The carved symbols pulsed beneath her feet, steady as breath.

A thought surfaced, unrelenting. This was no longer simple surrender. This was the shape of it, the outline of something that had claimed her, a form she could not turn away from.

Her voice trembled, though not with weakness. "What is between us now?"

Lucas's fingers brushed her jaw, gentle yet immovable. His eyes held hers with a weight that neither faltered nor soothed.

"The darkness," he said.

The glow dimmed. The air pressed close, heavy with unseen presence. And from somewhere deep within the stillness, her name was spoken again. Ethan's voice, or something wearing it. The sound curved around her like a tether reaching back across distance, across time.

Cassandra closed her eyes. The whisper folded into her, not as fear, but as a reminder of what she had stepped past.

She had crossed the threshold. Whatever lay beyond it, she could not return.

And inside, that truth did not summon dread.

It stirred wonder.

It thrilled.

9
TO NAME THE SHADOW

For a long moment, she remained still. Not from sleep. Not from fear. But because the quiet seemed to hold her in place, as if the room itself remembered what had passed.

Cassandra lay on her back, eyes following the pale lines etched into the ceiling. The morning light pressed faintly through the curtains, uncertain and cool, as though it had arrived too early and was still deciding whether to stay.

But it was not the light that stirred her.

It was the low current within her. Constant. Rising softly in her chest, as though something buried deep inside had woken before her and refused to be stilled.

It had not left.

Lucas lingered in her body like heat after flame. Not burning, but vivid. Her wrists tingled faintly, not from pain, but from the silk and what it had meant to give herself so completely.

And then, cutting through the warmth like breath in winter, a whisper.

Ethan.

Not angry. Not pleading. Simply there.

She turned slowly onto her side, her hand reaching for the robe folded at the foot of the bed. It felt heavier than before. Not in fabric or thread, but in memory, as if it carried more than she was ready to hold.

Her other hand drifted toward the phone on the bedside table. The screen blinked once. A missed call.

His name on the screen.

He was not gone. Only further. Still real. Still tethered in a way that would not unravel quietly.

Her thumb hovered over the call log, but she did not press it. Not yet. Her hand lowered slowly, resting against her sternum, where the current continued, low and steady.

It was not fading.

And that, more than anything, unsettled her.

The screen illuminated her face in the dim room, casting uneven shadows across the walls. She stared at it, unmoving. For a moment, the air changed. She imagined Melbourne again, sunlight through gum trees, the echo of his laugh outside a café. There had been a time when that life had felt complete. Now, it seemed far away, tucked behind a door she was not sure she could open again.

She searched for his name in her messages. The blank space waited, quietly pulsing with expectation.

What would she even say? That she missed him? That she was sorry? That something had changed and she no longer knew how to explain what she needed?

A single tear slipped down her cheek. She brushed it away.

Her thumb hovered, then lowered.

Still, her hand lingered, resting on the device like a lifeline to something both comforting and unreachable.

Though she could not see it from here, she felt the book's weight in the room. The memory of it pressed at the edges of her thoughts. Its leather cover, dulled in the morning light, had once looked inert, but Cassandra knew better now. Pages that had vanished were returning, sometimes one at a time, as if biding their moment.

Perhaps it would offer more. Perhaps not. A mirror of her confusion. A keeper of riddles she was not sure she wanted solved.

She rose slowly, brushing her hair back from her face. As she moved, she pulled the robe around her and let it settle over her shoulders. The silk lining grazed her skin, warm and remembering. One side slipped low, revealing the place where the heat had gathered the night before. Her skin was still flushed there. She touched it absently. It did not burn, but something beneath it stirred.

The quiet stretched. Even the air seemed to pause, listening for her decision. She drew the robe tighter, her eyes drifting once to the book resting across the room. Its stillness anchored the silence, patient and unyielding.

The silence was broken by a knock.

"Cass?" Miranda's voice muffled and tentative. "You awake?"

She nodded before remembering Miranda could not see her. "Yeah. Come in."

The door creaked open, and Miranda stepped into the room, two cups of tea in her hands. Her hair was piled messily on her head, and the cardigan wrapped around her made her look soft, unguarded.

"I thought you might want this," she said, offering one cup.

Cassandra took it, her fingers curling around the warmth. The first sip did not settle her, but it helped her breathe.

Miranda sat on the edge of the bed beside her, their shoulders nearly touching. She did not ask what had happened. She did not need to.

For a while, they drank in silence. Then Miranda stood and crossed to the window, pulling the curtain back just a little. Grey sky. Light rain. The world going on, as if nothing had changed.

"It was real, wasn't it?" Cassandra asked. Her voice sounded small, even to her own ears.

Miranda did not answer at once. She let the silence linger, perhaps to give the words weight.

"Real enough to change you," she said at last.

Cassandra looked down at her tea, then back at Miranda. "That ritual… have you done it before?"

Miranda's shoulders stiffened, but she did not turn. "I have been part of many rituals," she said carefully. "Each one different. Each one meant to reveal something."

Cassandra's throat tightened. "And what did yours reveal?"

Miranda finally turned to face her. "That we all carry truths we spend most of our lives avoiding."

The room fell quiet again. Rain whispered against the glass. Miranda did not speak. She only stayed near, their tea cooling between sips. Outside, the rain softened to mist.

"How long have you known?" Cassandra asked quietly.

Miranda did not pretend to misunderstand. Her eyes stayed on the window. "Long enough to recognise the signs in someone else."

Cassandra lowered her gaze to her hands. "And you still let me go?"

"I didn't let you," Miranda said gently. "You chose to go. I only made sure the door stayed open behind you."

The words lingered between them like softened light. They carried no sting, only truth.

By the time Cassandra finished her tea, the rain had eased to a mist. Miranda glanced at the window, then turned back to her.

"Come on," she said, her voice low, almost coaxing. "Let's get some air. Walk a little."

Cassandra hesitated. Movement felt unnatural, as though she were stepping into a world that had kept turning in her absence. Still, she rose, the robe shifting as she moved, silk brushing her skin with a reminder she could not quite name.

Miranda opened the door, pausing with one hand on the frame. "We don't have to talk about it now," she said, leaving the words open, spacious. "But when you are ready... we can."

Cassandra met her eyes briefly, then lowered her gaze. Her reply was almost a breath. "Okay."

By late morning, they walked. Wrapped against the cold, they wandered the quieter streets of Camden. Cassandra carried a small notebook beneath her arm. She had not opened it in days, but the weight of it comforted her, as though it held fragments of herself she had not yet spoken aloud.

They stopped at a narrow café with fogged windows and ferns pressed close to the glass, their fronds slick with condensation. Miranda ordered black coffee. Cassandra chose tea. They shared fresh scones with cream and jam.

They sat near the window, steam rising from their mugs, ribbons of warmth curling between them. Outside, the street blurred to outlines in the mist, softened into impression.

"Do you want to talk about it?" Miranda asked gently.

"I don't know where to start."

Miranda nodded, following a raindrop down the pane. She left the silence open.

Cassandra turned toward the street, her voice low. "I feel like I crossed some kind of line. And I don't know what that means."

Miranda studied her for a moment before sipping her coffee. "Do you regret it?"

"I don't know." Cassandra exhaled hard, then leaned forward, resting her head in her hands. "It felt like I was choosing something. But I don't remember the exact moment I said yes. Not really. And now it's inside me."

"The current?"

Cassandra nodded. "And more than that. Guilt. Want. Doubt. As if I let something in that refuses to leave unnamed."

Miranda's voice lowered. "You let yourself in. The part you tried to quiet."

"But what if it was wrong?"

Miranda set her cup down, leaning slightly forward. "Wrong by whose rules?"

Cassandra had no answer.

"There is no wrong," Miranda continued softly. "Only truth. Even when it hurts. Even when it takes you apart before it gathers you again."

Cassandra lifted her gaze to the glass. The rain had eased to a mist, the city beyond reduced to shapes and shadows. "I kept feeling Ethan. Even while it was happening. His voice. His name. I wanted to reach for him, but I couldn't."

"And now?"

"I do miss him. But not the same way. I miss who I was when I was with him."

Miranda tilted her head, thoughtful. "That part of you is still here. But maybe now she stands beside someone you never expected to meet."

A pause stretched between them. A bicycle bell chimed faintly outside, then faded. The tea in Cassandra's hands had cooled, but she held it anyway.

"I feel like I'm changing," she whispered. "And I'm afraid of what it might cost."

Miranda reached across the table. She did not take Cassandra's hand, but the closeness steadied her. "You're becoming who you were always meant to be. Not someone else. Just... more."

Cassandra swallowed, her throat tight, her pulse loud. "And what of Lucas?"

Miranda hesitated, then answered carefully. "He's part of it. But not all. This is still your path."

Cassandra glanced at the notebook near her cup. She did not open it.

A familiar voice broke the quiet.

"Cass?"

She looked up. Lydia Hart, sharp and composed as ever, stood before her with a takeaway coffee in hand.

Cassandra straightened. "Lydia. Hi."

"Didn't expect to see you out in the wild," Lydia said with a crooked smile. Her gaze flicked to the notebook. "Working?"

"Trying," Cassandra replied, the word catching strangely in her throat.

"Good. I won't hover, but feel free to come by the office this week. There's something new coming in. It might suit you."

She glanced at Miranda, and Cassandra followed. "This is Miranda."

Miranda offered a polite nod. "Nice to meet you."

Lydia returned it with a small, knowing smile. "You too."

There was a pause. Then Lydia's gaze returned to Cassandra, lingering a beat too long, as though she had noticed something beneath the surface. Cassandra could not tell if it was intuition or her own unease.

She gave a brief nod, and Lydia slipped away.

Cassandra stared after her, the cooling tea forgotten in her hands.

"Did that feel strange to you?" she asked.

Miranda shrugged, though her eyes were distant. "The world hasn't changed, Cass. You have."

And for the first time since the night before, Cassandra did not feel entirely unmoored.

She was still divided, but she had begun to sense the shape of the break.

Her fingers tightened faintly on the cup. "I don't think I know who I am right now," she whispered. "It's like I'm watching myself from a distance, and she's different. Braver, maybe. Or reckless."

Miranda didn't answer at once. She stirred what was left of her coffee, the sound small but grounding.

"That distance you feel isn't proof you're lost. It's proof something inside you has woken."

She paused.

"And you're watching it happen."

Cassandra's eyes watered, though she blinked quickly to steady herself. "What if I don't like the version that wakes?"

"You don't have to decide that now," Miranda said gently. "You only have to let her speak. Let her move. Let her breathe. You can shape her as you go. Nothing is fixed."

"But everything feels so permanent."

Miranda nodded once. "That is how change feels. Heavy. As if it asks something of you. But sometimes the weight is only truth finding its place."

A tear slipped down Cassandra's cheek, and this time she let it fall.

"I betrayed someone last night," she said. "Even if Ethan doesn't know it… I do."

Miranda's expression remained calm, but her eyes softened. "Did you betray him, or did you meet a part of yourself that refused to wait any longer?"

Cassandra's throat clenched. She lowered her gaze to her lap.

"I don't want to hurt him."

"I know."

"But I feel like I already have."

Miranda set her mug aside and reached across the table, resting her hand over Cassandra's. "You love him. That doesn't stop being true. Even if something else is becoming true now."

Their hands remained linked for a quiet moment. Outside, the mist blurred the world into outlines and shadows.

"I just wish I understood what Lucas wants from me. From all of this," Cassandra said. "Sometimes it feels like he's showing me who I am. Other times it feels like he's unmaking me completely."

Miranda's thumb brushed across her hand. "Maybe it's both. Maybe becoming means setting aside what no longer fits. Even the safe pieces."

Cassandra exhaled unsteadily, but it eased her chest. The tea was cold now, yet she drank it anyway. A small act of anchoring.

"I didn't think I'd feel this much," she murmured. "I thought I could stay outside it. Observe. But now it's all inside me."

"You were never meant to be a bystander in your own story."

The words landed softly, but they carried weight. Cassandra looked at her again, truly looked, and something in Miranda's face told her she was not alone in this. That Miranda, too, had once stood at the same threshold and chosen to step forward.

They took the long way home. Past ivy-clad fences and brick terraces stained darker by the rain, past lampposts slick with mist that still clung to the air. The streets moved slowly through their Sunday hush, as if the whole city had pressed itself into quiet. Miranda didn't speak, and Cassandra didn't need her to. The silence between them was companionable, reflective, a pause large enough to let the world breathe for them.

As they rounded the bend near the canal, Cassandra slowed.

Across the water, something moved.

It was not clear. Only a figure. A shape cut against the cluster of trees. She froze, her stride broken, eyes narrowing against the drizzle.

A tall silhouette. A dark coat. Still.

She blinked, and it was gone.

Her pulse quickened. "Did you see that?"

Miranda followed her gaze, a faint crease in her brow. "See what?"

"There was someone... standing by the trees. Watching."

Miranda studied the empty bank for a moment before looking back. "It is easy to see ghosts when you are carrying one."

Cassandra didn't answer. The canal rippled blank, the branches unmoving, yet something clung to her skin as if she had stepped through a thin boundary. Invisible. Unnamed.

She drew her coat closer and crossed her arms.

They moved on. Their footsteps settled into rhythm once more. At the far end of the street, a door opened and the scent of baking bread spilled into the mist, warm and human, a reminder that ordinary things still waited. That not everything had changed.

But she had.

The flat greeted them with its familiar hush, a quiet that settled deeper after the outside chill. Cassandra slipped off her coat and hung it near the door, her scarf still damp from the rain. As she stepped further in, a faint thread of lavender met her. Subtle. Elusive. A lived-in presence woven into cushions, curtains, corners of air. It brushed against her like memory, not perfume.

Miranda moved into the kitchen. "I'll open a bottle," she called. "We deserve it."

Cassandra didn't reply at once. Her eyes had fallen to the book.

It rested on the coffee table. Closed. Waiting. Its presence no longer sharp with unease, but softened into something quieter. Curiosity, perhaps. Or recognition.

She crossed the room and lowered herself onto the couch, fingertips grazing the leather cover. Cool beneath her hand, yet not forbidding. No markings stirred, no pages shifted. It only waited, still and certain, as though it had always belonged.

She left it closed.

Not yet.

Her gaze drifted toward the hallway, where the faint glow from her bedroom spread across the floor. The flat felt suspended, like it was holding its own breath to give her time to catch up to herself.

Miranda returned with two glasses of red and offered one before curling into the other end of the couch.

"To truth," she said.

Cassandra raised her glass. "To still figuring it out."

They drank.

The wine was dry, its warmth spreading slow through her. Miranda rested her head back against the cushion, eyes closed but wakeful, her presence asking nothing more. Cassandra was grateful for that.

Her notebook lay across her lap where she had set it down when they returned. She opened it to a blank page, its weight both anchor and invitation.

"I think I want to try and write," she said, half to herself.

Miranda opened one eye, a smile tugging faintly. "Then write."

Cassandra pulled the pen free and paused, the stillness of the flat gathered close as if waiting. Then, with a quiet breath, she pressed ink to paper.

Winter Trends in Camden

When the city sheds its colours and dresses in greys, we learn who we are beneath the layers.

In Winter, Camden wears a second skin. Layers, yes. But not only of fabric. Of story. Of selves. You see it in the mismatched coats of market vendors. In scarves that look inherited, passed down or abandoned. In boots softened by years of pavement, in patched elbows carried with pride.

It isn't about style. Not really. It is about memory. About texture. About the way people armour themselves against the cold and carry their pasts openly.

Cassandra sat back and read it through. It wasn't the piece she had expected to write.

But it felt true.

Miranda leaned closer, her voice low and warm. "That's beautiful. It sounds like someone who has been paying attention."

"I've been carrying every moment as if it carved itself into me," Cassandra said.

Miranda smiled faintly. "Maybe that's the same thing."

Cassandra's lips curved in return, small but unforced, and she bent back over the page. Her pen moved more easily now, the words arriving without apology.

She kept writing.

She wrote of colour and of silence. How Camden's winter palette was never just grey, but deep ochres and muted reds, plum scarves and coats the shade of moss and forest shadow. She wrote how the people didn't follow trends so much as remake them. Every layer a story. Every stitch belonging to someone who had worn it before.

She wrote of breath visible in the cold, curling into small clouds before dissolving. Of shadows stretched long across the canal just before dusk. She wrote of being lost, and how the city never asked her to be found, only to keep moving, to notice, to belong without asking permission.

The pages filled, one after another. The wine loosened her hand, and something deeper in her chest. She didn't see Miranda watching her.

When she finally lifted her head, the flat had settled into a gentler hush. The world outside carried on, faint with traffic and time, but within these walls the air felt held.

Miranda rose and took her empty glass. "I'll let you finish," she murmured.

Cassandra nodded, her eyes already drifting back to the notebook. The pen moved again, this time without pause.

Transformation doesn't always arrive with thunder. Sometimes it comes wrapped in silk. In silence. In a robe you didn't choose but now cannot take off.

She set the pen down.

For the first time in days, she felt something close to peace.

She lingered there, letting the words soak into her like the last sip of wine. The flat remained quiet. Miranda had retreated to her room, her door left ajar, spilling a narrow band of light across the hall.

Cassandra closed the notebook gently and set it on the table beside her.

The article existed now. Not quite the one Lydia had asked for. But the one that had been forming all along, waiting. Since the last assignment. Since before. She hadn't been ready to write it until now, and yet it lived here, complete enough.

She rose, slow and thoughtful, and crossed to the desk near the window. Her laptop sat there, half-open from earlier in the week. She touched the trackpad. The screen lifted into a pale glow, her reflection washed in blue.

The blank document blinked, expectant.

She began to type.

Not word for word. Not a simple copy. A translation. Emotion shaped into sentences. She trimmed excess, left room for breath. Her fingers moved quickly, pausing only now and then to reread, smoothing a line, shifting a phrase that had fallen too raw.

As she typed, the city outside leaned into early evening. Light slipped from the windows, and the desk lamp quietly took its place. In the next room, Miranda turned a page, the sound soft as breath.

When the last line settled, Cassandra read the piece through once more.

It carried the title of *Winter Trends in Camden*, but beneath the fabric and colour, it spoke of transformation. Of how people revealed themselves layer by layer, how change lived in what they chose to wear and what they left behind.

Her cursor lingered over the subject line. Slowly, she typed:

Winter Layers: Camden in Mid-Transformation

She paused, drew a steady breath, and clicked Send.

The message vanished.

And it was finished.

Not just the article. The hesitation.

She closed the laptop and leaned back in her chair. The tightness in her chest eased, leaving a lighter space she hadn't expected. She didn't know what Lydia would make of the piece, or whether it would even find print. But it felt unguarded. It felt hers.

She had caught something true.

And for this night, that was enough.

The light in the flat had grown softer, slipping toward evening. Cassandra stood by the window, her fingertips resting on the sill. Outside, rooftops carried the sheen of rain, their edges hushed beneath the fading sky. The city had not changed, not really. But something in her had.

The book remained where she had left it. Unopened, but not forgotten.

Crossing the room, she lowered herself to the floor beside it. The leather was cool beneath her palm. She hesitated, then drew it open.

No flutter this time. No vanishing ink. Only a single line, centred and waiting.

To name the shadow is to see what still lives inside it.

She read the words again.

They did not strike like a warning. Nor like a riddle. They settled into her with the clarity of a mirror, spare and undeniable.

From Miranda's room came the faint rustle of a page, followed by the clink of glass. Cassandra closed the book and leaned back, the sentence anchoring itself in her chest. There were still parts of herself she had not faced. But they were no longer strangers.

Her eyes drifted to the desk near the window. The laptop sat closed now, the screen dark, but she could still feel the echo of what she had written. A new article sent. A truth offered, not out of duty, but because it had risen from her.

The book had answered in kind.

That felt like something.

She carried her glass back to the couch, pulling a soft throw across her knees. Beyond the windows, the last of the daylight folded behind the rooftops.

She did not light the candles. Not tonight.

A line of amber from the hallway lamp kept the flat from falling fully into shadow. Cassandra reached for the notebook and opened it once more. Her pen felt warm, familiar in her fingers. She did not write about winter or fashion this time, nor Camden's layered streets. She wrote what the message in the book had awoken.

There is a darkness that does not want to consume you. It only wants to be seen. To be given a place.

The words came slowly, deliberate, as if they had waited in silence until she was ready.

And in seeing it, I begin to forgive myself. For not turning away. For stepping toward it. For wanting more than safety.

The sentences rested on the page, plain and unadorned. She underlined the last line once, lightly.

Forgiveness, she realised, was not something granted from outside. It began here. In ink. In breath. In stillness.

From deeper in the flat, music began to play. Low, indistinct. Not a melody she knew, but steady enough to hold her.

She lifted her glass, drank slowly, and leaned her head back against the cushions.

The book had fallen silent again.

But she had not.

Something inside her remained open. To Lucas. To the shadow. To whatever waited.

Yet she wondered: was this opening, or unravelling?

A sound interrupted her thought. Miranda clearing her throat as she stepped into view, wine bottle in hand.

"Need another?" she asked gently.

Cassandra nodded. "Yes. I think I could."

Miranda poured with care, half-filling Cassandra's glass before her own. The wine caught the lamplight, dark and rippling.

They sat in silence, the warmth blooming slowly in Cassandra's chest. It did not chase away the chill entirely, but it softened it.

"I keep thinking about what he said to me," Cassandra murmured at last. "Before I left. 'We're not finished yet.' I've been trying to work out what that means. Whether it's about him and me. Or something else. Something larger."

Miranda set her glass down. "Maybe it's both."

Cassandra studied the surface of her wine. The words lingered, not like a question, but like a thread she had not yet pulled.

"Do you think this is leading somewhere? Or am I just lost inside it?"

Miranda's voice was quiet, steady. "I don't think you're lost. I think you're finding pieces you didn't know you had left behind. And Lucas... he isn't a map. He's a mirror. You don't need to follow him to find the way."

Cassandra's voice lowered. "I don't know what I'm walking into."

"Maybe you're not walking into it," Miranda replied. "Maybe it's walking into you."

No more words followed. Only silence, whole and unbroken. Cassandra felt it settle around her, not pressing but holding, elemental as flame, steady as touch, patient as truth.

Like awakening.

10
THE EDGE OF WILLING

A mirror, not a map.

The words lingered after Miranda fell silent, delicate as glass, sharp as a shard beneath the skin.

Cassandra let them remain. She didn't rush to fill the space they left behind. Something inside her needed to unfold around their shape, slowly, without forcing.

She drew a breath that reached deeper than the last, tilting her head against the cushion and lifting her gaze to the ceiling. The plaster lines were uneven in places, pale seams that caught the room's low light, but it wasn't them she saw.

"It's hard to know what's real," she murmured. "What part of this is truth, and what's just..."

She didn't finish. The words loosened at the edge of her voice, drifting away.

Miranda moved beside her. She didn't reach across. She didn't press. She only spoke with a softness that threaded through the hush like balm.

"Sometimes it's not about what's real," she said. "It's about what stays."

The sentence landed with more weight than Cassandra expected. Not heavy in a way that pressed her down, but in the way a memory returns, not to haunt, but to remind.

What stays.

The current in her chest.

The ache in her wrists where the fabric had lain.

The way her breath changed at the thought of his hands.

But also, the cool solidity of her notebook, resting open on the table. The certainty of the article she had sent. The strange calm that followed.

The sound of Miranda's breathing, steady and near.

The way she had not moved away.

Cassandra lowered her gaze, studying Miranda. Her expression was unreadable, yet unwavering, a stillness that held more than words could. In that constancy, Cassandra felt something unspoken begin to anchor. Not resolve. Not yet. But a quiet steadiness that returned her to herself.

The silence between them was no longer absence. It had become a presence of its own. Whole. Holding.

Cassandra felt it move across her skin, not as pressure, but as something elemental.

Like heat without fire. Like breath without sound.

And beneath all of it, the current that had remained since that night.

Not fading. Not waiting. Becoming.

She reached for her notebook and opened it again. Not to write, only to hold it.

Her fingers traced the words on the page she had left open. They felt different now. Not like something she had written, but like something she had accepted.

To name the shadow is to see what still lives inside it.

Was that what Lucas had meant? That she hadn't finished naming it?

She wasn't sure. For now, perhaps uncertainty was enough.

"I'm scared of what comes next," she said softly.

Miranda touched her arm with a gesture that was gentle, steady.

"Then something in you is awakening, Cass."

The breath she released felt lodged since morning.

Awakening.

The word lingered. What did it mean?

The room held her, muted and shadowed, as she leaned into the stillness and let the day slip.

When the light faded and evening gathered fully around the flat, Cassandra rose and moved to her room.

Later, when the quiet had deepened into night, she lit the lavender candle on the windowsill. The match flared softly, the wick catching with a slow bloom of light that trembled once before holding. Shadows flickered across the walls, drawn long by the flame. Its scent rose gently, curling through the air like something remembered.

She sat on the edge of the bed and watched it burn. The glow brushed across her hands, across the fabric pooled at her legs. Lavender had always reminded her of home, of calm mornings and towels warmed on radiators, of the reassuring cadence of her mother's voice in another room.

Of all that once felt safe.

But even that comfort had changed. Now it held questions, woven through the scent like threads she could no longer ignore.

There was more to uncover. Not only in the symbols etched into the book, or the magnetism in Lucas's gaze, or the rituals that had drawn something unnamed to the surface.

But in the silent chambers within herself, the ones she had only just begun to unlock.

She lay back slowly, candlelight drifting in blurred gold across the ceiling. The scent lingered.

And in that liminal space where waking loosens, where the body softens and thought grows thin, something stirred.

Not a voice. Not exactly.

Just a sensation. A subtle press beneath the skin. A knowing that did not rise from thought.

No, we're not finished yet.

The words, or perhaps only the idea of them, lingered as she floated in the narrow passage between sleep and waking. A faint shift in the air drew her upright. When her eyes opened, the candlelight had dimmed and the room felt thinner, as though the night had already stepped aside to make room for what waited.

A signal moved through her before thought could. Low and insistent, it pressed in her chest with the muted persistence of a pulse beneath water. Distant, but impossible to ignore.

She stayed still, caught between sleep and waking, as if her body already knew something had shifted. The air felt suspended, listening. Not empty. Not at rest.

When she opened her eyes, nothing in the room had changed. The candle stood unlit on the sill. The robe hung untouched in its usual place. Yet beneath the surface, something had realigned.

Cassandra rose carefully, as if not to disturb the fragile balance. The floor was cool under her bare feet. The fabric of her nightshirt brushed lightly against her legs as she moved through the dim hall, guided by an impulse older than words.

And then she saw it.

Just inside the front door, waiting.

An envelope. Black. Crisp-edged, deliberate. Resting on the floor at a precise angle, as if placed rather than dropped.

Her name written across the front. *Cassandra.*

The script was unmistakable. The same sharp, elegant hand that had once marked the note The Hollow at midnight. Perhaps even the same presence that whispered through the book. Not entirely his, but touched by him. Or perhaps he had been shaped by it instead.

And something more.

The ink shimmered faintly, catching what little light the morning gave, a depth that recalled the unseen spaces of Lucas's world.

She crouched beside it, her breath faltering. The air around the envelope felt charged. Not cold. Not warm. Simply aware.

Her fingers brushed its surface.

It yielded slightly, almost imperceptibly, as though responding from beneath.

She opened it slowly.

Inside: a strip of deep red silk, folded with precision. A small card, cream-coloured, soft as worn linen.

Tonight. Wear the silk. Speak nothing until the mirror.

That was all. No signature. No explanation.

Not a request. Not a surprise.

A continuation.

The silk slipped into her palm as if it had been waiting. Warmer than fabric should be. Heavier, too, as though carrying something beyond itself. It unfurled across her hand with a gravity that felt alive.

She didn't flinch. There was no panic. Only the rhythm of something deeper. Not fear. Not resistance. Just a slow, tidal surrender she no longer tried to hold back.

She stood there a long while, the crimson binding in her hand, the card beside it like a breath unspent. The flat kept its watchful silence. That hour between night and morning when the world hesitates. The window above the street glowed faintly, mist softening the outlines beyond. She did not move.

Not until the silence loosened its hold.

Barefoot and still wrapped in thought, she crossed into the kitchen.

Miranda stood at the window, arms folded tight. Her gaze fixed beyond the glass, where rooftops blurred into pewter sky. Rain had not yet begun, but it hovered in the air, weightless and waiting.

She didn't hear Cassandra at first.

The soft tread of footsteps drew her attention, and she turned, faintly startled. Her brow tightened.

"You're up early," she said quietly.

Cassandra stepped further in, the envelope still in her hand. She placed it on the counter between them, the silk folded carefully beside it.

Miranda looked down.

Only after a pause did she speak.

"It's happening faster than I thought."

Cassandra leaned back against the tiled wall, the cool surface pressing faintly through her nightshirt.

"And do you think I'm ready?"

Miranda's fingers tightened around her own arms. Her voice was quieter still.

"I think you're already in it."

And something inside her, silent for so long, stirred as though it had been waiting for this very exchange. Not to speak. Not even to rise. Only to be recognised.

"It's not about Lucas, is it?" Cassandra asked. Her voice sounded thinner than usual, as if it had travelled from beneath the surface. "Was it ever?"

Miranda turned. Her eyes carried something ancient. Not aged or weary, but weathered in the way stone remembers storms.

"No," she said. "He is the doorway. Not the destination."

Cassandra folded her arms across her chest. The nightshirt clung faintly to her skin, still marked by the cool press of the wall. "Then what is?"

Miranda's gaze dropped to the envelope on the counter.

"Something you carry," she said. "Something that has slept in you longer than you've known. The book. The dreams. Even this." Her hand hovered over the silk but did not touch it. "They're only ways of waking it."

"Waking what?"

"I don't know," Miranda admitted, her voice softer now, though reverent. "But I think... you do."

Cassandra looked away. Her throat tightened. Not with fear, but with the brittle strain of something left unsaid.

"Did you walk away?" she asked.

Miranda didn't answer immediately. Her eyes returned to the window, where rain threaded against the glass and tangled in the ivy. Each droplet traced a delicate path, veins drawn by weather.

"Once," she said, barely above a whisper. "I left it all behind."

Her tone changed, more distant, though not unkind.

"I moved to Florence. Rented a flat above a piazza that smelled of coffee and stone. I met a man there. He taught Italian poetry. He was kind. Curious. Unaware of any world beyond the one we could touch."

A faint smile touched her lips, not at the memory itself, but at the version of herself it preserved.

"He left notes in margins, fragments of verse. Sometimes Dante. Sometimes his own. I pretended they were spells."

Miranda's arms loosened. She exhaled slowly.

"I told myself I could stay. That if I buried the other world deep enough, it would stop calling."

Cassandra watched her. The rain had thickened outside, blurring rooftops into shapes of shadow.

Miranda smiled faintly again, but her eyes stayed far away. "He used to read Neruda aloud while I painted. We drank wine on the balcony. Grew tomatoes in mismatched pots. He wanted something simple. A life. A future."

Her voice slowed.

"For a while, I believed I could have it. The current faded. The dreams stopped. I thought it had passed me by."

She turned to Cassandra, and her gaze held something more vulnerable than anything she had spoken.

"Then one afternoon, I opened a book I hadn't touched in years. A worn copy of the Divina Commedia."

Her eyes softened, not with fondness, but with recognition.

"Tucked inside was a sprig of lavender. Still fresh. Still soft. Not pressed. Not faded. As though someone had just placed it there."

She paused, her silence full of meaning.

"That night, I woke whispering a word I had never known. Not Italian. Not anything I recognised. And when I spoke it aloud, the mirror in the hallway split clean down the middle."

She looked away, her hand brushing the ledge.

"He said it was the heat. A crack from summer air."

Her voice carried a fragile reminiscence.

"I didn't tell him otherwise. The next morning, I left with one suitcase and no explanation." She ran a hand through her hair, not to neaten it, but to ground herself.

"You loved him," Cassandra said softly.

Miranda gave a small nod. "In a way that made me feel human again."

"Then why didn't you stay?"

Miranda traced the windowsill with her fingers. When she spoke, her voice was steady, though something lay just beneath it.

"Because I would have had to lie. Every day. About who I was. What I had seen. And he deserved more than that."

The truth hung between them. Firm, undeniable.

"Do you ever wonder what would have happened if you hadn't opened the book?"

Miranda's hand stilled. "Sometimes. But it would have found me anyway. It always does. You can't close off that part of yourself forever. Not without losing something else."

Cassandra let the thought move through her before asking, "Did you try to go back?"

"I wrote him a letter once," Miranda said. "But I never sent it. I keep it in the book. Some nights I read it and pretend he is still there, on that balcony, waiting."

"Do you think he would have waited?"

Miranda's voice caught, just slightly.

"No," she said. "And I'm glad. Because if he had, I might have returned. And I wouldn't be here now."

Outside, the rain pressed harder against the glass. Ivy trembled once, then stilled.

Cassandra raised her eyes.

"Did you ever wish you had been chosen instead?"

Miranda turned more sharply this time.

"I was chosen," she said. "I just wasn't ready."

Her breath left her slowly. "And maybe I never wanted it as much as you do."

Cassandra didn't answer. Her throat tightened, though she let it remain. Because Miranda was right.

Beneath fear, beneath the questions, something older had begun to move. Not sudden, not wild, but steady. Certain. And hungry.

The hush between them was no longer fragile. It carried weight now. The kind that made space for truths that should not be spoken too soon.

Cassandra's gaze fell to the silk again. Its colour startled her still. That deep ceremonial red. It did not belong to the world she had imagined.

Not to the soft linen sheets she had once pictured. Not to the little house by the sea. Not to Ethan's laugh carrying through a kitchen as he burned toast, cursing while the smell of coffee lingered in the light.

"I had plans too," she said, almost to herself. "With Ethan."

Miranda turned slightly, but said nothing. Her presence didn't push. It remained.

"I thought I knew what it meant to build a life. Something small enough to hold. Something that asked for nothing but love and time."

Her voice thinned, the last word slipping through her throat like a thread too fine to hold.

"Do you still want that?" Miranda asked.

Cassandra hesitated. The question pressed into her, not to wound, but to reveal.

"I don't know," she said. "Sometimes I think I do. But then I remember how it felt the first time I opened the book. The first time the air shifted. The first time I looked at Lucas and felt as though I had seen him before."

Her breath caught.

"And that feeling doesn't belong in a beach house with crossword puzzles."

"I think part of me still wants it," she said. "The part that believes in Sunday mornings. In someone waiting when you come home."

Her chest tightened.

"I just don't know if that part will survive what is happening now."

Miranda's features softened, not in pity, but in recognition. Her gaze held a gravity free of distance. Not instruction. Only truth.

"It isn't about what you want," she said gently. "It's about what you can live with, once you've seen the truth."

Cassandra looked at her hands. They did not tremble. They did not feel unfamiliar. Yet they no longer felt entirely hers, as though something beneath the skin had begun to reshape them.

"Do you think I could ever go back?"

"You might," Miranda said. "But not as the same woman. And not to the same life. And neither would the people waiting for you."

The words did not cut. They landed lower, settling in her chest with a quiet finality.

She closed her eyes. The garden. The crosswords. The warmth of Ethan after a swim. They lived still, but softer now. Like half-remembered songs.

So did other things.

The silk slipping over her wrists. The silence that had once unnerved her and now felt like a threshold. The sense that none of this had ever been a choice, only a recognition of what had waited.

"I wanted to believe I could have both," she whispered. "That I could keep one foot in each world. But I don't know which part of me is choosing anymore."

Miranda's hand found hers across the counter. The touch was cool, steady.

"So did I," she said.

The touch was brief. Not reassurance. Not comfort. Only truth, exchanged and understood.

Then Miranda drew back, exhaling as though something beneath her ribs had altered. "I should get ready. The gallery wants me to do inventory. Sculptures, mostly. Another shipment. L.A again."

Her tone carried a quiet uncertainty, as if such details already felt irrelevant.

Cassandra nodded. The moment between them no longer fragile. It held.

Miranda stepped toward the hall. "I won't be long. A few hours. Call if you need me."

Her footsteps moved through the flat. Boots across floorboards. The weight of a coat lifted. Keys clinking against each other.

When the front door opened, it did so without hesitation. When it closed, it left no echo.

Cassandra remained at the counter. The silence was not empty. It filled the space differently now, weighted as though the air itself had begun to listen.

Something in her had turned.

The part that had stopped waiting.

She gathered the red strip and the envelope from the counter, her hands moving with a sense of tranquillity. Nothing about the objects felt ordinary. Not the smoothness of the fabric, not the weight of the card. She held them close as she walked slowly down the hall, each step deliberate.

The bedroom door clicked shut behind her, soft and certain.

She crossed to the bed and lowered herself onto the edge. Her legs folded beneath her, the ribbon settling in her lap like something alive and listening.

The book waited on the bedside table. Its cover sat slightly open, not wide enough to reveal the text, but just ajar, as if it had stirred in her absence.

Cassandra reached for it. Her fingertips grazed the edge of the cool leather binding, and the instant her skin met its surface, something shifted.

Not the air. Not the light.

Only a sensation, low and precise, moving beneath her skin like a current she had known before.

She opened the book slowly. One of the previously blank pages now carried writing. At the centre, a single sentence had formed.

The ink was neither fresh nor faded, but settled into the fibres of the paper as though it had always belonged there, simply waiting to be revealed.

It is not the silk that binds you.

She stared at it. The words did not vanish at once, as they sometimes had. They lingered, long enough to settle into her, long enough for her to recognise that they were not a command but a reminder.

She turned the page.

Blank.

Then, with a slow pull that felt like breath being drawn back into lungs, the ink receded. Not scraped away or erased, but absorbed, as if the book had reclaimed its own language.

Cassandra let her hand fall to her side. The book stayed open, its spine relaxed, its pages unmoving.

She lifted the ribbon again.

It felt changed in her grasp, as though the night ahead had already pressed its shape into the fabric. As if tonight would not only carry forward what had begun, but seal it. Alter it. Perhaps even claim something in return.

She drew the silk slowly across her palm, the texture alive against her skin, as though it remembered her too.

Beyond the glass, the city began its morning. The muffled hiss of tyres on wet bitumen carried upward. Somewhere, a siren rose and fell. Footsteps passed overhead, a reminder that another life was unfolding just above her own.

Yet all of it felt impossibly distant.

She set the fabric aside and rose. The floor's chill bit more sharply now. The air had thickened, as though the walls had drawn inward. She moved to the window.

The street below looked unchanged. Cars lined the curb, their windscreens beaded with mist. A bus turned the corner with a mechanical sigh. Yet the scene felt paler, as though its colour had drained, leaving only a faint impression of morning.

She pressed her palm to the glass. The chill met her skin but barely registered.

Something in the air was gathering. Not with force, but with the inevitability of a tide that could not be turned back.

She turned her head slightly. The book lay open, unguarded. The silk waited beside it, deep as the moment before surf breaks.

Returning to the bed, she lowered herself with intention, her legs folding beneath her. Her hands hovered above the fabric without touching. She drew a breath, then another, until the rhythm steadied.

Her eyes closed.

The air turned.

It was no longer silence, but something entering.

Heat stirred across her skin, faint at first, as though light had filtered through blood before reaching her.

She could not tell whether she had drifted into sleep or slipped into something deeper, something that moved alongside it. Behind her closed eyes, a flicker surfaced. Gold. Shifting. Waiting.

A hand emerged from the dark. Her hand, yet not entirely hers, reaching toward a slow, deliberate pulse.

The outline of a symbol surfaced, its curves carved with an age older than stone. It did not glow so much as breathe, carrying an intention that seemed to know her. To remember her.

She drew nearer without moving, the space between collapsing as if it had never truly been there.

The air surrounding the symbol thickened, not with wind or sound, but with presence.

Then a voice came, low enough to feel more than hear.

It was not Lucas.

It belonged to something older. Something she recognised without knowing why.

You have already stepped through.

The pause that followed felt like a held breath. Then another whisper, closer still, settled through her like a truth that needed no language.

The door was not the beginning.

Images rose slowly, layered one over another. The silver ring on her finger catching muted light. The taste of wine lingering on her tongue, shared across a table where silence had spoken more than words. Miranda's hand enclosing hers, steady and certain, as though guarding what they both understood.

Moments she had never expected to keep. Small enough to vanish, yet now returned with deliberate clarity.

A page turned somewhere inside her, the sound soft as breath at her ear.

A name followed, present for only a heartbeat before it slipped away, leaving its weight without its sound.

And then a gaze, held too long in a room that had swallowed its own light, yet never turning aside.

She stood before the symbol once more. Its pulse was not outside her but within, deeper than thought, older than memory. There was no need to reach for it. The recognition was already shared.

One final beat.

Then stillness.

In that calm, something unfastened. A layer she had carried without knowing it existed. The sensation was not loss or gain, only the awareness that it was gone.

Her eyes opened to the same room. The robe remained on the chair. The candle sat unlit. Yet her heart moved faster now, not with fear but with the undeniable press of knowing.

Her fingers brushed her wrist. No mark showed, no trace on the skin, but the shift was there all the same, settled beneath the surface.

A question rose without words.

Is this who I am meant to become?

No reply came, only the muted pulse of the city through the glass, familiar yet distant, as though it belonged to another world.

She no longer needed to ask what would come. The only choice was whether she would walk toward it.

She reached again for the ribbon. This time she did not simply let it rest in her hands. She wound it once around her wrist, loose enough for the skin to breathe yet close enough to feel its weight marking the rhythm beneath. A quiet tether. A reminder that the crossing had already begun.

Across the room, the small mirror above the dresser caught a pale slant of light, persistent enough to draw her forward. She rose, unhurried, stepping as though the space had already narrowed between her and the glass.

Her reflection met her gaze. The same lines. The same eyes. Yet something beneath them had changed, not fractured and not emptied, but altered in a way that could not be undone. She saw it, even if no one else ever would.

She lifted her bound wrist to her collarbone, holding it there as she watched herself. In that stillness, warmth brushed faintly against her neck, where none should be. Not real, not imagined, but undeniable.

His mouth against her skin had been unhurried and certain, a prayer spoken into flesh. Each movement carried intent that reached deeper than touch alone.

The heat of him, the steady press of his chest against hers, the rhythm that had drawn them together until the world dissolved, returned now with a vividness almost tangible.

His fingers had traced the lines of her body with the patience of someone learning a language, following every curve as though each one held meaning. Not only touching, but claiming. And in that claiming, she had felt herself surrender into a longing without words.

Her back had arched, her wrists bound, the ribbon slipping against her skin as their breaths mingled until it seemed they drew from the same air. The sound that had risen from her when their bodies met had been low and involuntary, and even now it echoed beneath her ribs, steady and insistent.

She remembered the way he had stilled then, forehead pressed to hers, as though in that instant he had found something sacred in the space between heartbeats. Something neither of them could deny.

Her pulse quickened beneath the binding, the memory blooming with a sharp sweetness that left warmth trailing through her. She wondered if tonight would carry the same weight. If it would feel like surrender again, or become something she could not yet comprehend.

Because some part of her already knew they were not finished. And she knew that if she kept stepping toward him, there would be no return to who she had been before.

She did not look away. Not yet. The reflection held her steady, unflinching in its truth. She saw herself as both afraid and altered, the woman in the glass already carrying the shadow of what was to come.

In that gaze, a thought settled with the inevitability of tide against stone.

She was not ready.

Yet she would go to him regardless.

Because whatever waited beyond this moment was already moving toward her.

And all that remained was the moment she chose to step forward.

11

THE MIRROR HOLDS

The car arrived a little after ten.

Cassandra had been waiting by the window, though she had not meant to. She did not dress quickly. She did not rush. Yet something in her had been leaning toward the moment before it came, as if she had already heard its approach long before the sound of tyres touched the street.

The robe wrapped around her again, the red ribbon of fabric hidden beneath the sleeve, its quiet weight resting against her skin. She carried nothing with her. No bag. No book. Nothing except herself. Even that felt uncertain now, as though her body had become a vessel she had only begun to understand, capable of holding more than she once believed.

She moved slowly across the flat, letting her steps find their rhythm without hurry. Each sound drifted softly through the air, as though the rooms had widened in her absence, the walls leaning back to watch her pass.

When she stepped outside, the air greeted her with the muted tones of late night. It was not silent, but attentive, the kind of calm that seems to hold the moment in place.

The car waited at the kerb, just as before. Dark. Sleek. Silent. The driver met her gaze through the glass and nodded once. There was no smile, no gesture of welcome, only recognition, as though nothing more were required.

She slid into the back seat. The leather carried the faint scent of warmth, not from the day but from presence. The door closed behind her with a soft, deliberate thud, a sound that seemed to carry its own decision, as though nothing would be the same when it opened again.

The city began to move around her.

It was the same route as before. The same turns. The same blur of traffic lights and half-lit shopfronts, their windows casting fragments of colour into the darkness. Yet the air inside the car felt altered. Still, but not stagnant. A stillness alive with something unspoken, moving without sound, carrying itself like a thought that had been waiting for the right moment to emerge.

Outside, the streets stretched like veins through the city's sleeping body, carrying its slow pulse beneath the muted glow of lamps and signs. Cassandra watched them pass, slower now, each one slipping away as if the night were folding inward. The shimmer of rain caught in the beams of passing headlights, scattering light in shards across the wet asphalt, as though the road itself had been paved with broken glass.

A man stood alone at a bus stop, his forehead pressed against the metal pole beside him. He did not move. Nothing around him moved. It was as though time had passed him over entirely.

She rested her cheek against the window. The glass was cool, steady in its stillness, grounding her, though not enough to hold her fully.

The city drifted past on the other side of the glass, blurred and liquid, shapes dissolving into one another in the wash of light and shadow.

For a moment, she saw herself. A pale face. Eyes watching too closely. And behind them, or perhaps within them, something else. Not another face exactly, but a flicker, a shimmer beneath the surface, a movement too fluid to hold and too ancient to name.

She blinked, and it was gone.

But the sensation remained.

A hush gathered in her chest, not born of fear but of a heightened awareness, as though the air itself had adjusted to meet her.

She drew the air in slowly and found it waiting, steady and sure, a rhythm she recognised without knowing how.

The car turned down the gravel road.

The trees closed in, their branches arching above like the curved bones of a ribcage, the road a spine leading deeper into the dark. The tyres crunched softly over stone, the sound absorbed by the dense air as the world outside narrowed into shadow and bark.

She remembered this road. The way the woods seemed to seal behind her once she entered, the way the silence here grew heavier, more complete.

But tonight was not the same.

It was not a return. Not a repetition.

Something in her bones had altered, a silent current moving through her, measured and sure. The ribbon wound at her wrist seemed to answer the rhythm of her pulse, its presence no longer passive but aware. The robe lay differently across her shoulders now, as though it had learned the shape of her.

Tonight was not only about touch.

It was about what could be seen.

The car began to slow.

Gravel shifted beneath the tyres in a softened cadence, each turn of the wheels deliberate, almost ceremonial, as if the road itself recognised the nearness of this place.

They came to a halt.

The driver did not turn. His posture remained composed, hands resting neatly, gaze fixed ahead.

Cassandra reached for the handle, then stilled. Her fingers hovered, curling back to her lap as she turned to the window once more.

The trees here pressed closer, their darkness layered, their branches bending in shapes that recalled outstretched hands, not grasping, but beckoning forward.

She let the air move into her slowly. Not to steady herself. To clear the space within her.

Then she stepped out.

The night closed around her like a fine veil, cool against her skin, carrying the scent of damp earth threaded with the barest sweetness beneath it. Not floral. Not smoke. Something older, carrying the memory of seasons long past.

Lucas's house stood where it always had, half concealed by the tangle of trees, its stone walls softened under the slow climb of ivy. Yet the light was changed. Only a few windows glimmered now, none of them at the front.

It did not feel deserted.

It felt intent.

Her steps were near silent along the path. The robe shifted lightly against her legs, the fabric at her wrist settled like a secret she had agreed to keep.

The front door stood slightly ajar. Not wide. Not careless. Open just enough to allow the night to slip inside. Or perhaps to let something unseen drift out.

She looked up at the house.

The stone seemed to hold its own shadow, as though it had drawn the dimness closer, gathering it against the walls. Vines clung to the surface in long, twisting lines, catching slight traces of light from somewhere she could not see. The windows were unlit except for a single glimmer far to the side, a pale suggestion rather than an invitation.

It watched her. Not with hostility, but with the patience of something that had seen her coming for far longer than she had known to arrive. An uneasy shiver traced her spine, not from cold, but from the sense that the house itself had been waiting.

She hesitated at the threshold, not out of doubt, but with the recognition that crossing it would mean more than entering a room. It would mean stepping further into something that had already begun to alter her.

Her feet carried her forward.

The room seemed to contract around her the moment she passed through the door. Not with a rush or sudden gust, but with a quiet compression, as though the space within had been holding itself in readiness.

The scent reached her first. Ivy and iron. No sweetness, only the sharp green of earth layered over something metallic, like stone that had weathered centuries of rain.

It was an old scent. Rooted. Certain of its place.

She took another step, then another, until her feet came to rest at the base of the staircase.

Wooden steps rose ahead, wide and curved, their grain polished smooth beneath a quiet sheen of candlelight. The banister beside them was finely carved, but not in a way that felt made by hands alone. It had the slow, deliberate shape of something that had grown into its form over years, its lines following a pattern older than the house itself. The light gathered in small pools along the walls, not illuminating so much as breathing warmth into the air, like the inside of something living.

She had climbed those steps before, but tonight they seemed altered. Not strange, yet carrying a depth she had not noticed, as though the staircase itself had learned more of her since her last ascent.

Cassandra lifted the hem of her robe and began to climb.

The sound of her steps did not ring out into emptiness. It was caught and held by the space, taken into the wood and walls as if they were listening. Something in the air moved differently here, drawing close around her in subtle threads that reminded her of water in a slow current.

She reached the first landing. The curve ahead drew her upward toward the second.

And there he stood.

Lucas leaned against the wall at the bend of the staircase, the light touching one side of him while the other remained in muted shadow. His robe was black again, though it seemed to hang with a softer ease, the fabric folding and falling as if it remembered movement. A single curl of hair had slipped forward across his brow, and his gaze met hers without command. There was only an unbroken awareness in it, a steady regard that made the air between them feel heavier and more precise.

She stilled on the stair, one hand resting lightly against the banister. The rhythm in her chest shifted. Not faster, not louder, but clearer, as though it had aligned with something he carried.

Moving once more she stopped a few steps below him.

"I've been trying to understand," she said. Her voice carried the weight of the hours before this, each word shaped by thought that had not been hurried. "Why this? Why now?"

Lucas's head tilted slightly. "Do you mean, why you?"

"I mean all of it." She took another step toward him, the robe brushing against her legs in a whisper. "The robe. The book. The rituals. The silk. The silence. Is this something you chose for me?"

"No." He descended one step, slow and soundless, the fold of his robe barely shifting with the movement. "I, didn't choose you."

Something inside her tightened. "Then who did?"

Lucas's mouth curved, not enough to soften the edge of his words, yet far from malice. "You did."

Her eyes searched his face, waiting for more.

He closed the distance between them one measured step at a time until they stood level. "Not here. Not in this room. Perhaps not even in this life. But somewhere… before you ever crossed into this, you opened the door."

She shook her head, the denial quiet but instinctive. "That doesn't make sense."

"Most truths don't," he said, and the words seemed to belong to a place older than the two of them.

His hand lifted, not toward her, but past the line where robe met flesh, indicating a narrow turn she had never noticed. Or perhaps it had never been revealed to her. The shadow there felt deliberate, like a withheld breath.

The corridor sloped gently away from the staircase, its walls flanked by a series of archways. Beyond each arch the darkness breathed differently, as though each space carried its own temperature, its own kind of waiting. The air here was cooler, touched with something mineral, like water drawn from stone.

They began to walk.

The silence between them did not strain. It shaped itself around them, holding back the rush of questions, letting the steps themselves carry her forward. Too many answers would have been noise.

When she finally spoke, her voice felt quieter than she expected. "What am I becoming?"

Lucas glanced toward her, his eyes catching the low candlelight.

"You're remembering," he said, the words almost indistinguishable from the air. "And remembering always looks like becoming."

The shape of that truth pressed into her, settling somewhere deeper than thought.

Her next question rose slowly, as though she feared its answer. "Will I lose myself?"

He slowed his pace, and for a moment they simply stood in the half-light.

"I think," he said at last, his voice unhurried, "you already have."

Her steps faltered. The space around her seemed to lean closer, as though it had been waiting for this moment.

Lucas faced her fully. "But that is not always a loss. Sometimes it is the only way forward. To let dissolve everything that was never truly yours."

Her fingers slipped beneath the sleeve of her robe until they found the silk. She pressed it lightly against her skin, feeling its coolness anchor her.

"And if what comes next is not what I want?"

His gaze held steady, unreadable yet absent of cruelty. "Then you will know."

The hallway curved ahead, its narrowing walls drawing her onward. A finer current moved through the space, subtle but certain, like the measure of something unseen. What waited there had no name, but it had been waiting for her.

Lucas moved aside, no longer in the place of a guide but of someone who understood that the next step was hers alone.

Her foot found the first board of the floor beyond.

Beneath her, the surface changed. The muted warmth of wood gave way to something colder, smooth beneath her soles, dark as water before dawn. Stone or glass, she could not tell. It did not give back her reflection, yet a faint shimmer lingered there, as if fragments of memory had been pressed into its surface and were now shifting just out of reach.

The chamber opened round before her, its walls curved in quiet containment.

Mirrors stood in a perfect ring, tall and unbroken, their surfaces darkened as though veiled. None returned her image. Not yet. They seemed to hold their breath, each one carrying a muted awareness, like closed eyes behind which something stirred.

She crossed further into the space. The red binding at her wrist drew closer around her skin, not in warning, but as if acknowledging that this was the place it had been meant to bring her.

Behind her, Lucas lingered at the edge of the chamber, the dim light holding him there, watching and waiting.

Cassandra turned in place, her gaze sliding from shadow to glass.

The first pane shifted. A ripple, faint and quick, as though the surface had been disturbed from within. Then another. And another. Until the circle around her glowed with an almost-hidden light, each pane trembling with the promise of revelation.

They showed her. But not as she was now.

In one, she wore the weathered coat she had left behind in Melbourne, its collar turned up against a wind she could almost feel. Her eyes in that version were unguarded, open with a hope she barely recognised.

In another, she stood with the book spread in her hands, her lips shaped around words that she seemed to be reading for the first time, though some part of her already knew them.

A third caught her mid-movement, both wrists bound in silk, her posture curved toward something unseen, her mouth open as if the moment had taken even her own breath from her.

She stilled.

Each reflection was a thread, a truth she had lived, a possibility not yet reached, a path waiting in the folds of time.

And then she saw the one that stopped her completely.

Lucas was there. Behind her. His hands resting over her shoulders, his head lowered to her neck. In that mirror, she leaned back into him, her body shaped to his without a question, without the thought of turning away.

Her chest tightened. She stepped back from it, the movement small but decisive. Yet the next mirror met her with equal force.

This time, she stood alone. The woman in the glass was stronger, her gaze steady, her presence carrying a quiet gravity. There was an age to her that had nothing to do with years. Shadows touched her, but they no longer claimed her.

Cassandra could not tell if that self was waiting ahead of her or if she had already walked that path and left it behind. Only that it was real, and that it was watching.

The mirrors glimmered dimly around her, their light folding into the silence until it felt almost tangible. She moved toward them. The chamber seemed to grow as she moved, the air thinning yet becoming more present, as if it had widened so it could hold this moment. Nothing else existed here. Only her and the reflections.

She approached the nearest one. Its frame was etched with deliberate care, every line and curve shaped with patience. Vines wound through the carving, curling into symbols she almost recognised. Ivy traced a near-invisible line across the grain, like something meant to be hidden until the right eyes found it.

Nestled between the patterns lay sprigs of dried lavender, their pale buds flattened with age. A faint fragrance rose when she leaned closer, carrying the weight of memory, something once held close and now pressed into stillness.

The surface deepened as she neared. At first, her reflection was her own, unaltered. Her eyes searched back at her, shadowed with unspoken questions. Her lips parted slightly, as if the act of drawing air had momentarily slipped from her.

Then the surface changed. Not a ripple, not a blur, but a quiet and deliberate shift.

Melbourne emerged. The old apartment she had shared with Ethan, drawn in such detail that she could almost feel the air within it. The kitchen stood behind her reflection, the worn table where they had sat with morning coffee waiting in its place, familiar in every line. A golden shaft of sunlight reached across the tiled floor, warmer than she remembered, softer, as if the light itself had been told to be gentle.

And there he was.

Ethan.

The curve of his smile. The way his hand reached for hers without hesitation. His face unchanged, unaware of the distance that had grown between them. He was laughing, his head tilted back, his eyes crinkling at the corners the way they had when the world still felt simple. She had not seen that look in a very long time.

Something rose in her throat, too soft to escape. Her fingers lifted without thought, drawn toward the glass as though the image might meet her halfway. She felt the soft fabric at her wrist shift, a slight tightening that made her pause.

The silence here deepened. It was not the silence of an empty room, but of a space that was listening. Watching. Waiting for her to remember something she had been told. A rule. A boundary. An instruction.

Do not speak until the mirror.

The words moved through her like a breath she had not realised she was holding, steadying her hand before it could touch the glass.

She pressed her palm to the glass. The surface was cool beneath her skin, but in her mind it yielded warmth. She imagined the weight of his hand against hers, the gentle press of his fingers, the scent of coffee curling through the air. Somewhere behind it all, the faint ghost of the music he used to play while they cooked, a song whose melody had faded yet still lingered in the quiet spaces of her mind.

A tear slipped from her cheek and fell without a sound. Another followed, unhurried, carrying no demand for attention. These were not the sobs of grief in its sharpest form, but the slow ache of a life paused too soon. A door never fully closed.

This was not only memory. It was a tether. A truth. A love that had not unravelled, only been folded away in a place she rarely dared to touch.

Her hand trembled as she lowered it from the glass. The air seemed denser now, pressing gently at the curve of her arm. Her lungs moved slower, as if keeping time with an older rhythm that did not belong to this room. She did not want to leave the image behind, yet she knew she could not remain in it. Not fully. Not now.

The surface smoothed again, returning her reflection. Her face was pale, her eyes bright with the trace of tears, her lips closed as if the mirror itself had sealed them. She held that silence within her, not forced but chosen, as though the glass had reminded her what it meant. To carry presence without words. To listen instead of speaking. To know that silence was not absence, but a vow.

She let the image fade, though it clung to her in the quiet behind her ribs. The light in the glass thinned, releasing her reflection back to her, and she stepped away with the sense that the room had shifted in her absence.

Another pane waited ahead, pale against the curve of the chamber, drawing her forward before she realised she was moving. It rose like a narrow window, carved from pale, unpolished wood. The surface held the faint scent of sap and earth, as though it had been taken from a living tree and shaped without stripping away its memory.

Something in her leaned toward it before she moved, and when she did, her fingers hovered just shy of the frame. The glass caught the low light and deepened, then bloomed with a soft, molten gold that seemed to come from within rather than from the room around it.

She was younger, though no longer a child. Perhaps fifteen or sixteen. Her hair was pulled back in a loose knot, a few strands falling into her face. Dirt streaked the knees of her jeans, a scrape marked her elbow, and the quick rise and fall of her chest told of something sharper than fear.

A cliff face towered before her. Tall. Uneven. Relentless.

Miranda was there beside her, just as young. Her voice carried a playful challenge, but something steadier ran beneath it.

"Come on," she joked. "Unless you want to climb back down and admit I'm braver."

Cassandra watched her younger self roll her eyes, mutter something inaudible, and reach for the third handhold. Then the next. And the next.

The image shifted.

Now she stood at the top. Wind tugged strands of hair loose from their tie. Her arms were stretched wide, her face lifted to the sky, her mouth open in a cry that carried no trace of fear.

It was freedom.

In that moment she had known something, not in thought or in language, but in the quiet defiance rooted deep within her. She could face what unsettled her. She could rise.

The wind in that memory moved through her hair again, cool and unhurried, carrying a hint of salt and rock dust. Her pulse had been quick from the climb, yet her breath had steadied, settling into the same rhythm as the horizon in front of her. She remembered the way Miranda had laughed beside her, not unkindly, the sound rising into the open air as if it had nowhere else to go.

A coil drew in beneath her sternum. She had not remembered the climb in this way for years. She had never thought it mattered. But the mirror had.

She touched the glass briefly. "Thank you," she murmured, though she had no idea who she was speaking to. The sky and wind blurred into stillness, the cliffside sinking back into the glass as if it had never been there.

The air between her and the next mirror felt closer, charged, as though each step toward it would draw her deeper into a truth that remained just beyond her grasp. Its frame was smaller, rougher, the uneven edges catching her eye as though it had been waiting for her alone.

Cassandra paused before it, letting calm settle around her, then stepped into its waiting pull.

The surface stirred with a darker glow. This was not the warm light of the cliffside, nor the golden hush of remembered laughter. It spread like ink in water, filling the glass until only a shadowed scene remained.

She recognised it instantly.

The ritual. The one where the lines had begun to blur, when her skin had recalled more than her mind could claim.

Her body arched beneath Lucas, the red length falling in a loose ribbon from her wrist. Heat moved between them, skin against skin, the steady weight of his hands at her waist. She saw the moment her head tilted back, the low sound that escaped when their bodies found the same rhythm. Her lips were parted, her eyes closed in that threshold between yielding and wanting more.

She studied herself as if seeing a stranger. And she saw him.

The way his gaze held her, the hunger tempered by precision, the control that didn't need force. The way she had offered herself to it. The choice she had made without hesitation.

A pull formed inside her, not in resistance, but in recognition of what it meant to give so fully. Guilt stirred, sharp and warm, not born of regret, but of knowing she hadn't yet measured the cost.

Her hand hovered, close enough to feel the heat rising from the glass, yet she couldn't bring herself to touch it.

She eased back, the heat in the glass fading as though the moment itself had chosen to release her, retreating into the depths of its own silence. The air in the chamber adjusted around her, not with a breeze but with a slow rebalancing, as if the room had been holding its breath and was now letting it go.

Light shifted across the curve of the mirrors, altering in ways she couldn't measure, and in that change came the faintest trace of movement at her back. It wasn't a sound, not even the disturbance of fabric, but the quiet pressure of awareness. She knew before she turned that he was there.

Her gaze dropped. For a moment the glass filled with light, the vision dissolving into it. The moment was gone.

And then she felt him behind her.

Lucas.

His presence came without sound, unfolding beside her like a tide slipping in at night. No footsteps marked his approach, only the slow awareness of him in the air. A touch followed.

His hand traced the line of her arm with deliberate care, pausing where the robe met skin. He rested there, the faint warmth of his palm steady against her shoulder. His voice came close, the words brushed in quiet certainty.

"Do you see more clearly now?"

She didn't speak. Her eyes stayed on the reflection as it steadied to plain glass, the last trace of the image gone.

Lucas moved to stand at her side.

"Every mirror in this room shows a truth," he said. "Not always the whole of it, but enough."

She swallowed. "Is that what this is for? To look back?"

"No," he said softly. "To look through."

She turned to him then, not with accusation, but with something closer to ache.

"Then what do I do with what I've seen?"

He met her gaze, and for the first time, his eyes looked almost human.

"You remember it," he said. "You let it shape you. And then you keep walking."

Cassandra turned back to the mirrors. She wasn't sure she wanted to see more, but she also knew she wasn't done.

Lucas didn't speak, but his hand stayed at the small of her back, a steady presence, guiding without pressure. She followed him from the mirrored chamber.

The air altered as they stepped into the corridor again. It felt warmer here, heavier, like something caught between walls that had been listening for too long. The wooden floor gave way to a softer surface beneath her feet, rugs laid in overlapping layers, their intricate patterns bending and twisting as though they had been woven with stories rather than thread.

They advanced without hurry. The silence carried a pulse of its own, faint yet steady, echoing somewhere deep inside her chest. A subtle fragrance lingered, wax mingled with resin, the scent of pages left to age in closed rooms. Shadows reached differently in this part of the house, stretched long and uncertain, their edges blurred as if unsure where to end.

They turned a corner where the light thinned to a pale seam across the floor, spilling from some unseen source hidden behind the walls. Doors appeared at intervals, each one sealed. Some were plain, their grain dark and close; others bore carvings so delicate she could not tell if they had been shaped by hand or time itself. None opened. None invited.

The path ahead narrowed, then widened again without warning, as if the house itself were adjusting around them. Her steps found the same rhythm as Lucas's, each one carrying her deeper into the stillness until she could no longer measure how far they had come.

They paused when the atmosphere thickened once more, denser, as though the air itself had been waiting.

Lucas set his palm to a door carved from dark wood. A sound resonated through the grain, low and resonant, not quite a groan, not quite a sigh. The door eased inward, and Cassandra crossed the threshold.

The chamber was circular, like the mirror hall, though smaller. More intimate. The walls were the same dark stone, but smoother here, curving inward toward a domed ceiling that lifted with the quiet reverence of a cathedral.

Candles lined the perimeter. Hundreds of them. Each flame quivered only faintly, their glow laying a soft mantle over the stone until the surface seemed almost warm to the touch. The air carried the trace of wax, layered over something older beneath it, a dust that felt undisturbed for years.

At the centre stood two mirrors.

They faced one another, tall and unbroken, their frames darkened with age, the wood worn where countless hands might once have steadied themselves. Unlike the mirrors she had already encountered, these surfaces neither shimmered nor wavered. They revealed no image, no suggestion of what might come. Only the stillness of something waiting.

Lucas stepped aside, his silence unbroken.

Cassandra's feet carried her forward as though they already knew the path. The space between the mirrors tightened around her, their silent weight pressing in from either side.

She stopped at the very centre.

Her reflection appeared in both, caught from opposite angles, as though one revealed the face she offered the world and the other held the truths she kept hidden behind her eyes.

The fabric at her wrist pulsed once. Lucas's gaze lowered to it. A single fingertip traced the air just beside the knot, not making contact, only marking its presence.

Then his voice came, low and unhurried. "Do you know why you were asked to wear it?"

She shook her head slowly. "No."

"It marks you," he said. "Not as owned. Not as claimed. But as willing."

A sharp stillness tightened in her chest.

"The silk is a thread," he continued. "One that ties this moment to every one that came before it. Every step you took. Every choice. And now, it binds nothing except your own becoming."

Her fingers found the end of the ribbon, tucked beneath the robe's sleeve. She pulled gently.

The silk loosened, slow and soundless, like the release of air from a held note. It slipped free, pooling in her palm.

Lucas stepped closer. His fingertips brushed the edge of her robe just above her shoulder.

"May I?" he asked.

She nodded.

He drew the robe from her body in a single motion, not abrupt but reverent. The fabric fell, folding around her ankles with the softness of something that had learned her shape. Warmth gathered between them, touched with the faint memory of his breath against her skin, the same deliberate heat she remembered from the night their bodies had found one rhythm.

Cassandra stood still, the silk resting loosely in one hand. Her skin tingled under the candlelight, not from cold but from sharpened awareness.

Lucas didn't reach for her again. He only gestured toward the mirrors.

"Two paths," he said. "Both are real. But only one belongs to you."

She turned to the first.

The mirror brightened, and then an image formed.

Cassandra stood at the mouth of a long hall, her hand outstretched, surrounded by people whose faces were cloaked in shadow. They bowed to her. The silk had become a sash, dark red and gleaming, drawn tightly around her waist. Power radiated from her, quiet and complete.

Cassandra didn't appear cruel in that reflection, yet the woman staring back no longer looked like herself.

Her gaze shifted to the other mirror. This image carried a gentler light.

A garden stretched in the frame, sunlit and calm. A book rested across her lap while ivy trailed over the curve of a wooden bench. Her fingers lay over another hand. Ethan's. Their heads leaned close together. Laughter touched their faces, and the warmth between them held the scene still, as though time had chosen not to pass.

There was no silk.

She lingered between the mirrors, her heartbeat steady at the base of her throat. Bare feet adjusted against the stone while the ribbon slipped free from her hand, curling to the floor.

Eyes closed, she waited. Lucas's voice reached her across the quiet.

"Which is the mask?" he asked. "And which is the truth?"

"I don't know," she whispered.

"Then let the mirrors show you."

Her lids lifted.

This time, both mirrors wavered.

Each held her image, yet neither was complete. One trembled at the edges as if waiting to be chosen. The other blurred at its centre, already sliding away like a dream on waking.

She stepped forward until she stood precisely between them. The length of fabric lay at her feet, still now, its quiet presence emptied of any beat. She bent, lifted it with care, and tied it once more at her wrist. The knot she made this time was deliberate.

Lucas watched without moving.

She turned to face him, her voice even. "I don't choose tonight."

He inclined his head in slow acknowledgement. "That's also a choice."

Her gaze returned to the mirrors. Neither stirred now. Each held only her, not as she had been, but as she was becoming.

She stayed there, suspended between the two reflections. Not fractured. Not divided. Whole. The chamber's silence didn't strain. It was alive with a quiet that rose from the stone beneath her feet.

The fabric at her wrist remained knotted, a subtle tether that didn't bind but reminded.

Lucas stepped forward. Not to speak and not to lead, only to witness. His presence no longer felt like a question. It felt like part of the answer.

Cassandra raised her hand toward the nearest mirror, stopping just short of the surface, close enough for her warmth to brush the image without disturbing it.

She no longer needed to see another version of herself. She had seen enough. What mattered now was what she would carry, which parts would remain, and which would be left behind.

The mirror stayed quiet. Behind her, Lucas waited. She stepped back from it, her heartbeat steady in the stillness, stronger than the hush around her.

Her gaze dropped to the silk. Its red edge caught a thread of light, unyielding in its knot. It held. And so did she.

"I'm not the same as when I arrived in London," she said quietly.

"No," Lucas replied, his voice low. "And you won't be the same when you leave."

The silence between them wasn't hollow. It carried every version of her that had ever dared to look more closely.

Cassandra turned once more toward the chamber. Toward the mirrors. Toward herself. Then she walked forward, not away from anything, but into what waited next.

The door closed behind her with the subdued certainty of something returning to its place. Lucas did not follow her down the corridor. He remained within the chamber, a still figure as candlelight traced the stone and shadow.

Her steps along the passage were even, unforced. The robe brushed her ankles once more, though she scarcely felt it now. The ribbon stayed knotted at her wrist, a small weight she no longer thought of loosening.

Beyond the threshold, the night had deepened. The trees seemed taller, their branches silvered under the moon, unmoving as if holding their vigil. At the end of the path, the car waited. The same shape. The same driver. The same quiet.

She entered the back seat without speaking. The interior held its warmth, but it no longer touched her. A presence lingered in the air, faint and altered. Not anticipation.

Completion.

As the engine stirred and the woods fell behind them, she leaned her head lightly against the window. A pale ghost bloomed across the glass, then faded with the sweep of the headlights.

The road was familiar. The city rose again like a mirage, its lights pulsing slowly through mist. Buildings stood as they always had. Nothing outside had changed. And yet everything had.

She watched her reflection in the glass. It surfaced, then vanished between the rhythm of passing beams. Not entirely her face. Not wholly a stranger's.

Somewhere along the drive, she stopped looking.

Back at the flat, the hallway light flickered when she closed the door behind her. The robe felt heavier in her hands. She slipped it from her shoulders, folding it across the arm of the couch before walking barefoot into her bedroom.

After closing the door, she struck a match and touched it to the candle's wick, watching the flame bloom and steady as the scent of lavender filled the air, warm and familiar.

The mirror stood silent, framed in soft wood, its surface dulled by the dark. No shimmer. No visions. Just her shape, gently lit by the candle on the sill.

Drawn closer, she leaned into its quiet. No ghosts waited. No hidden truths. Only her own eyes, shadowed but steady. The silk circled her wrist. She lifted it slightly, watching how the knot had held. Her fingertips traced the edge of the fabric without untying it.

Then she looked deeper. Not to uncover what had been hidden.

But to see what had endured.

Her reflection answered, moving with her in calm accord. There was no blur, no flicker. Only stillness.

On the table beside her bed, the book rested with its cover closed, yet not cold. She picked it up, her thumb along the spine, and opened to a waiting page.

At first, there was nothing. Only the faint grain of paper beneath her fingers, bare and expectant.

Then the words formed.

All answers will come soon.

When the last shadow lifts and the light finds you.

The breath she had been carrying since the mirrors slipped free, the sound small and sure in the quiet. The candle's flame trembled, casting shifting gold across the walls as the shadows leaned closer.

With care, she closed the book, not with reverence but with certainty. The flame wavered once, a spark lifting from the wick before sinking into darkness, and the room received her like a presence long known.

She stood before the mirror, her posture steady, gaze clear. Not searching. Not fearing. At her wrist, the silk gave a subtle thrum beneath her skin, and something within her answered.

The silence was no longer empty. It leaned toward her, not as shadow, but as something alive, patient, and near. Words were no longer needed.

She had stepped fully into what she was becoming.

And somewhere beyond the night, it was already moving toward her.

12
THE STEP BEYOND

T he glass doors of Vanguard Publishing hissed closed behind her. Cassandra stepped inside as if crossing into a memory that did not belong to her.

The light was sharp and deliberate, cast from ceiling panels that revealed every surface without mercy. Clean-lined desks stretched in ordered rows, each one curated with the careful disorder of coffee mugs, stacked folders, and pens aligned at precise angles. The air was cool and processed, its stillness broken only by the faint hum of ventilation that could not disguise the scent of paper and toner.

It all felt arranged, as though a set designer had worked late into the night to convince her the world remained intact. That the familiar was still safe to touch. That this place still belonged to her.

But every sound arrived unsoftened.

Phones rang in quick, staccato bursts. Keyboards clattered without rhythm. Laughter lifted and collided with the glass partitions, scattering in jagged echoes before falling away. Even the light click of footsteps against polished tiles struck her as intrusive, a reminder that she had been somewhere where sound lingered differently, where every note carried space to breathe.

She moved forward slowly, her back held straighter than intended, her smile arriving a fraction too late. It was the posture of someone performing a role they no longer believed in.

Behind her, a measured rhythm of heels crossed the floor, confident and unhurried.

Lydia approached with her usual precision, each step as exact as a final mark on a page. The sharp tailoring of her jacket seemed to cut its own line through the light, her presence both controlled and undeniably seen.

"Look at you, Cass," she said, tilting her head with a smile that reached her eyes just enough to suggest it had been rehearsed elsewhere. "You look like someone who's been somewhere wild."

The words carried a note that might have been curiosity, or might have been calculation.

Cassandra's mouth tugged into something resembling a smile she had almost forgotten how to use.

"Come on. Let's go to my office." Lydia's hand brushed her arm, brief but deliberate, before she turned, her movement as exact as her voice.

Cassandra followed, her steps clicking in quiet rhythm along a hallway lined with framed posters and awards she had once passed without thought. Their glossy surfaces caught the light as she moved, turning each image into a shifting reflection that did not quite let her see herself.

Inside the office, the brightness softened. The lamps cast a warmer glow, as though the room had been designed to offer relief from the rest of the building. Lydia gestured to the chair opposite her desk.

"Sit. Coffee?"

"Please. Triple shot."

One eyebrow lifted as Lydia crossed to the corner bench and reached for the French press. "That bad, huh?"

Her voice carried an undercurrent that reached further than her words, a warmth threaded with concern, carefully balanced beneath her polished professionalism. She pressed the plunger with deliberate slowness, the scent of dark roast blooming into the air, curling through the quiet with a weight that felt older than habit.

With her back still turned, Lydia said lightly, "Whatever it is... I hope it's something you chose. Not something that's choosing you."

The words touched something deep within her, a place she had not realised was waiting to be found.

Lydia returned, setting the mug in front of her before lowering herself into the chair behind the desk. She folded one leg beneath the other in a movement so practised it might have been ritual.

"I read your article," she said, her gaze lifting to meet Cassandra's. "Camden in Winter has never sounded so raw. Or so... haunted."

Cassandra's fingers curved around the ceramic mug, the heat sinking slowly into her palms. She did not lift it to her lips.

"I loved it," Lydia added quickly. "Don't get me wrong. But it had teeth. There was something beneath the surface. A kind of hunger."

Cassandra let the words settle before answering, her voice quiet. "Thank you."

Lydia studied her for a long moment, then eased back slightly in her chair.

"I have something I think you'll like," she said, tilting her head as if to draw Cassandra a fraction closer into her confidence. "Unusual. A bit of a deep dive. There's a reclusive sculptor in Highgate who only works at night. He lives and works in an old chapel in the woods. It's barely marked on any map."

She paused, her eyes still on Cassandra, measuring the space between them.

"His last exhibition caused quite a stir. Some called it dangerous. Others refused to speak of it at all. Sound intriguing?"

An image formed at once: weathered stone half-hidden by trees, a doorway where the light thinned. Another place at the edge of the known, another figure wrapped in myth and shadow.

She exhaled slowly, the vapour rising from her cup and blurring the space between her and the room.

Why was she always drawn into places like these, pockets of the city that seemed to exist just beyond the reach of ordinary time?

A wry curve touched her mouth. Why could none of these stories ever unfold in daylight?

Just once, she thought, she would like to meet someone fascinating at a café at noon, somewhere with croissants and sunshine.

Lydia watched her closely. "You've changed," she said, her tone almost kind. "Not in a bad way. Just... more depth. More shadow."

Cassandra let the words pass without answer.

She could still feel the impression of stone against her skin, as if something sacred had marked her and refused to let go. Lucas's voice lingered, coiled low in her chest, like a verse that would not fade.

Her shoulder warmed beneath the seam of her blouse, not with pain but with the echo of something once stirred there, settling again like an ember beneath ash.

The warmth from her coffee rose in curls towards her lashes. It smelled wrong. Too clean. Too bright.

She took a sip anyway, just to feel something warm that did not belong to candlelight or touch.

Lydia settled against the back of her chair, arms folded, her gaze narrowing with the quiet precision of an editor deciding where to cut. It was half assessment, half guard raised. She looked like a woman who had already read the first draft and was weighing whether to shape it with care or let the knife slide in without hesitation.

"Long night?" she asked.

"Something like that." Cassandra set the mug down and glanced toward the window. "Things have just been... intense."

Lydia gave a slow nod, tapping the side of her cup. "Whatever it is, just make sure it's worth losing yourself for."

Cassandra didn't reply, because part of her was already elsewhere.

She had begun to write differently. To dream differently. To feel the glide of silk where there was none, to sense the heat of candlelight even in the brightest of rooms.

Lydia hesitated, then leaned forward, her polished tone softening. "He is the kind of subject that gets under your skin. I thought of you straight away."

Cassandra's voice was cautious. "Who is he?"

Lydia's smile was faint, almost secret. "That's the thing. No one really knows."

Cassandra traced a finger along the rim of her mug. Her reflection trembled there, blurred and distant, as if belonging to someone else.

Something in it caught her. The timing. The place. The way Lydia spoke, as though unknowingly reciting lines from a dream Cassandra had never shared.

It was like a door easing open, just wide enough to step through.

And from somewhere deep within, she felt it.

Not a memory. Not a voice. More like an echo that had wound itself through everything since that first night.

She exhaled slowly, completely still, her eyes locked on the dark coffee as if it held the answers. But the pull remained. Quiet. Constant.

A part of her wanted to walk away, to take an easier assignment, something neutral, something without edges.

But this one had already found her.

She did not say yes.

And yet, she did not say no either.

Lydia waited, as though she sensed the shift in the silence between them. She reached to one side of her desk and drew out a slim grey folder. The paper was smooth and crisp, the kind she reserved for stories that carried power. She slid it across the polished surface.

"I thought you might want to see some of his work," she said. "These aren't official press shots. An insider at the gallery took them. Off the record."

Cassandra opened the folder with care. The images inside were printed in black and white, their grain softening edges as though each had already been weathered by time. The first showed a sculpture rising from the centre of what appeared to be a chapel altar, its form twisting upward. Curved stone swept into shadow, and the arms did not end in hands but in something that might have been wings.

The next was quieter in its impact but no less striking. A woman's torso half-emerged from what looked like molten wax, the surface rippling around her as though still soft. Her eyes were closed. Her lips parted just enough to suggest prayer. Or warning.

"He doesn't title them," Lydia said, her tone low. "At least, not publicly. They simply arrive. Appear in galleries without fanfare. Sometimes there's no one there to speak for them. The pieces do all the talking."

Cassandra turned the pages slowly, letting her gaze rest on each image before moving to the next. Every sculpture felt like an entrance to somewhere unseen. Each seemed to carry words she could almost hear, if only she leaned close enough.

"What's the angle?" she asked.

Lydia lifted one shoulder in a measured shrug. "Art as ritual. Creation as compulsion. Maybe even transformation. Whatever speaks to you. Just follow it."

Her fingertips brushed lightly over the final photograph. This one was darker than the rest, not because of the sculpture itself but the space that held it. Long bars of shadow stretched across a stone floor. Behind the piece, a tall window rose toward the unseen roof, framed thickly in ivy. The faint glow of candlelight touched the edge of the lens, barely there yet impossible to ignore.

Something turned inside her. Not sudden, but steady, like a wheel beginning to move. It felt less like the start of an assignment and more like the next step of something already set in motion.

"I'll take it," she said.

Lydia smiled, but it was measured. Not triumphant, more like relief softened by caution.

"I hoped you would," she said. "But I wanted you to choose it. For your own reasons."

Cassandra closed the folder. Its weight felt tangible in her hands, grounding her.

"I'm not sure I even know what the right reasons are anymore."

"That's all right," Lydia replied, her voice gentle. "Just make sure they belong to you."

Beyond the window, the light had tipped. Not quite grey, not yet gold. That strange hour when the city seemed to be letting go.

Cassandra rose, tucking the folder beneath her arm.

"Do you know how to find him?" she asked.

Lydia's smile returned, touched this time with something unreadable.

"Apparently there's a gate at the back of Highgate Wood. No sign. Just a path that curves right and disappears behind a grove. People say it leads to the old chapel. If you find it, you'll know."

Cassandra inclined her head. The description sounded more like a story than a set of directions, but she understood it all the same.

"They say he doesn't do interviews," Lydia went on. "But maybe that's only to keep the amateurs away. If anyone can draw him out, it's you."

As Cassandra reached the door, Lydia added, "Take your time. But not too much. He's not the sort to wait."

Her hand rested on the handle for a moment.

"I didn't think he would be. Do you mind if I use the bathroom before I go?"

"Of course," Lydia said, already reaching for her phone. "And Cass…"

Cassandra paused in the doorway.

Lydia's gaze lifted, steady and intent. "Be careful. Some stories you don't just tell. You step inside them."

Cassandra gave a slight nod, then moved into the corridor.

The walk to the bathroom felt longer than it should have. The lights overhead burned with a cold clarity that made the air seem too thin, too exposed. She pushed open the door and slipped inside.

The scent of disinfectant hung in the stillness. She crossed to the sink, placing her hands on the cool edge of the counter. The mirror reflected her face in sharp detail, every angle caught under the unflinching glare of fluorescent light. Yet the longer she stared, the more her features seemed to lose their certainty, as though the surface of the glass could not quite decide what it wanted to hold.

She leaned in, her breath barely stirring the space between her and the reflection. It was a deliberate movement, the kind made when expecting to find something or someone else staring back.

The lights above gave a brief, silent tremor. A thin pulse of shadow moved across the walls. When her eyes opened again, her reflection had not shifted position, yet it no longer felt entirely her own.

A flicker in the glass drew her eyes lower, to the line of her blouse. As she adjusted, the collar slipped slightly, the fabric brushing against her skin.

There.

Just visible at the edge of the opening, where the cloth had fallen aside.

A mark.

Not red, not bruised, not painted. Etched.

It shimmered faintly, as if lit from within. A shape she could not quite name, curling along the curve of her left shoulder like a memory made visible.

Her lungs stilled.

She reached up slowly, fingers trembling as she loosened the top buttons of her blouse. The fabric gave way, sliding enough to reveal it more clearly. The mark was neither ink nor scar. It pulsed softly, like a heartbeat remembering something hers had forgotten.

The bathroom seemed to lean closer around her.

The mirror did not lie.

Touching the mark hesitantly, warmth spread beneath her fingertips, not painful but deep, reaching further than the skin. It had not been there yesterday.

Or had it?

The door creaked as someone entered. Cassandra fastened her blouse quickly and turned back toward the sink, lifting her hands to her hair in an absent gesture.

The other woman nodded politely before disappearing into a stall.

Cassandra let out a long, measured sigh. She ran cool water over her hands, then pressed her palms to her face, letting the sensation hold her steady.

She left the bathroom quietly, her reflection lingering behind her, carrying an awareness she was not ready to claim.

The flat was quiet when she stepped inside, though the scent of wine and the faint trace of warmed cushions told her someone was home.

Miranda was curled into the corner of the couch, a half-full glass in her hand, her legs tucked beneath her. Relief flickered in her gaze the moment Cassandra entered.

"There you are," she said softly.

Cassandra set her bag down, releasing a long breath as she toed off her boots. "Yeah. Sorry. I needed time to… think."

Miranda tilted her head, studying her. "I haven't seen you for days. You were gone when I got home last night and again when I woke this morning. Is everything okay? Do you want to talk about what happened?"

Cassandra hesitated in the hallway, her hand brushing her shoulder before falling away. She crossed into the kitchen and poured herself a glass of wine. The bottle's neck tapped lightly against the rim, the sound familiar yet strangely distant.

For a moment she stood there, glass in hand, then carried it back to the couch and lowered herself beside Miranda. The cushions yielded between them.

The air held the low hum of the heater and the soft press of dusk against the windows.

"There's so much," she said at last. "Most of it I don't even understand myself."

Miranda's silence felt like permission.

"I think I need to tell you anyway."

She began slowly, letting the words shape themselves, each one as fragile as something newly unearthed. She spoke of the chamber, the circle of mirrors, the way Lucas had guided her through them, each reflection altered, each whisper clinging rather than fading. She told Miranda about the final mirrors, how they had drawn her deeper, showing not only who she was, but who she had been and who she might yet become. A hall of versions. Not a performance, but a reckoning.

Her voice lowered. "And then there was the mark. I only noticed it today."

She touched her shoulder lightly through the blouse, then unfastened the top buttons. The fabric loosened, falling aside just enough to reveal the curve of her left shoulder.

The sigil caught the fading light, its faint shimmer alive against her skin. It looked less placed than awakened, as if it had surfaced from beneath, waiting for its moment.

Miranda leaned closer, her gaze steady, her expression carrying something more than surprise. "That's not just a mark," she said softly. "It's a seal."

Cassandra let the blouse fall back into place, her eyes dropping to her hands. "I know."

"It feels like it was always there," she added quietly. "Not drawn. Not cut. Just awakened. It doesn't hurt. But something has changed."

Miranda's expression held, still and heavy with weight. She leaned back slowly, her glass tilting slightly as though she had forgotten it.

Cassandra watched her closely, noting the flicker in her eyes as though she was searching for something she might not find. The air between them thickened, taking on its own shape.

Only then did Cassandra reach for her wine. She took a sip, the taste grounding her, then set the glass aside. Her hand lingered on the stem for a heartbeat before releasing it.

"I saw Lydia today," she said at last. "She gave me something I thought you might find interesting."

She drew the folder from her bag and placed it on the table. Opening it with care, she spread the photographs across the surface in muted black and white. Marble and shadow. Human forms caught in transformation. One seemed to hold light differently, glowing as if it carried its own source within.

Miranda leaned in, her hand hovering above one photograph before her fingertips grazed the edge. Recognition cut through her features with sudden clarity.

"I've seen this," she murmured. "Not the photograph. The sculpture."

Cassandra's head turned sharply, the memory of their earlier conversation about the gallery rising to the surface.

Miranda kept her gaze fixed on the image. "Remember when I told you about those new pieces that appeared at the gallery? No paperwork. No artist's name?"

Cassandra nodded slowly, already anticipating what was coming.

"This was one of them. It appeared one morning, standing in the middle of the floor. No one knew who had brought it in. It wasn't part of any delivery we expected. It felt... different, like it didn't belong to us."

Her fingers drew back, as though the photograph still carried the cool weight of stone.

"And then it vanished. Overnight. We assumed someone collected it, but there was no record. No courier, no signature. Nothing. Just gone."

Cassandra lowered her gaze to the image again. The twisted form. The curve that suggested life without living.

"I know how to find him," she said quietly. "But walking straight in doesn't feel right."

Miranda studied her, then reached for the photograph. She turned it over, her eyes narrowing. In the bottom corner, faint and almost hidden, was a line of handwritten scrawl.

"There's an email address," she said.

Cassandra leaned closer. The letters wavered for a moment before settling into focus. They were not printed or stamped but written with a slow, careful hand, as though meant to be found only by those who knew to look.

"What do I even say?" Her voice was almost inaudible.

Miranda's answer came without hesitation. "Then say the truth."

The words lingered. Cassandra kept her eyes fixed on the address, the slope of the handwriting already etched into her mind. It felt like an opening. A test.

Miranda leaned back against the cushions, reaching for the novel on the arm of the couch. She opened it but did not turn a page. Instead, she gave Cassandra a small nod, quiet permission to choose.

Cassandra rose and disappeared into her bedroom. The sound of a zipper broke the hush. When she returned, she carried her laptop under one arm, her glass of wine in the other.

She set them both on the coffee table and sat cross-legged on the rug, the photographs spread around her like fragments of something half-remembered.

The screen glowed to life. Her fingers hovered over the keyboard, caught between starting and staying silent.

She opened a new message and typed the address with care, each letter deliberate. Then she stopped, fingertips resting against the keys.

What do you say to someone who might not want to be found?

Her pulse slowed as she began to write.

Subject: Inquiry

Dear Sir,

My name is Cassandra Moore. I am a freelance writer currently researching contemporary sculpture and its intersections with myth, memory, and identity.

Your work has recently come to my attention. I encountered it briefly through a gallery and again through a private reference, though no clear attribution was listed in either case.

I understand this message may be unexpected. If you are indeed the artist connected to these pieces, I would be honoured to learn more, whether through a brief correspondence or, if agreeable, a short visit at a time of your choosing.

Please know that I approach this with respect and curiosity. No assumptions. No pressure. Only a wish to understand more about the story behind the work.

Kind regards,

Cassandra Moore

She read it twice, then once more, the rhythm of the words settling into her like the echo of a step taken in a darkened hall. The cursor blinked steadily at the edge of the final line. Her finger hovered for a heartbeat before pressing Send.

The screen refreshed, and the message disappeared into the unseen spaces between them.

Miranda glanced up from her book. "Did you do it?"

Cassandra gave a slow nod. "It's sent."

The room quieted around them. The heater's low murmur blurred into the hush. Outside, dusk pressed itself against the glass, its colour deepening with every moment.

Neither of them spoke. The stillness in the flat felt less like absence and more like a threshold, waiting.

♥

Her phone buzzed shortly after six.

The sound cut through the quiet like something misplaced, a note that did not belong in the stillness of the room.

Cassandra blinked against the pale grey of morning, her eyes dry and heavy with sleep. For a moment she lay unmoving beneath the weight of the doona, the faint vibration pulsing against the wooden surface of the bedside table.

She reached for it slowly, her pulse quickening, the air thinning with each second. A part of her already knew what she hoped to see.

The sculptor. A reply. A summons.

Or Lucas. A word. A thread drawn tight again in the dark.

But it was neither.

Ethan.

Her chest tightened. She stared at the screen before unlocking it. The message was short, still caring, yet marked with a distance that startled her.

Hey, just checking in. Hope London isn't swallowing you whole. Miss you.

No photo. No call to follow. Only space. She read it twice, as though repetition might uncover something hidden between the words. Tapping the screen gently, she watched the letters dissolve back into the pale white light. The room seemed altered, the silence less forgiving than it had been.

Had she really not spoken to him properly in days? The last full conversation blurred, details fading like fragments of a dream. Something about deadlines. Something about being busy. None of it clear.

She had meant to call. She always meant to.

But the days folded in on themselves now, collapsing into hours that vanished before she could grasp them. And the nights stretched wide, holding her with a force she did not resist.

The phone slipped from her hand onto the mattress. The screen glowed a few seconds before dimming, Ethan's words swallowed by the dark.

Her fingers drifted unconsciously to her shoulder, brushing the warmth that lingered there. The mark had faded from sight, yet it remained, as though her body still carried the echo of a touch that had never truly left. For an instant she wished Ethan's message could anchor her as it once might have, but the pull beneath her skin refused to quiet.

The message waited, unanswered. She did not know what to write back. Not yet. Perhaps not at all.

In the shower, the water came too hot, striking her skin with a sharpness that forced a sudden gasp. She let it run anyway, eyes closed, forehead resting against the tile, steam curling upward around her. The sound filled the room, relentless and steady, drowning out everything else. For a while it was almost cleansing, almost ordinary. The heat grounded her, if only because it was simple. No candles. No silk. No symbols. Only water.

She wanted that simplicity to be enough. To let the steam rinse her clean of questions, to leave the morning unmarked. But even as she tried to surrender to the steadiness of it, her mind slipped elsewhere. To the sculptor. To the fragments of stone that shifted even in stillness. To the photographs that revealed nothing and yet unsettled everything. To Lucas, whose presence refused to release her, even when oceans and silence should have made forgetting possible.

It had been days since his last message. Since the silk. Since the ritual of mirrors and the voice that lingered like smoke at the edge of hearing.

Was it strange he had not reached out again?

Or was this part of it, too? The silence. The waiting. The test of how far she might lean forward without being called.

Soap slid slowly across her skin. Her fingers paused when they skimmed her shoulder. The mark stayed quiet, unburned, yet never forgotten. A seal, Miranda had said. And what had it sealed her into?

When she stepped out, steam still clinging faintly to her body, the air beyond felt cooler, sharper, as though she had crossed from one chamber into another. Wrapped in a towel, she moved through the flat with an unmeant stillness. The bedroom waited in pale silence, light pooling faintly across the floorboards. Morning had begun again, grey dissolving into a bleached gold that flattened edges and left everything too exposed.

She dressed in soft layers, grounding ones. Cotton, wool, fabrics that gave no suggestion of ritual. Something ordinary, she told herself, though her reflection in the mirror still seemed to carry traces of something else.

The flat kept its hush. She padded barefoot into the kitchen, the floor cool against her soles, and filled the kettle. The rush of water broke the silence briefly, then subsided into waiting. She made tea more from habit than desire, each movement performed with the steadiness of routine.

Her phone lay silent on the counter beside her. No new messages. No replies.

Not from him.

Not from the sculptor either.

She carried the mug to the lounge, the warmth fading quickly against her palms. The laptop rested where she had left it, lid half-open, its black screen catching the faintest outline of her face. A thin draft slipped through the sash frame, curling at her ankles and sending a shiver through her. She pulled the cardigan closer, not for comfort so much as to keep herself anchored.

If she lingered too long in stillness, her thoughts would scatter. They always did.

She eased the laptop open, the hinge groaning faintly, and the blank document rose before her. The cursor blinked like a pulse against the pale screen, patient and insistent.

The Shape of Silence: Sculpting the Unseen in London's Fringe Art Scene.

The title glowed at the top, tentative but steady. She wasn't sure it would remain, not yet, but it gave her something to lean into, a place to begin.

Her fingers hovered over the keys. Then, as if momentum had chosen her rather than the other way around, she began to type.

A few works arrive with no explanation. No title cards. No artist statement. Only the significance of stone and the way light bends itself across the surface, gathering in hollows, clinging to edges, vanishing where shadow takes hold. Figures without names. Fragments without origins. And yet something in them insists on being remembered.

She paused. The words hung on the screen, raw but alive. She lifted the mug, tasting tea that had already cooled into something muted and thin. The silence pressed in again. Still no message. Still nothing.

Setting the cup aside, she let her hands fall back to the keyboard. A sentence became another, then another, until three short paragraphs filled the page.

Then the quiet shifted.

A sound, slight but insistent. The soft ping of an arriving email crossed the room, sharp and bright, like a match catching in the dark.

The half-formed sentence blinked faintly at the top of her screen. She turned toward the notification.

Re: Your enquiry.

There was no name. No greeting. Only a reply.

She clicked.

Ashmere Chapel. Midnight tonight. You know the way.

A stillness passed through her, tightening the space around her ribs.

She studied the words, letting them settle.

No address. Only the name, the time, and that quiet insistence. You know the way.

And she did.

Lydia had mentioned the place, describing it as a chapel hidden deep in the woods at the edge of Highgate. Last night, unable to sleep, Cassandra had searched for it.

Ashmere Chapel was absent from any official registry. No website. No photographs taken in daylight. But it lingered in the margins of other stories, scattered through fragments of local history and the darker corners of fringe art blogs.

Writers spoke of it with odd precision, as though they were not describing a building so much as recalling the aftertaste of a dream. Half-remembered. Rarely named aloud. Always just out of reach.

Midnight. Never daylight. Never ordinary.

She closed the laptop softly. Not with finality, but with something like reverence.

The tea beside her had gone tepid. Outside, the light was shifting again.

But tonight, it would all lead to the chapel, and she would follow.

The flat was quiet again when Miranda emerged from her room. She moved softly through the space, her hair tousled from sleep, a scarf wrapped loosely at her throat. Cassandra hadn't heard the door or the creak of floorboards, only the subtle change in air and the rustle of movement in the hallway.

Miranda peeked around the corner, her eyes landing on Cassandra, the laptop closed beside her.

"You're up early," she said.

"I got a reply."

Miranda paused mid-step. "From him?"

Cassandra nodded. "The sculptor."

She reached for the laptop and opened it again, turning the screen gently toward her. The message sat there, still illuminated.

Ashmere Chapel. Midnight tonight.

You know the way.

Miranda's brow furrowed as she studied the words, then lifted her gaze. "No name. Just that. That's all."

Her expression steadied into something unreadable. Not worry, not quite, but close. She crossed into the lounge and sank into the cushions beside Cassandra.

"Well," she said at last, "at least he's consistent."

Cassandra gave a dry, soundless laugh and lifted her glass, swallowing the last of her cold tea. "I looked it up last night," she said. "Ashmere Chapel. I know how to get there."

"Of course you do." Miranda's voice was gentle. "You wouldn't have been called if you didn't."

That word, *called*, lingered between them.

Miranda reached for the book she had abandoned the night before. She flipped it open, thumb holding her place, her eyes lowered. "If you need anything before tonight," she said, "I'll be here."

Cassandra touched her arm lightly. "Thanks."

Miranda only nodded, gaze drifting back to the page, though the weight of it seemed to remain.

Cassandra rose, stretched, and padded back to her bedroom. The door clicked softly behind her.

She stood in the middle of the room, uncertain what to do with her hands. The daylight felt sharper here, less forgiving.

Her gaze drifted to the wardrobe, then to the chair where she had returned the robe. She did not touch it. Not yet.

Instead, she crossed to the vanity and slid open the drawer. Soft fabrics. A few necklaces. The silver ring she had bought in Camden, resting in its small pouch. She slipped it onto her finger, the cool metal a reminder. Of beginnings. Of something chosen.

A fresh jumper followed, black and soft at the cuffs, and she tied her hair loosely away from her face. Her reflection in the mirror looked back at her, thoughtful but calm. No flickering images now. No shadows bending close.

She crossed to the desk, opened her notebook, and turned to a blank page.

What are you becoming?

The words stared back, stark and unadorned. She left them unanswered. For now.

The rest of the afternoon moved slowly. She tried to eat but left most of the plate untouched. She brewed more tea but let it cool before she remembered it. Miranda kept mostly to herself, appearing now and then to sit beside her for a few minutes before retreating with her book or the faint clatter of something simmering on the stove.

Outside, the light began to slip. The city dimmed. Windows across the street turned gold. Headlights slid past in quiet flashes.

She showered again, slower this time, letting the water run over her like a secret pressed close. Heat traced down her spine, curling against her skin, the rhythm steady but unrelenting. For a while she simply stood there, forehead resting lightly against the tile, letting the sound fill the space until it became its own kind of silence.

Her eyes drifted shut, and with the darkness came memory. The mirrors. The shifting glass that had shown her not only who she was but who she might have been, who she still could become. Lucas's voice, quiet and certain, still lingered in her chest like a verse that refused to fade. The silk binding, red and absolute, pulsing against her wrist. The dreamlike chamber where choice had felt heavier than stone.

Her mind slipped further, to Ethan's message on the screen that morning, brief and caring, yet distant enough to sting. She had not replied. She was not sure what she wanted to say. His face had appeared in one of the mirrors too, unchanged, laughing the way he once had, before London and the hunger it carried had touched her. For a moment she had almost reached through the glass, almost pressed her hand to his. But even then, something else had held her back.

The steam curled upward, softening the edges of thought, but nothing erased the mark she had seen on her shoulder. Not ink. Not bruise. Something alive beneath the skin, awakened. Miranda's words echoed: a seal. She touched the spot lightly with her fingertips, water slipping down her arm, and still she felt it there, as though the heat only deepened its memory.

She thought of Camden too, the market stalls, the silver ring she had chosen, the scarf slipping from Miranda's shoulders, the city's shadows shifting in rhythm with her. And The Hollow, with its music and its smoke, the moment she had first stepped into a room where silence was treated as invitation, not absence.

The water poured on, threading through her hair, sliding across her chest, as if carrying every place she had walked through since the beginning. Each moment layered over the next until she could no longer separate what belonged to waking and what belonged to something else.

She opened her eyes at last. The glass shower door was blurred with condensation, her reflection fractured and faint behind the fog. A woman was there, but not the same one who had arrived in London.

Steam clung to the mirror when she stepped out, blurring the surface until her features dissolved completely.

Back in the bedroom, her hand drifted toward the robe.

This was an opening. A question offered. And she reminded herself again that this was only an interview. Words, not vows. A story to chase, not a rite to enter.

She let the robe fall gently back onto the chair.

Instead, she opened the wardrobe and pulled out a long black coat, thick enough to cut the wind. Beneath it, a dark jumper and jeans. Practical. Grounded. Human.

She laced her boots slowly, the sound of each loop and pull centring her in the room. When she stood, the mirror caught her full height.

No sigil. No silk.

Just a woman who could still choose.

She turned off the light and stepped into the hallway.

Miranda stood waiting near the door, as if she had known the moment would come. A scarf was wound loosely at her neck, her hand resting on the knob.

"I'm not going to ask if you are ready for this," she said.

Cassandra gave a small, crooked smile. "Thanks. I don't know if I'm ready, but I'm willing."

"Then that's enough." Miranda's voice stayed even, but her eyes caught the light, shimmering the way they always did when words carried more than she wanted to admit.

Cassandra nodded. She reached for the door handle, then paused.

"I don't know what I'll find there."

Miranda looked at her, steady and sure. "That's the point."

Then, before Cassandra could move again, Miranda stepped forward and drew her into a gentle hug. It was not long or heavy, only warm and certain, as if to remind her she was not walking into the unknown alone. Cassandra let herself hold that closeness for a moment, then eased back with a faint exhale.

She opened the door.

The night air met her, icy and restless. The scent of damp stone and faraway woodsmoke clung faintly to the breeze.

She stepped out onto the landing, pulled the coat tighter around her, and began to walk.

It was only an interview, she told herself. Nothing more.

And yet, the city seemed to dim around her, the night pressing in as though it had been waiting.

Somewhere ahead, Ashmere Chapel waited.

And something in her moved with it, already knowing the way.

13
THE SILENCE OF CHOICE

The air outside was brittle, the kind that made the city smell of wet concrete and static, sharp against the back of her throat.

London moved around her as though she were not part of it, its rhythm indifferent to her presence. Cars hissed past on damp roads, headlights flashing across her face without recognition. Footsteps trailed behind for a moment before dissolving into silence, leaving only the steady tap of her own boots.

Her reflection surfaced in the darkened shop windows, a step out of time, as if the city could not decide where she belonged. Glass showed her face, pale and watchful, but always a half-beat behind, a shadow of the woman she thought she was.

She crossed Junction Road as the streetlights flickered awake, their hum faint and irregular, struggling to claim the dark. Above, the sky was an iron-grey expanse, colourless and heavy, the shade of forgotten things.

And that was when she saw him.

Across the street, beneath the weak circle of a failing bulb, a figure stood. *Ethan.*

Her chest tightened, breath faltering as though the simple act of recognition had dislodged her from herself.

He had his hands in the pockets of his jeans, shoulders tilted forward against the cold, a posture so familiar it made her ache. That grey hoodie, the one she used to steal on Sunday mornings, still lived in her memory, soft and creased from wear. The tilt of his head, the faint forward lean, the almost-ready words shaping silently behind his mouth.

It was unmistakable.

But he did not smile. He did not lift his hand in greeting, did not speak her name across the narrow distance of the street. Instead, his hand rose slowly, palm out, not beckoning, not calling, just reaching, as if recalling the shape of something once held and now irretrievable.

Her body leaned before she could stop it. A part of her wanted to cross, to touch, to let her hand rest in his the way it once had. The distance between them seemed so slight, a single step that might collapse everything she had carried since leaving him behind.

Something inside her answered. Not fear. Not grief. Recognition, yes, but also something deeper, more ancient. Because she knew.

The angle of his mouth was not right. His eyes held too much shadow. He was not waiting for her. He was remembering her, remembering them, holding on to a version of her that no longer existed.

She understood it in her ribs, in the place where silk had once bound tight, in the pulse that had learned to carry silence as though it were language. He

159

was not Ethan as he lived, but Ethan as he lingered.

The hand that reached toward her wavered, fingers thinning against the air, as if they were made of smoke unravelling into night. His outline shimmered faintly, his face a shade too pale, and the space between them grew heavier with the certainty that she was seeing not the man himself but the echo of what he had been.

She blinked. A car passed between them, lights flaring and scattering against the wet air, momentarily blinding.

When the beam slipped away, the pavement was empty.

The space where he had been remained charged, heavy and unyielding, as though the air itself remembered his outline.

Cassandra's breath left her in a long, uneven thread. The street felt thinner without him, stretched taut around the absence. She longed to look back, to search the shadows for proof that he had not dissolved entirely. But she did not turn. She stepped forward, her boots meeting the curb, coat drawn close, hands gripping the fabric at her chest as if to anchor herself to the present.

Her stride was steady, but inside her ribs something trembled, a faint shiver no rhythm could disguise. Seeing him, even as an echo, pressed into her like a question without answer. Was it memory shaping itself into form, or had she truly brushed against some part of him that had refused to let go?

The thought unsettled her, not as fear but as longing. A tenderness worn thin with time, still aching, still alive. Ethan lingered in her not as proof of nearness but as a reminder of the part of herself that reached still, even when she told herself she had moved beyond.

The city thinned as she walked. Buildings receded, lights scattered into distance, and silence drew closer with every step. The night seemed to wait for her, the streets narrowing toward something inevitable.

Ashmere Chapel lay ahead.

And though she told herself this was only an interview, a story to write and nothing more, a part of her already knew she had crossed into something she would not easily leave behind.

The train ride to Highgate was silent. Cassandra sat by the window, her coat drawn close, though she could not feel the cold. The hum of the carriage pressed faintly against her, a rhythm that failed to anchor her to the moment.

She did not bother with music, nor podcasts, nor the quiet scroll of news at the edge of distraction. Her phone stayed in her pocket, the screen dark, its weight slight in her coat yet somehow heavier than before, as if it held messages she would never open and answers she was not ready to read.

Her hands rested in her lap, fingers loosely laced, unmoving, as though they belonged to someone else entirely, as though she were only borrowing them for this journey, a stillness held against the blur of the city rushing by.

In the window's reflection, she watched herself drift along the glass, pale and just a blurred shimmer, a ghost superimposed on the city as it swept past in darkened shapes and fractured light. Her features dimmed whenever the train entered shadow. When the lamps returned, the glass wavered, fragmenting her into panes of light, as if showing the outline of what waited beyond this journey.

She was no longer a woman on her way to a job, nor someone heading toward an ordinary evening or even a destination she could explain. Not even a woman, really. Just a presence now, one shape among many, a shadow with a name she was not sure still belonged to her. Cassandra.

The name echoed faintly in her thoughts, distant and soft, like a trace of someone no longer fully here. It trembled at the edge of her awareness, the way a voice does in a dream, familiar yet already receding, and the more she tried to hold to it, the more it slipped.

Her gaze fell back to the glass, and for a moment she thought she saw someone else staring back. Not Ethan, not herself as she remembered, but something caught between. The sway of the train made the reflection waver, fragmenting her features into shifting panes of light, until she almost believed the glass was not reflecting her at all but showing her the outline of what waited beyond this journey. She blinked, but the impression lingered, quiet and insistent, like a whisper she could not yet decipher.

It lived within her, not as a word or a sound, but like a current folded deep in her frame, waiting for its moment. It pressed between her ribs like an intake she had not meant to draw.

What would Ethan feel if his hand rested on her shoulder now? Would he sense the mark still warm, still hidden? Would his fingers recoil before he understood the reason?

Would he even recognise her? Or would he see only what she had glimpsed on the street earlier, not a man she could reach, but a figure carried by recollection, a presence remembered rather than alive?

Her thoughts turned again to his message. It had been brief, touched with concern, but careful in its phrasing, as if he were guarding something fragile that no longer belonged to him.

Had he felt the same shift she carried, or had she simply thinned in his world, fading the way distance and silence erase people when too much time has passed between them?

A swell rose inside her chest, not grief and not desire, but something more elusive. It resembled mourning, though not for Ethan. It was a mourning for a self she could no longer return to.

Ashmere Chapel. The name pressed against her mind, heavier now. What was it truly? And beneath that question, deeper still, what was she becoming?

The thought slipped through her like smoke, impossible to hold.

She let her eyes fall closed. Not in sleep, only to halt the city for a while, to still its restless passing around her.

She did not open them again until the train's doors hissed apart and the platform voice whispered Highgate into the air, as if it had been speaking directly to her.

Cassandra stepped out of the train into the chill, her coat pulled close as the doors sealed behind her. The platform stretched nearly bare. A girl in headphones hurried past without a glance, her pace fading quickly toward the exit. At the far pillar, a man in a crumpled coat leaned against the stone, his eyes lowered, unmoving.

The night received her in silence as she crossed toward the steps. She did not follow the main road. Instead, her feet found the side path Lydia had mentioned, the one that curved toward the woods. With every stride beyond the last of the streetlamps, she felt herself drift further into something unnamed.

The air altered, still and sharp, like the pause between notes in an old hymn.

She paused at the corner where the path began. The trees arched overhead, their branches knitted together as though forming a gaze she could not turn from. A thin cloud of warmth slipped from her lips, vanishing almost at once.

It was not fear. But it was close.

Her pulse rose in her throat. She adjusted the strap of her bag, cast one glance back at the quiet road, and then stepped forward.

The houses fell away. The woods gathered thick around her. Frost silvered the grass at the edge of the path. Somewhere in the branches, a bird stirred and went still again.

Her pace slowed, deliberate now, her boots finding stone where the dirt thinned. She became aware of the ribbon circling her wrist, soft against her sleeve. She had tied it on again before leaving the flat, almost without thought, as if it belonged to her more than anything she chose.

She could not see far ahead. The trees pressed close, the moon gave only the faintest trace of light. Still, she followed the winding path, one step at a time, her movement dissolving into the hush of the woods.

Her eyes adjusted, and shapes began to emerge from the dark. Each shadow seemed to shift as she passed, as if the woods themselves weighed her presence. A question flickered at the edge of her mind, urging her to turn back, but her feet carried her on, slow and unwilling to stop.

Her skin prickled, every nerve awake to the silence. She thought of the distance behind her, the emptiness of the road, the man still leaning against the pillar. If she went back now, she would return with nothing. If she continued, she did not know what she might find. The thought pressed like a stone inside her, heavy and uncertain.

Then the trees gave way.

And the chapel appeared.

It was older than she had imagined. The roof dipped slightly to one side, and the stone walls looked as though they had risen out of the woods rather than been built there.

No light glowed behind its windows. No name marked the entrance, yet the air felt charged.

Alive.

She halted a few metres from the door as the stillness closed in around her, thick and insistent, like the held moment before a flame catches wick. The trees behind her had gone utterly silent. Even the night itself seemed to pause, as though waiting for her next step.

Her inhale faltered, not from exertion but from the awareness that she had crossed a threshold she might not easily return from. The chapel seemed to know she was there.

The ribbon at her wrist caught the moonlight, its surface glinting as if it shimmered with a life of its own. It had not slipped nor loosened, but lay against her skin with an intent that felt deliberate, as though it belonged here, waiting for this exact night.

Her throat constricted when she swallowed, the air sharp and thin. A pressure coiled inside her, not pain, but something old and unspoken, like recognition hidden deep within her bones.

Turning back tempted her. The thought pressed at her with the weight of relief, promising the station's pale lamps, the empty platform, the safety of retreat. Yet another part of her, the one that had leaned into every whisper, every ritual, every secret sign, rooted her in place. That part refused to let her go.

Reason offered its counterbalance. This was only another assignment. Just another story to follow through to its end. Nothing more than an abandoned chapel, weathered by time and embellished by rumour. She was letting the night play tricks on her. She was being silly. With a small shake of her head, she tried to laugh at herself, though the sound never came.

She drew in a careful breath, steadier by choice than by ease, and stepped forward. The gravel shifted beneath her boots with a brittle crunch. The night air brushed her cheek, neither warm nor cold, more like a hand testing her resolve. Somewhere close, damp stone gave off a faint earthy scent, mingled with the sharper trace of old wood, as if the building itself exhaled around her.

Her palm lifted, fingers hovering an inch above the chapel door. The wood was darkened by years of rain and wind, its grooves worn deep like channels carved by time itself. As she pressed her hand against it, warmth stirred beneath her skin, as though the building itself carried a pulse.

The moment stretched, as though the night itself had stilled for her. Then the pressure shifted, and the decision was hers alone.

For an instant she hesitated, palm still against the wood. Then she pressed. The door gave way without resistance.

It was ancient, yet quiet, the hinges releasing not with protest but with a whisper, as though they had been waiting for this touch, long prepared for her arrival.

The air that spilled out was cool and damp, like stone kept too long in shadow. It drifted low, curling around her ankles as she stepped forward, brushing her skin as if to test the depth of her resolve. There were no lanterns, no candles, no faint glow to guide her path. Only the unbroken dark, and whatever waited inside it.

The step carried her inward, and the door eased shut behind her, though no hand had drawn it closed. The sound carried softly, not warning, not finality, but something that felt like reverence.

The chapel did not greet her. It offered no welcome. The stillness here was different, weighted, the kind that settles in places where prayers once gathered and linger even after the voices are gone.

Stone arches rose overhead, ribbed and vaulted, their lines vanishing into the blackness. The scent of moss traced along the edges of the walls, cool and earthen, mingling with the faintest memory of incense and something older still. Not decay, not dust, but a presence that pressed quietly at the edge of recognition. Perhaps it was memory. Perhaps it was longing.

Her steps carried softly into the nave, each one muted by the stone beneath her. It did not echo. Instead, the floor seemed to draw her weight into itself, as though it remembered the press of those who had come before. The hush did not yield. It gathered around her, patient and listening, as if the walls themselves were waiting.

Shapes took form ahead. At first only shadows, then edges, then presence, silvered faintly where moonlight pierced the high windows and spilled across the floor in narrow bands.

Sculptures. Dozens, perhaps more. They lined the nave like a congregation held in eternal witness. Some rose in towering bronze, greened with time, while others crouched small and pale, their surfaces bone-white, luminous where the light touched, ghostlike where it did not.

Not one of them smiled. Their faces lingered just shy of human, as if shaped by a hand that had once studied life closely, then stopped short of granting it. Eyes hollow, mouths closed, expressions stalled on the edge of speech that never came.

She passed a woman draped in robes that seemed to ripple despite their rigid cast. The figure's head tilted upward, toward a heaven erased by shadow. Her arms extended, palms open, caught between the posture of surrender and offering. Cassandra slowed beside her, gaze caught by the curve of those fingers. The gesture was too familiar. She had mirrored it herself once, submerged in water, when dream and waking blurred into one, her hands raised in that same uncertain balance between giving and yielding.

The deeper she walked into the chapel, the quieter the world became. It was not only the absence of sound, but the slowing of thought itself. The current of her mind, so often restless, stilled as though it, too, had been summoned into silence.

Step. Silence. Step. Silence. Nothing more.

Moonlight fell in fractured shafts through the high windows, narrow beams that cut across the nave and lingered only where it chose. It did not flood the space. It selected. It revealed. And what it revealed, it revealed with purpose.

At the far end, where once an altar might have stood, a single figure waited apart. Taller than the rest. Draped in red velvet. The cloth poured heavy over its form, still and suffocating, a weight of silence in the shape of fabric. The light touched its edges but never its face, as though what lay beneath was forbidden to be seen too soon.

Her eyes lingered, caught by the impossible sense that the statue leaned toward her. No shift, no sound, yet something in its bearing seemed to bend closer, aware of her presence, expectant. The air gathered tight in her chest, her body stilled as though she were the one being studied.

She did not approach. Not yet. Something in her recognised the gravity of this instant, knew it was not meant to be hurried. It carried the hush before a vow, the space before surrender, a moment stretched so thin it seemed it might tear with one more heartbeat.

The silence shattered. A voice came from behind her, sudden enough to make her start.

"You're early."

The voice was male, low and deliberate. It did not intrude on the silence. It seemed born of it, shaped by the same stillness that pressed against her skin. She did not need to turn. She knew it was Lucas.

Her chest loosened on a long breath she had not realised she was holding. The pull of the figure before her was stronger now, drawing her toward it as though the chapel itself wished her to continue. At her wrist, the silk shifted against her skin, not with force but with memory, as if it remembered what came next more surely than she did.

She reached for the velvet. The fabric was cool beneath her fingertips, heavy with dampness, its weight carrying the patience of years held in shadow. With a single motion she drew it back. The cloth slid away, slipping through her hands and collapsing at her feet in a soft, defeated heap.

What stood beneath it held her still. A woman, tall and unyielding, carved with precision that bordered on reverence. Every line of her face, every tilt of her shoulders, every delicate curve of her hands was achingly familiar. It was not merely likeness. It was recognition.

The eyes, though made of stone, met hers as though they had waited. The mouth, unparted, seemed caught on the edge of a vow never spoken. And in that frozen silence, she understood.

The statue was her.

The self she had been. The self she was becoming. The curve of the neck, the quiet strength carried in the shoulders, the arms folded across the body in a gesture that was not closure but protection, it was all there.

And there, carved into the marble near the shoulder, was the mark. Her mark. Not painted, not scorched, but etched into the stone itself, as if it had always belonged there, waiting to be revealed.

The sight of it struck her with a force that unsettled the air in her chest. Something fragile and restless stirred awake inside her, a trembling recognition she could neither resist nor name. She stepped back, as though distance might steady her.

The voice came again, nearer now, threaded with a gravity that allowed no space for doubt.

"You're finally here. I hoped you would come, Cassandra."

Her name was not a summons. It was an invocation.

She turned slowly, as though the moment had been rehearsed in uncounted dreams and only now remembered. He stood before her, elegant, composed, yet altered. Too still, too precise, as if flesh had given way to form, as if he had been shaped not from blood, but from desire made solid.

He didn't smile. He only looked at her, and in that look she understood. He wasn't here to answer questions with facts. He was here to show her what the questions had always meant.

He watched her like someone who had been waiting a long time for something that could not be hurried.

Her lips parted before she even realised she had spoken. "It's you." The words slipped out unbidden, less a declaration than recognition given voice. Her voice felt strange in the stillness, too human, too warm, as though it might startle the silence into retreat.

"Yes," Lucas replied, the word carrying the weight of something long ago decided.

A beat passed. Then another. Her gaze drifted to the sculpture again.

"What is this place?"

Lucas didn't look away from her, but she felt his attention deepen, as though the surface of his gaze gave way to something older beneath.

"This," he said, "is where memory lives. Not memory as in the past, but what the past shapes when it's buried long enough."

She turned to the statue, her statue, the one carved from marble and uncertainty. "And this?" she asked, gesturing to the sigil.

Lucas stepped beside her now. His presence was close but never touching. He didn't reach for her. He didn't need to.

"That mark," he said, "was never mine to give you. It was written in you long before this. The rituals, the bindings, none of them were meant to change you. They were only meant to uncover what had always been yours."

Cassandra's throat constricted.

"So, I *was* chosen."

His face shifted, carrying something between sorrow and restraint, a flicker that was neither denial nor affirmation.

"No," he said. "You chose. Each step you took. Each time you let the word 'yes' leave your lips when no one was listening."

A tremor passed through her voice when she spoke again.

"All of this, the book, the rituals, the others, it wasn't about power."

"It was about recognition," Lucas said. "About remembrance."

She edged back, her heel brushing the velvet that had fallen in a dark spill at the base of the statue. "I don't understand. Why me? Why now?"

Lucas inclined his head with deliberate care, as though the answer itself had waited centuries to be spoken. "Because you were ready. Not to become someone different, but to stop pretending you were not already this."

Her chest tightened until the words came out raw. "And what of Ethan? I don't understand."

Lucas's voice softened. "He was the light you held to when you believed the dark was only danger. He was the part of you that longed for safety, for simplicity, for a path already marked."

"And you?" she asked.

He grew still, the silence itself shaping the weight of his reply. "I'm the darkness between dreams. The threshold that opens only when you stop fearing what waits on the other side."

She swallowed, her throat tight. "Are you even real?"

Lucas did not answer directly. His gaze shifted to the pool of dark velvet gathered at the statue's feet.

"Does it matter?" he said at last.

Cassandra followed his eyes, and something shifted inside her. Not understanding. Not peace. But a certainty that steadied her bones. This was not something done to her. It was the path she had always been moving toward.

Lucas stepped back, his voice lowering. "There's one more place."

She didn't ask what he meant. She only followed.

They passed beneath a stone archway, low and worn by time. The air shifted as they crossed, growing cooler, denser, saturated with the kind of silence that feels preserved rather than empty. The passage narrowed, shadows gathering close around them.

At its end, another chamber opened. Not grand. Not hidden behind veils. Simply waiting.

Lucas halted, then moved aside.

She entered alone.

The ground beneath her was not stone but something softened by age, earth pressed flat under countless unseen steps. At the centre stood another sculpture. This one was unfinished.

The body had been shaped from rough stone, its outline already hers, but the face remained untouched, a blank surface waiting for definition. Tools rested nearby: a chisel, a cloth, a basin of water. Nothing else. Only the stillness, and the weight of a moment that seemed inevitable now.

She stepped closer, and in that hush something cleared. She was not here to be chosen. She was here to choose.

The silk at her wrist remained, the same ribbon Lucas had once placed upon her, but it no longer felt like a gift from another hand. It had become her own.

She touched it lightly, a quiet acknowledgment. Not a ritual. A recognition.

Lucas did not speak. He did not move. His part was finished.

This was hers.

Cassandra lifted the chisel. Its weight settled into her palm as if it had been waiting for her, as if the shape of her grip had been carved long before she reached for it. She turned to the stone.

The unfinished figure stood before her, its body already traced into form, its face still untouched, suspended in possibility.

She smiled. Not because she knew what would come, but because at last it would belong to her.

Her free hand pressed against the surface. The stone was cool, but not empty. There was a pulse beneath it, a presence waiting to be released. Not crafted. Not invented. Simply uncovered.

The stillness around her shifted, delicate as a ripple through water. Not broken. Only deepened, as though the chamber itself held its breath before a vow.

She did not hurry. Her fingers lingered over the smooth blank where eyes would be, where a mouth had yet to take shape. She no longer feared what would emerge.

When she lowered the chisel, it was with reverence. Not as a sculptor. As someone holding a mirror to her own becoming.

Every motion would be slow. Careful. Not to create perfection, but to honour the self she had always carried.

This was not an ending. It was a beginning.

And when she finally stepped back, when the dust had begun to settle and her reflection lingered in the softened edge of the stone, she understood something else.

The carving was never meant to be finished.

It would go on becoming, just as she would.

From the shadows behind her, the chapel waited without watching. Silent. Whole.

She stood there for a long time, the chisel still warm in her palm, the faint outline of her presence softening in the cool air. The unfinished sculpture stood before her like a question that no longer needed an answer.

Her gaze fell to her wrist.

The silk.

It had remained with her through every turn, every silence she had chosen to enter. It had bound her to the path, not as a chain, but as a promise. It had reminded her of where she had been, and of what waited in the spaces she had yet to touch.

Now, it was time.

Her fingers moved slowly, loosening the knot. The fabric slipped free with a whisper, trailing against her skin like the trace of something once lived.

She turned to the figure. The stone was still cool, still rough where the carving had not reached. She lifted the silk, and as she placed it gently around the statue's wrist, she lowered her head in quiet gratitude. Thanks not for what she had been given, but for the choice itself, for the chance to step forward and claim it as her own.

The gesture was not dramatic. It was not loud. It was quiet. Deliberate. Final.

She tied it gently, letting the ends fall where they would. Not as a binding. Not as a mark. But as a gift.

The part of her that had carried the vow no longer needed to wear it.

She stepped back and looked at the sculpture once more. Not for confirmation. Not for closure. Simply to remember it.

The silk lifted faintly, stirred by the stillness itself, before settling again as though it had found its place.

And then all was still.

14
WHAT WAITS BEYOND

T he sound came first.

Not a voice. Not footsteps. Something older. A stirring at the edge of her awareness, like air curling through a half-open window at night.

Cassandra kept her eyes closed.

The chisel's weight still lingered in her hand, the earth steady beneath her feet, but the chamber was shifting. The heaviness of what had just been done loosened, lifting like mist dissolving at dawn. The air thinned. The walls seemed to draw in a breath and then release it.

When she opened her eyes, she was no longer standing before the unfinished figure. The sculpture had fallen away. She was facing the Book.

The Book she had left behind.

It rested upon a pedestal of stone. Not the bedside table she half remembered from the flat. Not the desk where she had once tried to force her words into shape. The Book was open, waiting, its pages turning in a current she could not feel.

Letters were not written, but unfolding, as though the paper had kept them hidden until now.

A single line appeared, luminous as if traced by firelight:

The key was never in the rituals. It was always in you.

Cassandra stared. Her hand lifted as if summoned, the ache of all she had carried inscribed across her palm.

The Book pulsed beneath her touch. Not cold. Not inert. But steady, alive, answering.

Another line surfaced, rising through the page like something pressing upward through soil:

Consent is the altar. Memory is the offering. You are both.

Her throat tightened and a tear slipped free. It was not sorrow that moved her. It was recognition. Clear. Vast. Irrefutable.

She stepped back, and the pages shifted once more. Not into words, but into impressions. Shapes drawn from places she had known, blurred at the edges like recollections half dreamed. A cityscape in shadow. A hand resting on a café table. A ring of smoke dissolving above a candle flame. A figure at the edge of water, turning before she could see his face.

Each image unfolded and dissolved in silence, as if the Book was not telling her but reminding her. Not leading, but returning.

She saw the velvet bindings. The Hollow. The chapel. The mirror that had once carried her mother's smile. The shore where she had almost remembered what it felt like to be free.

Each vision flickered and dissolved, turning like pages in a story she had lived but never wholly understood.

Through it all, Lucas's voice wove itself into the silence. Not a call. Not a guide. A thread in the air itself, quiet and unbroken:

You were never trapped. You were never lost. You were only waiting for yourself.

The ground beneath her seemed less solid now, as though the chamber was loosening its hold. Not gone. Not vanished. But thinned into something transparent, carrying her lightly, carefully.

She glanced around, half expecting the sculptures to rise again, the altar to return, the shadows to draw her back.

But only the Book remained.

And the door.

It stood open at the far edge of the space, spilling radiance that was not the colour of daylight but something more ancient, vibrating quietly in her bones.

Cassandra closed the Book with care. It did not resist. It had given all it could. She placed her hand upon its cover, steady and deliberate, a final gesture of thanks.

Then she turned toward the doorway.

Her steps made no sound. The air stirred in quiet spirals, drawing back as she passed, parting like fabric gathered aside. The chamber seemed to recognise her now, not as an intruder but as something returned. Fear no longer shadowed her. Hesitation no longer held her back. She moved with the calm of one who had awakened to a path carved long ago into her very being.

She lingered at the threshold and glanced back once. The chapel remained, yet it was already withdrawing, its outlines dimming, as though it wished to be remembered but not followed. It did not vanish. It receded, leaving her with what endured: the memory, the choice, the certainty that had taken root within her.

Her lungs caught at the quiet vastness waiting ahead. The light spilling from beyond was not sunlight, nor flame, nor any brightness she had ever known. It trembled with a promise she could comprehend.

Cassandra lifted her chin, steady, unflinching. And with a final exhale, she crossed into what lay beyond.

The café unfolded first.

The familiar corner booth appeared as if carved from the mist, the same place where she and Miranda had once sheltered from the dull strain of the city, pressed close to the window streaked with soft rain.

Two mugs waited between them, steam curling upward like the traces of laughter that had not yet arrived. The air carried cinnamon and something warmer still, the fragrance of comfort held in memory.

Cassandra slowed. The mist drew back in quiet deference, as if the world itself wanted the moment to fully reveal itself.

But this was more than recollection.

Miranda lifted her gaze, and their eyes met across the years. They were not dream eyes, not vague echoes. They held weight, steady and clear, alive with knowledge that felt older than either of them.

Her posture was unhurried, one arm draped along the back of the booth, the other curled easily around her mug. Yet there was gravity in her presence, as if she had been waiting here since the beginning, anchored in patience.

Cassandra moved closer.

"You found your way back," Miranda said softly.

Cassandra's throat tightened. "I didn't know I had gone."

Miranda's smile was different now. Not the sly tilt of mischief Cassandra had come to expect. Not the bright flash of humour shared in late hours. It was gentler. Fiercer. Protective, almost maternal in its depth.

"You had to go far enough to return freely," she said. "Without being pulled. Without being bound."

Her hand shifted, fingertip brushing the wood of the table. Cassandra's eyes followed. The surface rippled, not with water but with a shimmer that carried fragments of her own story. The velvet and its bindings. The hollow chamber. The chapel's fading light. Her mother's smile in the mirror. Her own face staring back.

Miranda's voice lowered, carrying the weight of something ancient, something that seemed to move through her rather than come only from her.

"There's one last passage," she said. "The final step before you see what waits for you."

Cassandra's eyes lifted, meeting Miranda's steady gaze. "Will it hurt?"

Miranda did not answer at once. She drew the cup closer, cradling it in both hands, letting the heat soak slowly into her fingers as though the warmth itself might shape her reply.

"Only what still clings," she said at last. Her voice was quiet and unshaken. "Purely what was never truly yours to bear."

Beyond the window, the city was gone. The rain-streaked glass no longer reflected streets or passing shapes. There was only light now, pulsing faintly, as if the world itself was holding its breath.

Miranda raised her mug, not as farewell but as offering, a gesture of quiet recognition that carried its own gravity.

"You were always meant for more," she said. The words were not echoes of memory. They fell with the weight of blessing, spoken as truth.

"Even when you couldn't see it."

Something within Cassandra opened at the sound. The pain that rose was sharp, yet it was not grief and not longing. It was love in its rawest form, the kind that reshapes rather than mourns.

She stepped forward and lowered her head until her forehead rested lightly against Miranda's, the touch both release and anchor.

"Thanks," she whispered. The words trembled, yet they held.

Miranda closed her eyes. For a moment they shared the same still air.

"Go," she said softly. "The rest of you is waiting."

The café began to waver. The booth, the window, the warmth of cinnamon, all thinned and drifted away, fading like warmth slipping from the skin.

When the last trace was gone, The Hollow revealed itself before her. When the last trace was gone, The Hollow revealed itself before her.

The street narrowed into shadow, its edges blurred by mist and lit only by the faint glow of distant lamps. Their reach faltered before the door, as if the light itself dared not cross.

Silence gathered first. Not absence, but a weighted stillness she remembered, the same presence that had once wrapped itself around her skin like a hidden garment.

She saw herself there again, a figure poised before the wooden door, hand lifted, hesitation coiled in her chest. The moment where retreat had been possible, where the familiar world still waited behind her.

Yet she had knocked. And the door had opened.

That memory pressed through her now, not as panic or longing but with the rhythm of a second pulse, steady and deliberate. The choice had been made, and it had marked her.

She felt the same hush enfolding her, the night close and attentive, the air alive with shadow and promise. She had not known then what waited inside, only that something rooted deep within her had refused to turn away.

Crossing that door had been more than stepping inside. It was the moment her life had turned toward what she was always becoming. The Hollow had not remade her. It had only unmasked what had been waiting.

Mist thickened at the edges of the vision, softening stone, swallowing lantern light, yet leaving the truth untouched.

The Hollow receded, but its gravity lingered, and in its place new shapes stirred.

Figures gathered. Cloaked in shadow, circling as they had that first night, their forms blurred at the edges as if wavering between presence and memory.

Cassandra slowed.

At first, she thought she recognised them, the Others she had once been amongst. James, Sophia, Victor. Silent. Watching. But the air shifted, and veils that had hidden them began to dissolve.

Beneath the hoods, she found no strangers. She found herself.

The girl trembling in the street.

The seeker whispering yes.

The one who had forgotten, and the one who had already begun to remember.

Each pair of eyes met hers, not with demand, not with accusation, but with recognition. With welcome.

It was her hand that had struck the door.

It was her face that had waited in the shadows.

The weight of it pressed deep into her chest, not as burden but as release. The truth rose within her like air after a long submersion, filling her with something wider, steadier, unbroken.

She walked among them, passing through the circle of her own lives. Each figure stood as she had once stood, cloaked in the weight of their time, silent but alive with meaning. None reached for her, none tried to hold her back. They only watched, steady as stone, their stillness carrying something fiercer than words. Pride. Permission. Belonging.

Her breath faltered at the understanding. These were not barriers set against her. They were not trials to overcome. They were steps, carved from her own becoming, each one necessary, each one flawed, each one sacred.

The girl trembling in the street. The seeker whispering yes. The one who faltered and rose again, the one who had almost turned away. She saw them all, felt them press into her like echoes returned to their source, and the acknowledgement struck sharp in her chest until she gasped.

Her vision blurred with tears that did not fall. It was not sorrow. It was awe. The holy ache of realising she had been walking beside herself all along, never alone, never abandoned, even when she thought she was missing.

As she moved forward, each figure bowed their head. Not in parting, not in mourning, but in quiet reverence, as if offering her back to herself. One by one they lowered, and with each gesture something inside her lifted, steady and sure, until she could almost feel the ground giving way to light beneath her feet.

Her chest rose on a shuddering breath. She did not try to hold it in. She let it move through her, raw and unbroken, and in the release, she felt herself become whole.

Cassandra kept moving, the circle of bowed figures dissolving behind her. The mist gathered, then thinned, parting with a slow shimmer like fabric being drawn aside.

Light shifted in its depths, soft at first, then hardening into shapes. White and grey. Paper and glass. The faint gleam of a desk.

Lydia's office emerged, though it was not the office she had known. It rose larger, stretched beyond its usual proportions, the glass walls reaching impossibly high as though they had no ceiling. The shelves were stripped bare. No scattered reports, no half-read journals. Only a single folder lay upon the desk, closed and waiting, its presence louder than any clutter could have been. Cassandra lingered at the doorway, her breath caught in her throat. The air inside vibrated faintly, a vibration just beyond the range of sound, as if fluorescent lights hovered somewhere out of sight. There was no scent of paper, no trace of coffee or perfume, yet the atmosphere felt saturated, heavy with words that had never been spoken.

Lydia sat behind the desk. She looked exactly as memory held her, sharp eyes fixed and calculating, hair pinned with that precise severity that allowed not a strand out of place. Her posture was still, though Cassandra knew the stillness was only the surface of thought turning in measured wheels.

She did not speak. Not yet.

Cassandra stepped forward. The door closed behind her without sound, dissolving into the air until there was no trace it had ever been there. Only then did Lydia's gaze rise to meet her, clear and unwavering.

"Do you understand now why I sent you?" she asked.

Her tone was neither warm nor cold. It carried no welcome, no threat. It hovered between, weightless as smoke, waiting to decide which way it would drift.

Cassandra felt the old hesitation coil within her chest. She forced it aside, steadying her voice. "You gave me the assignment, yes. But you were vague. It was as though you were holding something back."

Lydia lowered her eyes to the desk and tapped the closed folder once with the tip of her finger. The sound echoed sharper than it should have in the vast hollow of the room.

"I gave you all I was permitted to," she said quietly. "The rest you had to discover on your own."

Cassandra's breath stilled. "You knew it would lead here."

"I suspected," Lydia said. "But even suspicion carries risk. Truths revealed too soon can close doors as quickly as they open them."

Cassandra's chest tightened. "I wasn't ready."

Lydia inclined her head, and something in her expression softened. Just slightly. "Few are. Most never begin. You did."

Silence fell between them. Not empty. Not waiting. It simply was.

Cassandra reached for the folder. Her fingers hovered above the edge, uncertain.

"Do you want me to?" she asked softly.

Lydia folded her hands on the desk. "That's not the question."

Cassandra lowered her eyes, then looked up again. "Then what is?"

A flicker passed through Lydia's gaze, not mystery but something closer to mercy. "Are you willing to see what it asks of you?"

The weight of it settled then. Not from the folder, but from the recognition of every choice she had made. The articles. The assignments. The stories Lydia had chosen. They had never been only work. Each had opened a door.

And Cassandra had walked through.

She opened the folder.

There were no typed pages inside. No pitch. No notes. Only a scattering of photographs, square and glossy, their edges curled as though they had been carried too long.

The first showed herself as a girl, standing at the edge of a playground, her arms folded, her eyes turned not to the games but to the shadows between the trees. The next caught her years later, bent over a notebook in a dim café, the lamplight catching the crease of her brow as though she were already searching for something unnamed. Another revealed her arrival in London, suitcase at her side, gaze lifted toward the horizon of a city she had not yet stepped into.

Each image felt impossibly intimate, as if the camera had been placed not in front of her but inside her, capturing the exact moment she had chosen to see differently.

Her chest rose sharply, a soft gasp escaping before she could stop it.

She looked up, but Lydia was already standing.

"There's more beyond this," Lydia said. "You knew that before you stepped into the Hollow."

She turned another photograph.

This one showed her with Ethan, the two of them caught mid-laughter at a table outside some forgotten pub. His hand was reaching for hers, her face tilted toward him in unguarded joy. There was no weight in their expressions, no shadow. Only the easy light of something pure, untested, alive.

Her throat tightened, and for a moment she had to hold the picture still, as though it might dissolve if she let her breath stir it.

Beneath it lay one more.

A darker frame. The image blurred at the edges as if the light itself had resisted. Lucas stood alone in a narrow chamber, shadows clinging close around his figure. His face was half turned, unreadable, and yet his presence seemed to reach through the photograph as if it were more than paper. No name was written. No explanation given. Only the quiet certainty that this too was part of what had been placed before her.

Cassandra's hand trembled slightly. She lowered the photographs back into the folder, but their impression remained, pressed into her like words that could not be erased.

"Will it be different?" she asked, her voice little more than breath.

Lydia smiled. "Only if you are."

The office began to fade. The lights flickered. The shelves dissolved like smoke.

Lydia reached for the door, which had returned now. She opened it.

"Go on," she said.

Cassandra stepped through.

The mist brightened slowly. It did not rush. Instead, it unfolded with something more intimate, like breath drawn in before a song.

The clearing opened around her, soft and luminous.

And there, standing as if she had never left, was her mother.

She was not younger, and she had not changed. She looked exactly as

Cassandra remembered her.

Her apron was dusted with flour. Loose strands of hair escaped from the knot at the back of her head. A soft hum rose from her lips, tuneless but familiar, curling through the air like something warm and remembered. Her hands moved in a quiet rhythm, folding and shaping something unseen on the bench in front of her.

The scent of dough and comfort lingered in the air, catching gently at Cassandra's throat.

Her mother looked up.

And she smiled.

It was not just a memory. It was not a flicker or a ghost. It was a smile that cracked something open deep inside Cassandra, not to shatter it, but to let it exhale for the first time in years.

Her chest swelled with the sharp and tender, longing folded into love. She wanted to run forward, to bury her face against that familiar shoulder, to feel again the steady rhythm of safety that had once been her entire world. For an instant she could almost feel the significance of her mother's apron against her cheek, the warmth of flour-dusted hands smoothing her hair. She wanted to be small again, if only for a heartbeat, folded into the simplicity of that embrace.

But she did not move.

Her feet remained where they were, steady on the ground that seemed to vibrate with the moment. She let the ache rise through her like a tide, let it wash her clean. And when it ebbed, she found herself standing straighter, her shoulders no longer heavy but lifted.

Because she understood now.

She did not need to run to her mother. She did not need to grasp at the past. That love was already written into her, etched so deeply it could never be taken away. It had always been there, steady as a pulse, waiting for her to remember.

Her mother wiped her hands across her apron, the simple gesture filled with a grace that belonged to everyday moments, and stepped closer. The air between them seemed to hold its breath. She reached out, and with a tenderness that stilled everything around them, pressed a kiss to Cassandra's forehead.

The kiss was feather light, but it lingered, as if it carried more than comfort. It carried certainty. It carried blessing.

"You already know the way," her mother whispered. Her voice was gentle, grounded, carrying the warmth of a hearth that had never gone out. Her breath touched Cassandra's skin like something sacred, not fragile, but enduring.

There were no instructions. No warnings. No demands. Only the truth, given freely, placed into her hands like something she had always owned.

Cassandra's eyes fell closed, and for the briefest moment, she felt whole.

When she opened her eyes, the haze curled close again, folding over her shoulders like a shawl.

But this time, the light within it shifted. It deepened, darkened, not with threat, but with gravity. Like the pull of something remembered in the bones before the mind could explain it.

Cassandra stepped forward.

The air thickened, warm with the scent she had never been able to name. Ink. Ash. Salt. Something older still, like the trace of a fire that had once burned too close to the skin.

Lucas stood ahead, as if he had always been there.

He was framed by the suggestion of a room that was not entirely formed. Velvet curtains drifted behind him without wind. Candlelight flickered at the edges, casting long, soft shadows that refused to settle. His presence stirred something low in her chest. A hum. A tension. A thread still taut.

He did not speak at first.

His eyes found hers, and the silence stretched. Not empty. Full. It held every echo of what they had been, and what they had never said.

"You've come far," Lucas said eventually. His voice was low, shaped by something quieter than pride. "Further than I imagined."

Cassandra did not respond. She stood still, steady, though the air around her seemed to tremble.

"You let the darkness in," he continued. "And you did not break."

She looked at him, at the sharp lines of his face softened by the restless candlelight, at the restraint woven into his stance. He had not changed. But something in her had. She could feel it now, pulsing beneath her ribs like a second heartbeat. Not distance. Not detachment. Something deeper. A knowing that left no place to hide.

"You were never gone," he said. His words carried no judgment, only a quiet certainty that pressed against the walls of the room. "Only walking through the places no one else could follow."

He stepped closer.

Just one step.

The air thickened with it. Shadows bent across the velvet as if drawn to the motion. He did not reach for her. He only lifted his hand, palm up, open between them, steady and unshaken.

"And if you choose it," he said, his voice low, reverent enough to feel like a vow, "there is a world waiting. One that knows what you are. What you could become."

The chamber seemed to still around them. The velvet stirred as though it breathed. The flames bowed and rose again. Cassandra's eyes dropped to his hand, and her breath caught. Not from fear. Not from confusion. From the weight of choice pressing itself into her chest, as undeniable as her own pulse.

"You were always stronger than you believed," Lucas said. The words sank into her like water into dry earth. "And I never wanted to tame you. Only to show you what you already were."

His hand remained open. He did not press her. He did not plead. The silence between them held its shape like glass, fragile and unbroken, waiting for her touch.

Not final. Not yet.

Cassandra lifted her gaze. His eyes held hers, and in that long, unguarded stillness she felt both the peril and the promise of what waited if she reached across.

The moment stretched until it felt endless. Then, slowly, deliberately, Lucas lowered his hand. Not in defeat. In respect.

Whatever she chose, it would be hers.

He stepped back, and the shadows folded in behind him like a curtain falling at the end of a performance that had never been entirely an act.

"You were the one who lit the match," he said, just before the darkness claimed him.

And then he was gone.

Only the warmth of firelight remained, flickering across the edges of her path.

Waiting.

The firelight dimmed behind her, its warmth still curling faintly at the edges of her skin. The curtain of air thickened again, but this time it did not open with weight or wonder. It opened with quiet. With the hush of early morning. With the scent of eucalyptus after rain and the softness of cotton sheets still warmed by sleep.

The world shifted.

She was standing in the doorway of their flat in Melbourne. Not the one she had now. The one from before.

The kitchen glowed with late sunlight. Dust floated through the beams in unhurried circles. A radio murmured low in the background, playing something familiar, something that seemed to brush against memory without needing to name itself. She heard the faint clink of ceramic.

Ethan stood at the counter, barefoot, making tea.

Cassandra did not move. Not yet.

She watched as he stirred the cup, his movements unadorned, his face set in quiet concentration. There was no performance in it. No dream glow. Just Ethan, steady and real in the way only he could be.

When he finally turned, his smile struck her unprepared. It was not the grin he gave to strangers or the smirk he used to cover his nerves. It was the smile he saved for her. The one that reached his eyes and softened every line of his face.

"I made you one," he said, holding out the mug.

Her throat caught, the small sound trapped beneath her breath.

She stepped forward and took it from his hands. The porcelain radiated warmth against her palms. Exactly how she liked it. No lemon. One sugar. A whisper of milk.

"Thanks," she said softly. The words trembled, yet they felt whole.

He leaned back against the counter, watching her. His gaze moved over her as if reading more than just the shape of her. As if seeing what had changed. What had stayed.

"You've been on some kind of journey," Ethan said gently. Not a question. Just knowing.

Cassandra nodded. "A long way."

His hand reached for hers. Their fingers met between them, curling together like threads remembering how to be woven.

"You always said you were afraid of losing yourself," he said. "But maybe you just needed to find out who that was."

Cassandra closed her eyes.

"Do you still know me?" she whispered.

Ethan's thumb brushed hers. "I knew you even when you didn't."

A breath trembled loose from her chest.

He leaned in, pressing his forehead gently to hers. No pressure. Just presence. The kind that steadied her without asking anything in return.

They stayed like that for a long moment. She felt the mug warming her palm. She felt his breath. The way his other hand rested at her waist, not holding her back, only reminding her she was here, she was real, she was loved.

When she pulled back, she saw it clearly.

This was not a memory. Not quite. And not a vision of what would be. It was something deeper. A meeting place. Between who she had been and who she might still become.

"I don't know what happens next," she said.

"You don't have to," Ethan replied. His voice was steady, unshaken. "You just have to choose what matters."

Cassandra nodded. The ache in her chest was soft now. Not longing. Not regret.

Just love. Full and quiet.

He kissed her cheek. It lingered, unhurried, like the kind of touch that promised it would remain no matter what she chose.

Then he stepped back.

And the flat dissolved.

Not into mist this time, but into light.

A warm, amber glow that faded slowly until nothing remained but the sound of her breath.

The air stilled. It was not empty. Not silent. But waiting.

The mist parted as if with reverence, curling back around a single figure who had been standing there all along.

The Bookshop Keeper.

The mist thickened behind him, then slowly drew back like a curtain, revealing what had been waiting all along.

Two doors.

One stood to the left, framed by golden light that shimmered gently, warm and quiet as a memory held close. The figure beyond it was unmistakable. Ethan. He did not speak. He simply stood, waiting, hands at his sides, his gaze steady. The sea behind him rolled in soft, rhythmic pulses, familiar as breath, endless as devotion.

And then, as her eyes met his, he lowered himself slowly to one knee. Not in ceremony. Not in spectacle. But in quiet reverence, a gesture that held both promise and surrender. His head tilted up toward her, the golden light catching in his eyes, carrying the weight of everything they had already lived and everything they might still hold.

Cassandra's breath stuttered. Her hand trembled at her side, the ache rising sharp in her chest. For a moment she felt the echo of that first promise, the memory of the night she had said yes, the certainty that he would always kneel for her if it meant she would rise. Love pressed against her with such force it almost unmade her.

The second door stood to the right, carved in deep wood and velvet shadows. Candlelight flickered just beyond its threshold, restless and alive. And there, half in light and half in something darker, was Lucas. Still. Powerful. Unmoving. His eyes never left hers.

Unlike Ethan, he did not kneel. He did not bow. He stood with the gravity of one who would never yield, and yet there was no demand in him. Only invitation. His gaze carried the danger of fire and the promise of freedom, the fierce pull of a life that would never be ordinary. The shadows leaned toward him, stirred by his presence, as though even the darkness wished to be claimed.

Cassandra's chest tightened, the air between them charged with a hum that lived beneath her skin. She saw again his open hand, the silence that had waited for her touch. She felt the echo of his voice telling her she was more than she believed, that he had never wanted to tame her, only to show her what she already was.

Ethan's light burned steady to one side, golden and unshaken. Lucas's shadows breathed on the other, alive with possibility.

Both doors stood slightly ajar. Neither beckoned. Neither warned. The air thickened around her, holding its silence like a question. She drew in a breath and held it, as though even her lungs feared to choose between them.

Then a sudden gust tore through, rushing with the sound of wings and thunder, and both doors slammed shut at once. The echo shuddered through the mist, through her bones, sharp enough to stagger her.

Cassandra turned back to the Bookshop Keeper.

He stepped forward, the quiet of his movement like a page turning. From the inner pocket of his coat, he drew a single key.

It was silver. Familiar. But this time it gleamed as though it had never belonged to anyone else.

He held it out, resting in his open palm. Not as an answer. As an invitation.

Cassandra reached for it, and the heaviness settled into her hand like it had always been waiting. Solid. Certain.

The Bookshop Keeper nodded once, his expression unreadable, though something in his eyes lingered, an unspoken faith, quiet and steady as shelter.

"This next part," he said, "only you can do."

She turned back toward the doors. Though they had closed, she felt their presence still, pulsing like two hearts at either side of her. Her gaze lingered on each one, the golden glow, the velvet dark.

Her hand tightened around the key. Its weight pressed into her palm, neither heavy nor light, but certain. She felt the metal cool against her skin, as if it carried the memory of every threshold she had ever stepped across.

For a long moment she did not move. The ache of Ethan's devotion lingered in her chest, soft as breath, the vision of him kneeling still etched behind her eyes. The pull of Lucas remained just as fierce, a current thrumming in her ribs, a promise of fire that refused to be silenced. Both calls lived within her, neither weaker for the other's presence.

The air thickened, charged with waiting.

Cassandra drew in a steady breath. The key glimmered faintly in her hand, as though it recognised her hesitation, as though it had always belonged not to either door, but to her.

Her fears rose within her, sharp and familiar. The fear of losing herself. The fear of being swallowed by what she could not name. The fear of not being enough, or of being too much. Each one surfaced, pressing hard against her ribs. But this time they did not pull her back. They steadied her. They showed her how far she had already come.

Every step had led here. Every silence, every risk, every moment she thought she had been broken. They had not undone her. They had shaped her.

She stepped forward.

Her feet moved with quiet resolve, her body carrying her before her mind could argue. The mist shifted with her, drawing back in reverence, unveiling the doors once more. They stood tall, sealed now, no longer ajar. Their surfaces gleamed as if remade, one in gold, one in shadow, each alive with its own rhythm.

Cassandra lifted her chin. For the first time she felt no need to ask what lay beyond. The question itself no longer mattered. What mattered was that it was hers to choose.

She pressed the key into the lock.

It slid in as though the door had been made for this moment alone.

She turned it.

Click.

The sound rang out, soft and final, like a seal pressed into wax, like a story crossing the threshold into truth.

And with it, the choice was made.

The door shifted, its outline glowing faintly. The air stirred, alive with promise.

Cassandra's breath trembled, not with fear, but with clarity. For the first time, she felt the fullness of what she was becoming. Not bound to Ethan. Not bound to Lucas. Not bound to anyone's expectation. She was her own.

The path behind her uncoiled within her chest. The trembling girl at the door. The seeker whispering yes. The one who faltered. The one who rose. The one who had loved and lost and dared again. Every moment, every silence, every risk, had led here. Each had carved its place within her. None wasted. All hers.

She stepped forward, her hand brushing the edge of the frame.

The light beyond flared, neither golden nor dark, but something wider, something that seemed to draw both currents into itself. It pulsed through her bones, through her breath, through the steady rhythm of her heart.

She paused once more on the threshold, not in hesitation but in recognition. All she had feared, all she had doubted, all she had learned, was gathered here, resting steady within her.

And with a final breath, she crossed into what waited beyond, no longer searching, but stepping as who she had always been becoming.

15
THE CHOSEN PATH

T he first thing she noticed was the ceiling.
Plain white, faintly lined with cracks in the corners, a ceiling she could have sworn she had seen before. She let herself believe, for a heartbeat, that she was waking in Miranda's flat, safe in the old rhythm of mornings that had grown strangely familiar.

But then the light touched her. Not grey, not softened by rain, but gold, pouring through lace curtains that trembled with summer air. She turned toward the window and caught the green edge of ivy curling against the glass, alive in a way that Camden had never been.

Her gaze drifted further. A wooden dresser stood quietly against the wall, smaller than she remembered yet unchanged, its surface holding a glass jar with violet sprigs freshly cut, their faint fragrance seeping into the morning. Beside it lay a stack of old books, the spines bent and worn, one with a corner still marked by a ribbon she had once tied there herself.

Cassandra drew in a breath that caught halfway. She knew this place. Or thought she did. Yet her mind resisted, circling the recognition as if it were dangerous. She told herself it could not be. Not this room. Not now. The quilt covering her felt too present, its pale blue stitching pressing lightly beneath her fingertips as though the fabric itself remembered her. The faint scent in the air seemed too precise, too carefully placed to be real. Even the stillness carried its own weight, dense and attentive, as if the walls themselves conspired to convince her of truth.

Surely this was some extension of the dream. Another chamber conjured to test her, to see how far she could be led before doubt gave way to surrender.

Her hand pressed harder into the quilt, and with the pressure came memory she could not deny. The stitching was worn from years of washing, and she remembered lying beneath it as a child, her mother smoothing it over her legs with the absentminded care of someone who believed there would always be another morning.

The air carried the same lavender scent that had once slipped through the window at dusk, drifting in as her father watered the garden. She could almost see her younger self carrying flowers in from the yard, clumsy fingers dropping a petal as her mother laughed and found a jar to hold them.

Her chest tightened as memory unfolded around her. This was not Miranda's flat. Not Camden. Not the city at all.

This was her childhood bedroom.

For a moment she could not move. Her body seemed to know before her mind allowed it, every muscle aching with the weight of recognition. It felt like being returned to a place she had lost, but also like trespassing into a life that no longer belonged to her. The more she tried to deny it, the sharper the details grew, until disbelief no longer served her.

And yet the room did not settle into certainty. The ribbon-marked book on the dresser seemed to blur at the edges, as though it might vanish if she looked too long. The ivy at the window shifted in the light, green one instant, shadowed the next, belonging both to the garden outside and to some dream still clinging to her skin. She could not tell if the sparrow's call beyond the glass was part of this morning, or a fragment carried across from another world entirely.

The dream had not let her go. It pressed against her as if the walls of this room were made of it, as if every breath carried its residue. She saw the two doors again, one washed in light, the other in shadow, Ethan waiting, Lucas watching. The moment had balanced like a suspended note, trembling in the silence, until the key turned and the sound of it carried through her as if it would never stop.

The choice was made. Yet the echo of it remained, pulsing quietly inside her, not fading with the dream but settling deeper, as though it had always belonged.

The Bookshop Keeper's voice lingered most of all. It did not belong only to the dream. It spoke from some deeper place, patient and certain, as if he had not been a figure conjured by sleep but someone who had always been waiting.

Her hand rose to her shoulder without thought. The skin was smooth, unbroken, yet beneath it she sensed something permanent. Not scar. Not wound. A truth that pulsed quietly in her.

She lay still, her gaze fixed on the familiar ceiling above her, and tried to measure what was more solid, the room she could see, or the dream that refused to loosen its hold. Each detail shifted in and out of focus. The ivy at the window might have been real, or a fragment carried across the threshold of sleep. The birdcall outside could have been the echo of another voice. Even the light, golden and unbroken, felt too precise, too vivid, as though it belonged to some world half imagined.

She closed her eyes, waiting to fall back. When she opened them again, the ceiling had not changed. The quilt had not dissolved. And yet she wondered if waking was only another kind of dream.

This time, though, the thought did not frighten her. She felt the quiet strength of her own breath filling her lungs. The choice was hers now, and whatever world she woke into, she was no longer afraid of losing herself within it.

A soft knock at the door.

"Cass? You awake yet? Big day."

Miranda.

The sound startled her, though it landed with warmth, as if it belonged more to the present than to the haze that had clung to her. A smile curved her lips, slow and sure. She let out a breath she had not realised she was holding, letting it move through her and fill her lungs with the scent of old wood and morning air and the steadiness of home.

The floor was cool beneath her feet as she swung her legs over the edge of the bed. The earth beneath everything felt solid. Not heavy. Just true.

She stood.

Each movement was quiet. Intentional. A promise not spoken aloud, but carried in the way her body answered the room. Unwritten, undeniable.

She stepped toward the small mirror above the dresser. The glass caught her reflection. Familiar, and not.

Her hair was mussed, her eyes clear. Her mouth, though still, felt as if it carried a truth waiting to be spoken. Something final, and something beginning. The woman looking back at her was not the girl who had once woken beneath the quilt, nor the same Cassandra who had followed shadows through Camden's streets. She was a threshold, standing between what had been and what had yet to come, and in that stillness, she felt no fear.

She studied herself a moment longer, and calm spread through her, gentle as water settling after a storm. The uncertainty that had once clouded her gaze was gone. In its place was a quiet knowing, the kind that did not need to be defended or explained. Slowly, her lips curved, and the smile that rose was not tentative but whole, carrying the ease of someone who had chosen and would not turn back. She recognised herself in that moment not as someone waiting to become, but as someone who already was.

Just over her shoulder, she thought she saw something flicker. Not a face. Not a figure. But a warmth, like the shadow of someone turning away. A presence just out of sight.

It did not reach for her.

It did not ask her to stay.

Only watched.

A witness. A blessing.

She reached up and touched the mirror. The surface was cool beneath her fingertips, anchoring her in this moment. The smile lingered, not forced but natural, as though it belonged to her as much as breath. She felt it in her chest as much as on her lips. Steady. At peace. Certain.

The steadiness did not leave her when she dropped her hand. It lived in her now, quiet but unshakable, carrying her forward to what awaited beyond the door.

From the hallway, Miranda's voice called again, lighter this time, teasing.

"Come on, bride-to-be. You do not want to keep your groom waiting."

Cassandra smiled again. This time it reached deeper, as if it touched not only her lips but the quiet centre of her being.

Today was not about forgetting.

It was about carrying it all.

The strange, the sacred, the sorrowful. Every shadow and every light.

All of it was coming with her into something new.

She turned from the mirror and crossed the room. Her dress waited in the corner, hung on a simple wooden hanger. It seemed to hold its own breath, patient, as though it had been waiting only for her.

It was not the dress of a childhood fairytale. No jewelled hems. No stiff satin dreams.

This dress was hers.

Ivory. Flowing. Light. The cuffs trimmed in the faintest thread of dusky violet, not showy but true, a quiet nod to something remembered and cherished.

The ring was already on her finger. It had been there for months now, worn smooth by time and touch.

A silver band, delicate and strong. Ivy leaves etched along its curve. At the centre, a lavender stone, dusk-coloured and cool against her skin.

She brushed her thumb across it, feeling its weight, its memory, its steady presence.

Strange, she thought, how something chosen in waking life could still feel like the echo of a dream, or the first note of a song only just beginning.

Some promises, she realised, began long before they were spoken. And some, once made, sang quietly through every breath, waiting for the moment when they would be lived.

Miranda was waiting just outside the door, all warmth and quiet humour, a silver hairbrush in hand. When she saw Cassandra, she stilled for a moment before her face softened into something bright.

"There you are," she said. Her voice was thick with something like joy. "Thought you might have run off."

Cassandra shook her head.

"Not quite."

For a moment she only looked at Miranda, taking in the familiar shape of her, the steadiness she had offered when the nights were unsteady, the way her laughter had softened the edges of silence. Then she moved, sudden and certain, and threw her arms around her.

The hug was fierce, almost too much, as though every moment of doubt and longing had poured itself into the strength of her embrace. Miranda gave a small laugh against her shoulder, breathless with surprise.

"Goodness, Cass," she said, half teasing, half tender. "Are you trying to crush me before the wedding?"

Cassandra held on a moment longer before finally letting go, her smile brighter, steadier than it had been.

When they parted, Miranda gestured toward the little window seat.

"Sit. Let me make you more heartbreakingly beautiful than you already are."

Cassandra sat by the window, the early light pooling at her feet as Miranda brushed through her hair with careful, grounding strokes. Each motion was unhurried, the bristles moving like a kind of remembering.

The silence stretched between them, but it was not empty.

Cassandra let out a breath, slow and steady.

"I missed you," she said at last.

Miranda's hand paused for a fraction, the brush caught mid-stroke. "I wasn't gone," she murmured, though her voice carried a softness that betrayed the thought.

Cassandra's gaze fell to the wooden floorboards, tracing the pale seams of light across them. "No, but I think I was. In my dream."

The brush stilled again, quiet in her hair.

"You had a dream, do tell." Miranda questioned.

Cassandra nodded, her words hushed. "It wasn't like a normal dream. It felt... other. Like I had slipped into another life. One stitched to this one, but turned sideways. And there, I worked it out. All of it. The fears, the doubts, the choices I thought would undo me."

Miranda's hands resumed their rhythm, slower now, as though she was brushing through more than hair.

Her voice was gentle, almost tentative. "So, what happened in your dream?"

"There was this book," Cassandra said. "Old, strange. It changed every time I opened it. The pages disappeared if I went back. It only ever showed me what I was ready to see."

It stood open at the far edge of the space, spilling radiance that was not the colour of daylight but something more ancient, vibrating quietly in her bones.

Cassandra closed the Book with care. It did not resist. It had given all it could. She placed her hand upon its cover, steady and deliberate, a final gesture of thanks.

Then she turned toward the doorway.

Her steps made no sound. The air stirred in quiet spirals, drawing back as she passed, parting like fabric gathered aside. The chamber seemed to recognise her now, not as an intruder but as something returned. Fear no longer shadowed her. Hesitation no longer held her back. She moved with the calm of one who had awakened to a path carved long ago into her very being.

She lingered at the threshold and glanced back once. The chapel remained, yet it was already withdrawing, its outlines dimming, as though it wished to be remembered but not followed. It did not vanish. It receded, leaving her with what endured: the memory, the choice, the certainty that had taken root within her.

Miranda made a soft sound in her throat, not agreement, not disbelief. Simply listening.

"And there were rituals. Symbols. Candles. Silk. A robe left for me, a key that led me deeper. It should have felt strange, all of it. But it didn't. It felt sacred. Honest. Like I was being undone and remade at the same time."

The brush slowed, fingertips smoothing a strand of hair behind Cassandra's ear, grounding her in the telling.

Her voice dropped. "There came a point when I had to choose. Between what was real and what was only fantasy. Between darkness and light. Both called to me, but only one would carry me forward."

Miranda's voice was low, steady. "And you chose?"

Cassandra nodded. "Yes. And through everything I've lived, through every doubt and every lesson, I know now that I chose well."

Miranda let out a soft laugh, though her eyes stayed thoughtful. "That's full on. I hope you did."

The brush was set down with care, the faint sound of bristles against wood lingering in the stillness. Miranda reached for the delicate pins arranged neatly beside her, lifting them one by one as though each carried a quiet intention. She twisted Cassandra's hair slowly, fastening it into place with movements that were light but certain, the kind of touch that steadied rather than adorned.

Cassandra breathed out slowly, her words softer now but sure. "It was never about being chosen. It was about choosing. About trusting that when the moment came, I would be ready to stand in it."

Miranda's expression softened into something between affection and amusement. "Perhaps it was all just wedding jitters," she said lightly, though her eyes held more depth. "But either way, I've never seen you so sure of yourself as you are now, in this moment."

From outside, faint music began to rise, drifting through the open window with the morning air. It was not urgent, not commanding. More a quiet signal, a reminder that time was moving forward again, carrying them gently with it.

Miranda rose with a kind of grace that made the moment feel older than both of them, then extended her hand. "It's almost time," she said, her voice soft yet weighted, as though she were naming something sacred rather than announcing it.

Cassandra placed her hand in Miranda's, the steadiness of her breath carrying her as she turned toward the waiting corner of the room. The dress hung there in quiet suspension, as though it too had been holding its breath for this very moment.

"I dreamed of so many dresses," she whispered, her gaze steady on the fabric. "But none of them ever felt like this."

A knowing smile touched Miranda's lips, her eyes kind.

"Because this one's yours."

Together, they lifted the gown, their movements unhurried, reverent, as if taking part in an ancient rite. Miranda guided it carefully over Cassandra's head, her touch patient and sure, as though she were tending not only to cloth but to something within. The fabric settled against Cassandra's skin, cool at first, then warming gradually, almost as though it recognised her, as though it had been waiting to belong.

Light from the window caught in the folds of ivory, making them shimmer with quiet fire. At the cuffs and hem, threads of colour shimmered faintly, less lavender now than the memory of something carried forward, like the echo of a dream lingering just beyond reach. Miranda reached for the final piece, the deep red sash. She wrapped it around Cassandra's waist with measured precision, her hands sure, the knot tied with the solemnity of a vow.

For a heartbeat Cassandra thought of the ribbon she had once carried, another thread of the same shade, binding her then as it bound her now. The fabric gleamed in the light, rich as wine, bold as blood, a reminder of what had been lived and what was still to come.

"There," Miranda said, stepping back as though releasing her into the moment. Her eyes softened, her words carrying the weight of truth. "You look like the version of yourself you were always becoming."

The air seemed to hush. And then, a knock at the door. Gentle. Familiar. The door opened slowly, and Cassandra's mother stepped inside.

She did not speak at once. Her eyes lingered on Cassandra in the gown, light falling across her like a benediction, and then moved to Miranda, who was still smoothing the final fold of fabric with careful hands. For a long moment she simply stood there, one hand against the doorframe, her gaze shimmering with something quiet and whole.

"There you are," she said at last, her voice warm with pride. "My beautiful girls."

The words hung in the air, simple yet startling, as if they carried more than they first revealed. Cassandra felt their weight settle over the room, a truth spoken aloud as naturally as breathing.

Her mother stepped further into the room, her gaze moving between them, softened by memory.

"You both look so grown up," she said, her voice catching faintly. "I remember when you were just little things, wild with scraped knees and tangled hair. And now..."

Her words trailed off, heavy with love. Cassandra and Miranda exchanged a look that needed no explanation, a quiet smile that belonged only to sisters who had always walked together.

Miranda was not only Cassandra's closest friend but her sister, bound to her by both blood and a lifetime of laughter, quarrels, and secrets whispered in the dark. The two halves of her life stood side by side, reflected in her mother's eyes.

Her mother reached into the pocket of her cardigan and drew out a small, velvet-wrapped box. Her fingers lingered on it for a heartbeat before she held it forward.

"This belonged to your grandmother," she said. "She wore it on her wedding day. And I wore it on mine. I was not sure when I would pass it on, but..." Her eyes found Cassandra's, steady now, carrying both love and certainty. "Now feels right."

She opened the box with careful hands.

Inside lay a slender silver chain, its delicate charm circular, etched with a spiral motif. It was not the sigil that had once marked Cassandra's shoulder, yet it carried the same shape, the same weight, as though it echoed some older truth beneath the surface of things.

Cassandra drew in a breath that caught partway, her chest tightening with a rush of memory and meaning.

Her mother stepped closer. Miranda, without needing to be asked, reached out and gently brushed Cassandra's hair aside, her touch lingering for a moment against her sister's shoulder. The gesture was simple, but it carried the weight of years, of secrets shared and quarrels mended, of a bond that needed no words.

Their mother lifted the chain, her voice soft. "It always reminded me of something older than us," she said. "Like it came from somewhere quiet. But somehow, it always finds its way back to us."

With Miranda's hand still resting lightly against Cassandra, their mother fastened the clasp. The charm settled just above the neckline of the gown, cool against Cassandra's skin.

For a moment Cassandra thought she felt it stir, not with magic, but with knowing.

Her mother stepped back, her gaze moving between them, her eyes shimmering. "There," she whispered. "Now you're ready."

Cassandra stepped forward and folded herself into her mother's arms. The embrace was close and unhurried, a stillness that held more than words ever could.

Her mother's breath warmed her hair, and for a heartbeat the room felt suspended, as though it too was bowing into the moment.

Outside the window, the music shifted. Not a rush of sound, but a deepening, low notes settling into the morning air, a quiet summons that the day was beginning to turn toward its purpose.

When her mother finally released her, she caught Cassandra's hand and gave it a gentle squeeze, her eyes full. "Go on, sweetheart. They're waiting."

Cassandra nodded, but before her feet carried her toward the door, a faint vibration pulsed from the table by the window. Her phone lit softly in the half-light.

One new message.

Ethan.

I'm ready when you are. Let's do this together.

Her breath stilled, tender and sure. She pressed her hand against the screen, letting her fingertips rest there as if she could touch the steadiness in his words. He had never been lost to her. He had been waiting all along, patient in the shadows of every choice, every turn, until she was ready to step toward him. Not as dream. Not as fragment. Just Ethan, constant as he had always been. Real. Certain.

The necklace shifted at her collarbone, the silver charm warming against her skin. It was no longer the echo of a dream she might wake from. It was something carried into daylight, something chosen, something kept.

Golden light spilled from the hallway beyond, soft as honey, filling the air with promise.

At the far end, her father stood waiting. His hands rested loosely together, his shoulders calm, his presence rooted in the glow. When Cassandra looked up, his eyes shone with pride, carrying the weight of every step that had led her here. His smile deepened, quiet yet full, and in that single expression she felt the strength of all he wished for her.

His eyes shimmered, warm and unwavering, as if seeing her fully for the very first time.

Cassandra drew in a slow inhale, letting it move through her before taking another.

He looked unchanged at first glance, the same calm posture, the same gentleness in his bearing. Yet beneath it lived something more, something she had only ever glimpsed in fragments. The way he stood like the guardian of a threshold. The way he had always made space for her to become what she was meant to be.

Not only the man in the bookshop.

The keeper of it. The one who had always been there, in one shape or another, watching over the doorways she would cross.

She moved toward him, and he extended his hand. Not in silence, but in offering, as though the gesture itself carried its own language.

When she reached him, he squeezed her fingers with quiet strength, then lifted one hand to her cheek. His touch was soft, grounding, familiar.

"My Lass," he said, voice low. "You found your way, didn't you?"

Cassandra nodded, her eyes brightening.

His thumb brushed her cheek with a tenderness that reached deeper than words. Then he smiled, his expression touched with something timeless. "I always knew you would. Sometimes the path doesn't light until you're already walking it."

She let out a soft laugh, the sound like air released after being held too long. "You sound like someone I met in a dream."

He tilted his head, eyes gleaming. "Maybe dreams and fathers borrow from each other now and then."

They lingered in that quiet moment, the house seeming to hold its breath around them, attentive and listening.

Then he offered his arm. "Shall we?"

She slipped her hand into the crook of his elbow.

Together, they walked. The hallway stretched before them, washed in sunlight, dust motes drifting in slow spirals as if memory itself had taken form. The floorboards murmured underfoot, familiar and forgiving, carrying them forward.

At the far end, the light gathered as though it were more than morning, more than a house opening into a new day. It was a passage. A threshold. And her father, steady at her side, was both guide and witness as she stepped across into the life she had chosen.

Each step sounded louder than the last, not for the sound itself but for the weight behind it, as though the house remembered every version of her that had walked its corridors before.

They reached the end of the hall, where an old wooden door stood waiting, half-open, sunlight spilling through the crack and pooling across the worn timber floor. Beyond it, the garden revealed itself in full.

Lavender ribbons stirred on the breeze, tied to branches heavy with bloom. Ivy curled along the frame of the archway, its green deepened by the gold of morning. The scent of earth and summer drifted inward, carrying with it the hush of something both ordinary and sacred. And just beyond, gathered quietly beneath the trees, stood everyone she loved.

No longer echoes. No longer symbols. Just themselves.

Ethan waited at the front, his gaze already fixed on her, a smile rising as if it had been waiting there all along. He looked at her as though he knew every version she had ever been. Not only this woman. Not only the girl she once was. But all of her, held at once.

Her father leaned closer, his voice low and intimate.

"You look like your mother did on her wedding day," he said. "And maybe a little like someone older still."

She lifted her face toward him.

"What do you mean?"

His smile curved sideways, almost secret.

"Like you've walked through something ancient. And carried the light back with you."

Her chest swelled.

"I have," she whispered.

He didn't answer, only pressed her hand more firmly in his.

They paused together at the threshold. The doorway stood open, sunlight pouring through, the garden alive beyond it with colour and the quiet thrum of something holy. Cassandra stilled, not out of hesitation, but because something within her needed to bow to this moment, to honour the path that had led her here. Every shadow. Every choice. Every fragment of herself that had once seemed separate but now returned whole.

It was one final door. The last she needed to walk through. And this time, she carried no key in her hand. The key was her.

She closed her eyes. She thought of the silk and the book, of the rituals and symbols that had marked her skin and her spirit. She thought of the mirror that had not judged her, only revealed her. She thought of her mother, of Miranda, of Ethan, and of herself. She thought of that very first door in Camden, the night she had lifted her hand to knock, trembling yet unwilling to turn away.

Her breath steadied, deep and calm. She did not shape the words aloud, but she felt them fully.

I'm ready.

And she truly was.

When she opened her eyes, the light was the same, yet she was not.

Her father's arm was firm in hers.

She smiled.

And together, they stepped through the doorway, into the garden, into the beginning.

And the story she had carried, at last, became her own.

For in finding herself, she had found the strength to step into every choice that waited, ready at last to live them fully.

EPILOGUE

By evening, the garden had fallen into quiet. Petals drifted along the stone path like forgotten confetti, their colour softening in the last of the light. Above the archway, fairy lights glowed faintly, no longer celebrating but keeping gentle watch over the hush that followed joy.

Cassandra stood barefoot in the doorway, her dress gathered loosely at her sides. Inside, voices rose in familiar warmth. Her cousins laughed over half-finished champagne and stories too old to prove. Sofia had taken over the kitchen, claiming it as her own. James wandered to the piano, his music trailing through the walls like memory. Victor, as always, argued passionately about songs that only he could remember.

They were family. Not symbols. Not shadows. Just hers.

On the hallway table, beside her bouquet, rested the guest book. Bound in soft grey linen, unassuming, ordinary. Yet Cassandra's breath slowed as she opened it. The pages were simple, real.

The first lines were filled with love.

To Cass and Ethan, may your life be full of everything real and rare.
You always knew your way, even when you thought you didn't.
Keep choosing each other. Every day.
All our love, Mum and Dad x

Handwriting shifted with every turn. Some neat, some hurried. A sketch from Victor, wild and imperfect. A pressed petal from Sofia, pale but fragrant. And then Miranda's words, written in careful loops that carried both joy and the steadiness of sisterhood:

You were always the heart of us, the one who kept the threads together even when you thought you were unravelling. I love you endlessly, and I always will. Keep dreaming, Miranda xox

Cassandra smiled, the kind of smile that softened rather than stretched, as if it had been waiting all along. She traced the curve of the letters once with her fingertip, as though sealing the truth into herself, before she turned another page. Near the back, just before the end, her phone buzzed faintly on the table.

The screen lit with a message.

From Lydia:

This time, the story belongs to you. I'm sorry I cannot be there to celebrate with you both. But when you are ready, there is another chapter waiting. It begins in the hills above Hollywood. A reclusive artist. A forgotten melody. A house that watches. Let me know when you are ready to knock. Love, Lydia.

Cassandra held the phone for a long moment, her thumb hovering above the glass. She did not answer. Not yet. The words pressed gently into her, not as burden, but as promise. She set the phone aside, her hand lingering as if to seal the moment without rushing it.

The guest book's final page carried only one line, written in deep black ink, slanted slightly to the right and unmistakable.

Some stories live inside you longer than memory. You were always more than you believed, and your way home was already written within you. - L.A.

She knew that hand. She had seen it beyond ink, caught in mirrors, in dreams, in shadows. No flourish. No explanation. Only a truth she had already carried.

She did not look around. She did not need to. The moment was not meant to be solved, only felt. Her smile deepened, steady and knowing, because yes, she had found her way home. And her home was Ethan.

As though answering that truth, Ethan appeared in the doorway. His tie was loosened, his hair catching the last honeyed light. He did not speak. He simply reached for her, his palm steady, open, waiting.

She placed her hand in his. In that quiet touch, something inside her settled. Not with doubt. Not with ache. But with the certainty of what had always been hers.

Together, they stepped into the dusk, into the soft gold of a day almost ending. Behind them lay the path of pages already turned. Ahead stretched the unwritten road, waiting.

And always, a part of her would remember. Not as sorrow. Not as shadow. But as the thread that had led her here.

She had chosen well in the end. She had chosen herself.

And in choosing herself, she had found the truest beginning of all.

ABOUT THE AUTHOR

Gwendoline Vale is the pen name of the author. She writes of love, memory, and the unseen moments that shape who we are. Her pen name is a tribute to her mother, whose life taught her the importance of resilience. Trace learned strength in the spaces where her mother did not have it, and in doing so, discovered her own.

She believes that everyone has their own journey to walk, and that every story is a way of finding yourself. In writing, she hopes to show that the truest strength is not found in perfection, but in the choices we make, the paths we dare to follow, and the light we carry forward.

Through her work, she explores how shadow and light both shape us, and how, in the end, each of us discovers a way to call that path our own. And in sharing her stories, she hopes that you too can find your way home.

Her journey continues, and perhaps she will see you next in Los Angeles.

Thank You for Reading

Thank you for walking with Cassandra through the shadows of The Darkness Between Us.

Stories only live when they are shared, and I am deeply grateful you chose to share this one.

This book has been a labour of love and an act of self-recognition for me, and I hope that in some way it speaks to a part of you as well.

If her journey stayed with you, I would be honoured if you told a friend, passed the book along, donated it to a library or charity, or left a few words in a review, so that others who need to find the light can discover it too.

I hope to see you again soon.

Gwendoline Vale xox

www.ingramcontent.com/pod-product-compliance
Lightning Source LLC
Chambersburg PA
CBHW032124170626
46808CB00006B/2097